## PHILIP K. DICK

## CONFESSIONS OF A
## CRAP ARTIST

PHILIP K. DICK was born in Chicago in 1928 and lived most of his life in California. He briefly attended the University of California, but dropped out before completing any classes. In 1952 he began writing professionally and proceeded to write thirty-six novels and five short story collections. He won the Hugo Award for best novel in 1962 for *The Man in the High Castle* and the John W. Campbell Memorial Award for best novel of the year in 1974 for *Flow My Tears the Policeman Said*. Philip K. Dick died of heart failure following a stroke on March 2, 1982, in Santa Ana, California.

# CONFESSIONS OF A CRAP ARTIST

# PHILIP K. DICK

# CONFESSIONS OF A CRAP ARTIST

## —JACK ISIDORE
## (of Seville, Calif.)

### A CHRONICLE OF VERIFIED SCIENTIFIC FACT
### 1945-1959

VINTAGE BOOKS

A Division of Random House, Inc.

New York

First Vintage Books Edition, July 1992

Library of Congress Cataloging-in-Publication Data
Dick, Philip K.
Confessions of a crap artist—Jack Isidore (of Seville, Calif.):
a chronicle of verified scientific fact, 1945–1959 / Philip K. Dick.
—1st Vintage Books ed.
p.  cm.
ISBN 0-679-74114-3
I. Title.
PS3554.I3C6   1992
813′.54—dc20        91-50969
CIP

For information about the Philip K. Dick Society, write to:
PKDS, Box 611, Glen Ellen, CA 95442.

Manufactured in the United States of America
10   9

To Tessa,
the dark-haired girl who cared about me
when it mattered most; that is, all the time.
This is to her with love.

# CONFESSIONS OF A
# CRAP ARTIST

# 1

I am made out of water. You wouldn't know it, because I have it bound in. My friends are made out of water, too. All of them. The problem for us is that not only do we have to walk around without being absorbed by the ground but we also have to earn our livings.

Actually there's even a greater problem. We don't feel at home anywhere we go. Why is that?

The answer is World War Two.

World War Two began on December 7, 1941. In those days I was sixteen years old and going to Seville High. As soon as I heard the news on the radio I realized that I was going to be in it, that our president had his opportunity now to whip the Japs and the Germans, and that it would take all of us pulling shoulder to shoulder. The radio was one I built myself. I was always putting together superhet five-tube ac-dc receivers. My room was overflowing with earphones and coils and condensers, along with plenty of other technical equipment.

The radio announcement interrupted a bread commercial that went:

"Homer! Get Homestead bread instead!"

I used to hate that commercial, and I had just jumped up to turn to another frequency when all at once this woman's voice was cut off. Naturally I noticed that; I didn't have to think twice to be aware that something was up. Here I had my German colonies stamps—those that show the Kaiser's yacht the Hohenzollern—spread out only a little way from the sunlight, and I had to get them mounted before anything happened to them. But I stood in the middle of my room doing absolutely nothing except respiring, and, of course, keeping other normal processes going. Maintaining my physical side while my mind was focused on the radio.

My sister and mother and father, naturally, had gone away for the afternoon, so there was nobody to tell. That made me livid with rage. After the news about the Jap planes dropping bombs on us, I ran around and around, trying to think who to call up. Finally I ran downstairs to the living room and phoned Hermann Hauck, who I went around with at Seville High and who sat next to me in Physics 2A. I told him the news, and he came right over on his bicycle. We sat around listening for further word, discussing the situation.

While discussing, we lit up a couple of Camels.

"This means Germany and Italy'll get right in," I told Hauck. "This means war with the Axis, not just the Japs. Of course, we'll have to lick the Japs first, then turn our attention to Europe."

"I'm sure glad to see our chance to clobber those Japs," Hauck said. We both agreed with that. "I'm itching to get in," he said. We both paced around my room, smoking and keeping our ears on the radio. "Those crummy little yellow-bellies," Hermann said. "You know, they have no culture of their own. Their whole civilization, they stole it from the Chinese. You know, they're actually descended more from apes; they're not actually human beings. It's not like fighting real humans."

"That's true," I said.

Of course, this was back in 1941, and an unscientific statement like that didn't get questioned. Today we know that the Chinese don't have any culture either. They went over to the Reds like the mass of ants that they are. It's a natural life for them. Anyhow it doesn't really matter, because we were bound to have trouble with them sooner or later anyhow. We'll have to lick them someday like we licked the Japs. And when the time comes we'll do it.

It wasn't long after December 7 that the military authorities put up the notices on the telephone poles, telling Japs that they had to be out of California by such and such a date. In Seville—which is about forty miles south of San Francisco—we had a number of Japs doing business; one ran a flower nursery, another had a grocery store—the usual small-time businesses that they run, cutting pennies here and there, getting their ten kids to do all the work, and generally living on a bowl of rice a day. No white person can compete with them because they're willing to work for nothing. Anyhow, now they had to get out whether they liked it or not. In my estimation it was for their own good anyhow, because a lot of us were stirred up about Japs sabotaging and spying. At Seville High a bunch of us chased a Jap kid and kicked him around a little, to show how we felt. His father was a dentist, as I recall.

The only Jap that I knew at all was a Jap who lived across the street from us, an insurance salesman. Like all of them, he had a big garden out on the sides and rear of his house, and in the evenings and on weekends he used to appear wearing khaki pants, a t-shirt, and tennis shoes, with an armload of garden hose and a sack of fertilizer, a rake and a shovel. He had a lot of Jap vegetables that I never recognized, some beans and squash and melons, plus the usual beets and carrots and pumpkins. I used to watch him scratching out the weeds around the pumpkins, and I'd always say:

"There's Jack Pumpkinhead out in his garden, again. Searching for a new head."

He did look like Jack Pumpkinhead, with his skinny neck and his round head; his hair was shaved, like the college students have theirs, now, and he always grinned. He had huge teeth, and his lips never covered them.

The idea of this Jap wandering around with a rotting head, in search of a fresh head, used to dominate me, back at that time before the Japs were moved out of California. He had such an unhealthy appearance—mostly because he was so thin and tall and stooped—that I conjectured as to what ailed him. It looked to me to be t.b. For a while I had the fear— it bothered me for weeks—that one day he'd be out in the garden, or walking down his path to get into his car, and his neck would snap and his head would bounce off his shoulders and roll down to his feet. I waited in fear for this to happen, but I always had to look out when I heard him. And whenever he was around I could hear him, because he continually hawked and spat. His wife spat too, and she was very small and pretty. She looked almost like a movie star. But her English, according to my mother, was so bad that there was no use of anybody trying to talk to her; all she did was giggle.

The notion that Mr. Watanaba looked like Jack Pump-kinhead could never have occurred to me if I hadn't read the Oz books in my younger years; in fact I still had a few of them around my room as late as World War Two. I kept them with my science-fiction magazines, my old microscope and rock collection, and the model of the solar system that I had built in junior high school for science class. When the Oz books were first written, back around 1900, everybody took them to be completely fiction, as they did with Jules Verne's books and H.G. Wells'. But now we're beginning to see that although the particular characters, such as Ozma and the Wizard and Dorothy, were all creations of Baum's mind, the notion of a civilization inside the world is not such a fantastic one. Recently, Richard Shaver has given a detailed description of a civilization inside the world, and other explorers are alerted for similar finds. It may be, too, that the lost continents of Mu and Atlantis will be found to be part of the ancient culture of which the interior lands played a major role.

Today, in the 1950s, everyone's attention is turned upward, to the sky. Life on other worlds preoccupies people's attention. And yet, any moment, the ground may open up beneath our feet, and strange and mysterious races may pour out into our very midst. It's worth thinking about, and out in California, with the earthquakes, the situation is particularly pressing. Every time there's a quake I ask myself: is this going to open up the crack in the ground that finally reveals the world inside? Will this be the one?

Sometimes at the lunch hour break, I've discussed this with the guys I work with, even with Mr. Poity, who owns the firm. My experience has been that if any of them are conscious of non-terrestrial races at all, they're concerned only with UFOs, and the races we're encountering, without realizing it, in the sky. That's what I would call intolerance, even prejudice, but it takes a long time, even in this day and age, for scientific facts to become generally known. The mass of scientists themselves are slow to change, so it's up to us, the scientifically-trained public, to be the advance guard. And yet I've found, even among us, there are so many that just don't give a damn. My sister, for instance. During the last few years she and her husband have been living up in the north western part of Marin County, and all they seem to care about up there is Zen Buddhism. And so here's an example, right in my own family, of a person who has turned from scientific curiosity to an Asiatic religion that threatens to submerge the questioning rational faculty as surely as Christianity.

Anyhow, Mr. Poity takes an interest, and I've loaned him a few of the Col. Churchward books on Mu.

My job with the One-Day Dealers' Tire Service is an interesting one, and it makes some use of my skill with tools, although little use of my scientific training. I'm a tire regroover. What we do is pick up smoothies, that is, tires that are worn down so they have little or no tread left, and then I and the other regroovers take a hot point and groove right down to the casting, following the old tread pattern, so it looks as if there's still rubber on the tire—whereas in actual fact there's only the fabric of the casing left. And then we paint the regrooved tire with black rubbery paint, so it looks like a pretty darn good tire. Of course, if you have it on your car and you so much as back over a warm match, then boom! You have a flat. But usually a regrooved tire is good for a month or so. You can't buy tires like I make, incidentally. We deal wholesale only, that is, with used car lots.

The job doesn't pay much, but it's sort of fun, figuring out the old tread pattern—sometimes you can scarcely see it. In fact, sometimes only an expert, a trained technician like myself, can see it and trace it. And you have to trace perfectly, because if you leave the old tread pattern, there's a huge gouge mark that even an idiot can recognize as not having been made by the original machine. When I get done regrooving a tire, it doesn't look hand-done by any means. It looks exactly like the way it would look if a machine had done it, and, for a regroover, that's the most satisfying feeling in the world.

# 2

Seville, California, has a good public library. But the best thing about living in Seville is that in only a twenty-minute drive you're over into Santa Cruz where the beach is and the amusement park is. And it's four lanes all the way.

To me, though, the library has been important in forming my education and convictions. On Fridays, which is my day off, I go down around ten in the morning and read *Life* and the cartoons in the *Saturday Evening Post,* and then if the librarians aren't watching me, I get the photography magazines from the rack and read them over for the purpose of finding those special art poses that they have the girls doing. And if you look carefully in the front and back of the photography magazines, you find ads that nobody else notices, ads there for you. But you need to be familiar with the wording. Anyhow, what those ads get you, if you send in the dollar, is something different from what you see even in the best magazines, like *Playboy* or *Esquire*. You get photos of girls doing something else entirely, and in some ways they're better, although usually the girls are older—sometimes even baggy old hags—and they're never pretty, and, worst of all, they have big fat saggy breasts. But they are doing really unusual things, things that you'd never ordinarily expect to see girls do in pictures—not especially dirty things, because after all, these come through the Federal mails from Los Angeles and Glendale—but things such as one I remember in which one girl was lying down on the floor, wearing a black lace bra and black stockings and French heels, and this other girl was mopping her all over with a mop from a bucket of suds. That held my attention for months. And then there was another I remember, of a girl wearing the usual—as above—pushing another girl similarly attired down a ladder so that the victim-girl (if that's what you call it; at least, that's how I usually think of it) was all bent and lopsided, as if her arms and legs were broken—like a rag doll or something, as if she's been run over.

And then always there's the ones you get in which the stronger girl, the master, has the other tied up. Bondage pictures, they're called. And better than that are the bondage drawings. They're really competent artists who draw those . . . some are really worth seeing. Others, in fact most of them, are the run-of-the-mill junk, and really shouldn't be allowed to go through the mails, they're so crude.

For years I've had a strange feeling looking at these pictures, not a dirty feeling—nothing to do with sexuality or relations—but the same feeling you get when you're high up on a mountain, breathing that pure air, the way it is over by Big Basin Park, where the redwoods are, and the mountain streams. We used to go hunting around in those redwoods, even though naturally it's illegal to hunt in a state or Federal park. We'd get a couple of deer, now and then. The guns we used weren't mine, though. I borrowed the one I used from Harvey St. James.

Usually when there's anything worth doing, all three of us, myself and St. James and Bob Paddleford, do it together, using St. James' '57 Ford convertible with the double pipes and twin spots and dropped rear end. It's quite a car, known all around Seville and Santa Cruz; it's gold-colored, that baked on enamel, with purple trim that we did by hand. And we used molded fiberglass to get those sleek lines. It looks more like a rocket ship than a car; it has that look of outer space and velocities nearing the speed of light.

For a really big time, where we go is across the Sierras to Reno; we leave late Friday, when St. James gets off from his job selling suits at Hapsberg's Menswear, shoot over to San Jose and pick up Paddleford—he works for Shell Oil, down in the blueprint department—and then we're off to Reno. We don't sleep Friday night at all; we get up there late and go right to work playing the slots or blackjack. Then around ten o'clock Saturday morning we take a snooze in the car, find a washroom to shave and change our shirts and ties, and then we're off looking for women. You can always find that kind of women around Reno; it's really a filthy town.

I actually don't enjoy that part too much. It plays no role in my life, any more than any other physical activity. Even to look at me you'd recognize that my main energies are in the mind.

When I was in the sixth grade I started wearing glasses because I read so many funny books. *Tip Top Comics* and *King Comics* and *Popular Comics* . . . those were the first comic books to appear, back in the mid 'thirties, and then there were a whole lot more. I read them all, in grammar school, and traded them around with other kids. Later on, in junior high, I started reading *Astonishing Stories,* which was a pseudo-science magazine, and *Amazing Stories,* and *Thrilling Wonder.* In fact, I had an almost complete file of *Thrilling Wonder,* which was my favorite. It was from an ad in *Thrilling* that I got the lucky lodestone that I still carry around with me. That was back around 1939.

All my family have been thin, my mother excepted, and as soon as I put on those silver-framed glasses they always gave to boys in those days, I immediately looked scholarly, like a real bookworm. I had a high forehead anyhow. Then later, in high school, I had dandruff to quite an extent. And this made my hair seem lighter than it actually was. Once in a while I had a stammer that bothered me, although I found that if I suddenly bent down, as if brushing something from my leg, I could speak the word okay, so I got in the habit of doing that. I had, and still have, an indentation on my cheek, by my nose, left over from having had the chicken pox. In high school I felt nervous a great deal of the time, and I used to pick at it until it became infected. Also, I had other skin troubles, of the acne type, although in my case the spots got a purple texture that the dermatologist said was due to some low-grade infection throughout my body. As a matter of fact, although I'm thirty-four, I still break out in boils once in a while, not on my face but on my butt or armpits.

In high school I had some nice clothes, and that made it possible for me to step out and be popular. In particular I had one blue cashmere sweater that I wore for almost four years, until it got to smelling so bad the gym instructor made me throw it away. He had it in for me anyhow, because I never took a shower in gym.

It was from the *American Weekly,* not from any magazines, that I got my interest in science.

Possibly you remember the article they had, in the May 4th, 1935 issue, on the Sargasso Sea. At that time I was ten years old, and in the high fourth. So I was just barely old enough to read something besides funny books. There was a huge drawing, in six or seven colors, that covered two whole opened-up pages; it showed ships, stuck in the Sargasso Sea, that had been there for hundreds of years. It showed the skeletons of the sailors, covered with seaweed. The rotting sails and masts of the ships. And all different kinds of ships, even some ancient Greek and Roman ones, and some from the time of Columbus, and then the Norsemen's ships. Jumbled in together. Never stirring. Stuck there forever, trapped by the Sargasso Sea.

The article told how ships got drawn in and trapped, and how no one ever got away. There were so many that they were side by side, for miles. Every kind of ship that existed, although later on when there were steamships, fewer ships got stuck, obviously because they didn't depend on wind currents but had their own power.

The article affected me because in many ways it reminded me of an episode on Jack Armstrong, the All-American Boy, that had seemed very important to me, having to do with the Elephants' Lost Graveyard. I remember that Jack had had a metal key that, when stuck, resonated strangely, and was the key to the graveyard. For a long time I knocked every bit of metal I came across against something to make it resonate, trying to produce that sound and find the Elephants' Lost Graveyard on my own (a door was supposed to open in the rock somewhere). When I read the article on the Sargasso Sea I saw an important resemblance: the Elephants' Lost Graveyard was sought for because of all the ivory, and in the Sargasso Sea there was millions of dollars worth of jewels and gold, the cargoes of the trapped ships, just waiting to be located and claimed. And the difference between the two was that the Elephants' Lost Graveyard wasn't a scientific fact but just a myth brought back by fever-crazed explorers and natives, *whereas the Sargasso Sea was scientifically established.*

On the floor of our living room, in the house we rented back in those days on Illinois Avenue, I had the article spread out, and when my sister came home with my mother and father I tried to interest her in it. But at that time she was only eight. We got into a terrible fight about it, and the upshot was that my father grabbed up the *American Weekly* and threw it into the paper bag of refuse under the sink. That upset me so badly that I had a fantasy about him, dealing with the Sargasso Sea. It was so disgusting that even now I can't bear to think about it. That was one of the worst days in my life, and I always held it against Fay, my sister, that she was responsible for what happened; if she had read the article and listened to me talk about it, as I wanted her to, nothing would have gone wrong. It really got me down that something so important, and, in a sense, beautiful, should be degraded the way it was that day. It was as if a delicate dream was trampled on and destroyed.

Neither my father nor mother were interested in science. My father worked with another man, an Italian, as a carpenter and house-painter, and, for a number of years, he was with the Southern Pacific Railroad, in the maintenance department at the Gilroy Yards. He never read anything himself except the San Francisco *Examiner* and *Reader's Digest* and the *National Geographic*. My mother subscribed to *Liberty* and then, when that went out of business, she read *Good Housekeeping*. Neither of them had any education scientific or otherwise. They always discouraged me and Fay from reading, and off and on during my childhood they raided my rooms and burned everything in the way of reading material they could get their hands on, even library books. During World War Two, when I was in the Service and overseas fighting on Okinawa, they went into my room at home, the room that had always belonged to me, gathered up all my science-fiction magazines and scrapbooks of girl pictures, and even my Oz books and *Popular Science* magazines, and burned them, just as they had done when I was a child. When I got back from defending them against the enemy I found that there was nothing to read in the whole house. And all my valuable reference files of unusual scientific facts were gone forever. I do remember, though, what was probably the most startling fact from that file of thousands. Sunlight has weight. Every year the earth weighs ten thousand pounds more, because of the sunlight that reaches it from the sun. That fact has never left my mind, and the other day I calculated that since I first learned the fact, in 1940, almost one million nine hundred thousand pounds of sunlight have fallen on the earth.

And then, too, a fact that is becoming more and more known to intelligent persons. An application of mind-power can move an object at a distance! This is something I've known all along, because as a child I used to do it. In fact, my whole family did it, even my father. It was a regular activity that we engaged in, especially when out in public places such as restaurants. One time we all concentrated on a man wearing a gray suit and got him to reach his right hand back and scratch his neck. Another time, in a bus, we influenced a big old colored woman to get to her feet and get off the bus, although that took some doing, probably because she was so heavy. This was spoiled one day, however, by my sister, who when we were concentrating on a man across a waiting room from us suddenly said,

"What a lot of crap."

Both my mother and father were furious at her, and my father gave her a shaking, not so much for using a word like that at her age (she was about eleven) but for interrupting our mind concentration. I guess she picked up the word from some of the boys at Millard Fillmore Grammar School, where she was in the fifth grade at that time. Even that young she had started getting rough and tough; she liked to play kickball and baseball, and she was always down on the boys' playground instead of with the girls. Like me, she has always been thin. She used to be able to run very well, almost like a professional athlete, and she used to grab something like, say, my weekly package of Jujubees that I always bought on Saturday morning with my allowance, and ran off somewhere and ate it. She has never gotten much of a figure, even now that she's more than thirty years old. But she has nice long legs and a springy walk, and two times a week she goes to a modern dance class and does exercises. She weighs about 116 pounds.

Because of being a tomboy she always used men's words, and when she got married the first time she married a man who made his living as owner of a little factory that makes metal signs and gates. Until his heart attack he was a pretty rough guy. The two of them used to go climbing up and down the cliffs out at Point Reyes, up where they live in Marin County, and for a time they had two Arabian horses that they rode. Strangely, he had his heart attack playing badminton, a child's game. The birdie got hit over his head— by Fay—and he ran backward, tripped over a gopher hole, and fell over on his back. Then he got up, cursed a blue streak when he saw that his racket had snapped in half, started into the house for another racket, and had his heart attack coming back outdoors again.

Of course, he and Fay had been quarreling a lot, as usual, and that may have had something to do with it. When he got mad he had no control over the language he used, and Fay has always been the same way—not merely using gutter words, but in the indiscriminate choice of insults, harping on each other's weak points and saying anything that might hurt, whether true or not—in other words, saying anything, and very loud, so that their two children got quite an earful. Even in his normal conversation Charley had always been foul-mouthed, which is something you might expect from a man who grew up in a town in Colorado. Fay always enjoyed his language. The two of them made quite a pair. I remember one day when the three of us were out on their patio, enjoying the sun, when I happened to say something I think having to do with space travel, and Charley said to me,

"Isidore, you sure are a crap artist."

Fay laughed, because it made me so sore. It made no difference to her that I was her brother; she didn't care who Charley insulted. The irony of a slob like that, a paunchy beer-drinking ignorant mid-westerner who never got through high school, calling me a "crap artist" lingered in my mind and caused me to select the ironic title that I have on this work. I can just see all the Charley Humes in the world, with their portable radios tuned to the Giants' ballgames, a big cigar sticking out of their mouths, that slack, vacant expression on their fat red faces . . . and it's slobs like that who're running this country and its major businesses and its army and navy, in fact everything. It's a perpetual mystery to me. Charley only employed seven guys at his iron works, but think of that: seven human beings dependent on a farmer like that for their very livelihood. A man like that in a position to blow his nose on the rest of us, on anybody who has sensitivity or talent.

Their house, up in Marin County, cost them a lot of money because they built it themselves. They bought ten acres of land back in 1951, when they first got married, and then, while they were living in Petaluma where Charley's factory is, they hired an architect and got their plans drawn up for their house.

In my opinion, Fay's whole motive for getting mixed up with a man like that in the first place was to finally wind up with a house such as she did wind up with. After all, when he met her he already owned his factory and netted a good forty thousand a year (at least to hear him tell it). Our family had never had any money; we ate off a set of dime store blue willow for ten years, and I don't think my father ever owned a new suit at any time in his life. Of course, by winning a scholarship and being able to go on to college, Fay started meeting men from good homes—the frat boys who always horse around with big-game bonfires and the like. For a year or so she went steady with a boy studying to be a law student, a fairy-like creature who never did appeal much to me, although he liked to play pinball machines—to learn the mathematical odds, as he explained it. Charley met her by chance, in a roadside grocery store on Highway One near Fort Ross. She was ahead of him in line, buying hamburger buns and

Coca-Cola and cigarettes, and humming a Mozart tune which she had learned in a college music course. Charley thought it was an old hymn that he had sung back in Canon City, Colorado, and he started talking to her. Outside the grocery store he had his Mercedes-Benz car parked, and she could see it, with that three-point star sticking up from the radiator. Naturally Charley had on his Mercedes-Benz pin, sticking out of his shirt, so she and the rest of the world could see whose car it was. And she had always wanted a good car, especially a foreign one.

As I construct it, based on my fairly thorough knowledge of both of them, the conversation went like this:

"Is that car out there a six or an eight?" Fay asked him.

"A six," Charley said.

"Good god," Fay said. "Only a six?"

"Even the Rolls Royce is a six," Charley said. "Those Europeans don't make eights. What do you need eight cylinders for?"

"Good god. The Rolls Royce a six."

All her life Fay had wanted to ride in a Rolls Royce. She had seen one once, parked at the curb by a fancy restaurant in San Francisco. The three of us, she and I and Charley, walked all around it.

"That's a terrific car," Charley said, and proceeded to give us details on how it worked. I couldn't have cared less. If I had my choice I'd like a Thunderbird or a Corvette. Fay listened to him and we walked on, and I could see that she wasn't too interested either. Something had distressed her.

"They're so flashy-looking," she said. "I always thought of a Rolls as a classic-looking car. Like a World War One military sedan. An officer's car."

Consider to yourself if you've ever actually seen a new Rolls. They're small, metallic, streamlined but also chunky. Heavy-looking. Like some of the Jaguar saloon models, only more impressive. British streamlining, if you get the picture. Personally I wouldn't have one on a bet, and I could see that

Fay was wrestling with the same reaction. This one had a silver-blue finish with lots of chrome. In fact the whole car had a polished look, and this appealed to Charley, who liked metal and not wood or plastic.

"There's a real car," he said. Obviously he could see that he wasn't getting across to either of us; all he could do was repeat himself in his customary clumsy way. Beside his gutter words he had the vocabulary of a six year old, just a few words to cover everything. "That's a car," he said finally, as we got to the house we had come to San Francisco to visit. "But it would look out of place in Petaluma."

"Especially parked in the lot at your plant," I said.

Fay said, "What a waste it would be—putting all that money into a car. Twelve thousand dollars."

"Hell, I could pick up one for a lot less," Charley said. "I know the guy who runs the British Motor Car agency down here."

No doubt he wanted the car, and, left to himself, he possibly would have bought it. But their money had to go into their house, whether Charley liked it or not. Fay wouldn't let him buy any more cars. He had owned, besides the Mercedes, a Triumph and a Studebaker Golden Hawk, and of course several trucks for the business. Fay had told the architect to put radiant heating into the house, the resistance wire type, and up in the country where they were, it would cost them a fortune in electricity. Everyone else up there uses butane or burns wood. On the cow pasture Fay was having a swanky modern San Francisco type of house built, with recessed bath tubs, plenty of tile and mahogany paneling, fluorescent lighting, custom kitchen, electric washer and drier combination—the works, including a custom hi-fi combination with speakers built right into the walls. The house had a glass side looking out on to the acres, and a fireplace in the center of the living room, a circular barbecue type with a huge black chimney stuck over it. Naturally the floor had to be asphalt tile, in case logs rolled out. Fay had four bedrooms built, plus a study that could be used by guests. Three bathrooms in all, one for the children, one for the guests, one for herself and Charley. And a sewing room, a utility room, a family room, dining room—even a room for the freezer. And of course a tv room.

The whole house rested on a concrete slab. That, and the asphalt tile, made it so cold that the radiant heating could never be shut off except in the hottest part of summer. If you shut it off when you went to bed, by morning the house was like a cold-storage unit. After it had been built, and Charley and Fay and the two children had moved into it, they discovered that even with the fireplace and radiant heating the house was cold from October through April, and that during the wet season the water failed to drain off the soil, and, instead, seeped into the house around the frames holding the glass and under the doors. For two months in 1955 the house sat in a pool of water. A contractor had to come out and build a whole new drainage system to carry water away from the house. And in 1956 they put 220 volt wall heaters with manual switches and thermostats both into every room of the house; the damp and cold had begun to mildew all the clothes and the sheets on the bed. They also found that in winter the electric power was interrupted for several days on end, and during that time they could not cook on the electric stove, and the pump that pumped their water, being electric, failed to pump; the water heater was electric, too, so that everything had to be cooked and heated over the fireplace. Fay even had to wash clothes in a zinc bucket propped up in the fireplace. And all four of them got the flu every winter that they lived up there. They had three separate heating systems, and yet the house remained drafty; for instance, the long hall between the children's rooms and the front part of the house had no heat at all, and when the kids came scampering out in their pajamas at night they had to go from their warm rooms into the cold and then back into the heat of the living room again. And they did that every night at least six times.

Worse than anything else, Fay could never find a baby sitter up there in the country, and the consequence was that gradually she and Charley stopped visiting people. People had to visit them, and it took an hour and a half of difficult driving to get up there to Drake's Landing from San Francisco.

And yet, they loved the house. They had four black-faced sheep cropping grass outside their glass side, their Arabian horses, a collie dog as large as a pony that won prizes, and some of the most beautiful imported ducks in the world. During the time that I lived up there with them, I enjoyed some of the most interesting moments of my life.

# 3

In his Ford pick-up truck he drove with Elsie on the seat beside him, bouncing up and down as they turned across the gravel, from the asphalt, using the shoulders of the road. On the hillside sheep grazed. A white farmhouse below them.

"Will you get me some gum?" Elsie asked. "At the store? Will you get me some Black Jack gum?"

"Gum," he said, clutching the wheel. He drove faster; the steering wheel spun in his hands. I have to get a box of Tampax, he said to himself. Tampax and chewing gum. What will they say down at the Mayfair Market? How can I do it?

He thought, How can she make me do it? Buy her Tampax for her.

"What do we have to get at the store?" Elsie chanted.

"Tampax," he said. "And your gum." He spoke with such fury that the baby turned to peer fearfully at him.

"W-what?" she murmured, shrinking away to lean against the door.

"She's embarrassed to buy it," he said, "so I have to buy it for her. She makes me walk in and buy it." And he thought, I'm going to kill her.

Of course, she had a good excuse. He had the car—had been at friends, down in Olema . . . she phoned, said would he pick it up on his drive back. And the Mayfair closed in an hour or so; it closed either at five or six, he could not remember exactly. Sometimes one time, some days—week-days—another.

What happens? he wondered, if she doesn't get it? Do they bleed to death? Tampax a stopper, like a cork. Or—he tried to imagine it. But he did not know where the blood came from. One of those regions. Hell, I'm not supposed to know about that. That's her business.

But, he thought, when they need it they need it. They have to get hold of it.

Buildings with signs appeared. He entered Point Reyes Station by crossing the bridge over Paper Mill Creek. Then the marsh lands to his left . . . the road swung to the left, past Cheda's Garage and Harold's Market. Then the old abandoned hotel.

In the dirt field that was the Mayfair's parking lot he parked next to an empty hay truck.

"Come on," he said to Elsie, holding the door open for her. She did not stir and he grabbed her by the arm and swung her from the seat and down; she stumbled and he kept his grip on her, leading her away from the car, toward the street.

I can buy a lot of stuff, he thought. Get a whole basketful and then they won't notice.

In the entrance of the Mayfair, fright overcame him; he stopped and bent down, pretending to tie his shoe.

"Is your shoe untied?" Elsie asked.

He said, "You know god damn well it is." He untied the lace and retied it.

"Don't forget to buy the Tampax," Elsie told him.

"Shut up," he said with fury.

"You're a bad boy," Elsie said, beginning to cry. Her voice wailed. "Go away." She began to slap at him; he straightened up and she retreated, still slapping.

Taking hold of her arm he propelled her into the store, past the wooden counters, to the shelves of canned food. "Listen, god damn you," he said to her, bending down. "You keep still and stick close to me, or when we get back to the car I'm going to whale you good; you hear me? You understand? If you keep quiet I'll get you your gum. You want your gum? You want the gum?" He led her to the candy rack by the door. Reaching down he gave her two packages of Black Jack gum. "Now keep quiet," he said, "so I can think. I have to think." He added, "I have to remember what I'm supposed to get."

He put bread and a head of lettuce and a package of cereal into the cart; he bought several things that he knew were always needed, frozen orange juice and a carton of Pall Malls. And then he went to the counter where the Tampax was. Nobody was around. He put a box of the Tampax into the cart, down with the other items. "Okay," he said to Elsie. "We're through." Without slowing he pushed the cart toward the check stand.

At the check stand two of the women clerks, in their blue smocks, stood bending over a snapshot. A woman customer, an older lady, had handed it to them; the three of them discussed the snapshot. And, directly across from the check stand, a young woman examined the different wines. So he wheeled the cart back to the rear of the store and began unloading the different items from it. But then he realized that the clerks had seen him pushing the cart, so he could not empty it; he had to buy something, or they would think it was strange, him filling a cart and then a little later walking out without anything. They might think he was sore. So he put only the Tampax box back; the rest he kept in the cart. He wheeled the cart back to the check stand and got in line.

"What about the Tampax?" Elsie asked, in a voice so overlain with caution that, had he not known what word was meant, he would not have been able to understand it.

"Forget it," he said.

After he had paid the clerk he carried the bag of groceries across the street to the pick-up truck. Now what? he asked himself, feeling desperate. I have to get it. And if I go back I'll be more conspicuous than ever. Maybe I can drive down to Fairfax and get it, at one of those big new drugstores.

Standing there, he could not decide. Then he caught sight of the Western Bar. What the hell, he thought. I'm going to sit in there and decide. He took hold of Elsie's hand and led her down the street to the bar. But, on the brick steps, he realized that with the child along he could not get in.

"You're going to have to stay in the car," he told her, starting back. At once she began to cry and drag against his weight. "For a couple of seconds—you know they won't let you in the bar."

"No!" the child screamed, as he dragged her back across the street. "I don't want to sit in the car. I want to go with you!"

He put her into the cab of the truck and locked the doors.

God damn people, he thought. Both of them. They're driving me out of my cottonplucking mind.

At the bar he drank a Gin Buck. No one else was there, so he felt relaxed and able to think. The bar was as always dark, spacious.

I could go into the hardware store, he thought, and buy her some kind of present. A bowl or something. A kitchen gadget.

And the intention to kill her returned. I'll go home and run into the house and beat the shit out of her, he thought. I'll beat her; I will.

He had a second Gin Buck.

"What time is it?" he asked the bartender.

"Five fifteen," the bartender said. Several other men had wandered in and were drinking beer.

"Do you know what time the Mayfair closes?" he asked

the bartender. One of the men said he thought it closed at six. An argument began between him and the bartender.

"Forget it," Charley Hume said.

After he had drunk down a third Gin Buck he decided to go back to the Mayfair and get the Tampax. He paid for his drinks and left the bar. Presently he found himself back in the Mayfair, roaming around among the shelves, past the canned soups and packages of spaghetti.

In addition to the Tampax he bought a jar of smoked oysters, a favorite of Fay's. Then he returned to the pick-up truck. Elsie had fallen asleep, resting against the door. He pulled on the door for a moment, trying to open it, and then he remembered that he had locked it. Where the hell was the key? Putting down his paper bag he groped in his pockets. Not in the ignition switch . . . he put his face to the door window. God in heaven, it wasn't there either. So where could it be? He rapped on the glass and called,

"Hey, wake up. Will you?" Again he rapped. At last Elsie sat up and became aware of him. He pointed to the glove compartment. "See if the key's in there," he yelled. "Pull up the button," he yelled, pointing to the lock-button on the inside of the door. "Pull it up so I can get in."

Finally she unlocked the door. "What did you get?" she asked, reaching for the paper bag. "Anything for me?"

There was a spare key under the floormat; he kept it there all the time. Using it, he started up the car. Never find out where it went, he decided. Have to get a duplicate made. Once more he searched his coat pockets . . . and there it was, in his pocket, where it was supposed to be. Where he had put it. Christ, he thought. I must really be stoned. Backing from the lot, he drove up Highway One, in the direction that he had come.

When he reached the house, and had parked in the garage beside Fay's Buick, he gathered together the two bags of groceries and started along the path to the front door. The door was open, and classical music could be heard. He could see Fay, through the glass side of the house; at the dish drier she scraped plates, her back to him. Their collie Bing got up from the mat in front of the door to greet him and Elsie. Its feathery tail brushed against him and it lunged with pleasure, nearly upsetting him and causing him to drop one of the bags. With the side of his foot he pushed the dog out of his way and edged through the front door, into the living room. Elsie departed along the path to the rear patio, leaving him by himself.

"Hi," Fay called from the other part of the house, her voice obscured by the music. He failed, for a moment, to grasp that it was her voice he heard; for a moment it seemed only a noise, an impediment in the music. Then she appeared, gliding at him with her springy, padding walk, meanwhile drying her hands on a dishtowel. At her waist she had tied a sash into a bow; she wore tight pants and sandals, and her hair was uncombed. God, how pretty she looks, he thought. That marvelous alert walk of hers . . . ready to whip around in the opposite direction. Always conscious of the ground under her.

As he opened the bags of groceries he gazed down at her legs, seeing in his mind the high span that she reached, in the mornings, during her exercises. One leg up as she crouched on the floor . . . fastening her fingers about her ankle, while she bent to one side. What strong leg-muscles she has, he thought. Enough to cut a man in half. Bisect him, desex him. Part of that learned from the horse . . . from riding bareback and clutching that damn animal's sides.

"Look what I got for you," he said, holding out the jar of smoked oysters.

Fay said, "Oh—" And took the jar, accepting it with the manner that meant she understood that he had gotten it for her with such deep purpose, some desire to express his feelings. Of all the people in the world, she was the best at accepting a gift. Understanding how he felt, or how the children or neighbors or anyone felt. Never said too much, never overdid it, and always pointed out the important traits of the gift, why it was so valuable to her. She looked up at him and her mouth moved into the quick, grimace-like smile—tilting her head on one side she regarded him.

"And this," he said, getting out the Tampax.

"Thanks," she said, accepting it from him. As she took the box he drew back, and, hearing himself give a gasp, he hit her in the chest. She flew backwards, away from him, dropping the bottle of smoked oysters; at that he ran at her— she was sliding down against the side of the table, knocking the lamp off as she tried to catch herself—and hit her again, this time sending her glasses flying from her face. At once she rolled over, with stuff from the table clattering down on her.

At the doorway, Elsie began to scream. Bonnie appeared—he saw her white, wide-eyed face—but she said nothing; she stood gripping the doorknob . . . she had been in the bedroom. "Mind your own business," he yelled at the children. "Go on," he yelled. "Get out of here." He ran a few steps toward them; Bonnie remained where she was, but the baby turned and fled.

Kneeling down, he got a good grip on his wife and lifted her to a sitting position. A ceramic ashtray that she had made had broken; he began collecting the pieces with his left hand, supporting her with his right. She slumped against him, her eyes open, her mouth slack; she seemed to be glaring down at the floor, her forehead wrinkled, as if she were trying to make sense of what had happened. Presently she unbuttoned two buttons of her shirt and put her hand inside, to stroke her chest. But she was too dazed to talk.

He said, by way of explanation, "You know how I feel about getting that damn stuff. Why can't you get it yourself? Why do I have to go down and get it?"

Her head swung upward, until she gazed directly at him. The dark color of her eyes reminded him of that in his children's eyes; the same enlargement, the depth. They, all of them, reacted by this floating backward from him, this flying further and further along a line that he could not imagine or follow. All three of them together . . . and he, left out. Facing only this outer surface. Where had they gone? Off to commune and confer. Accusation shining at him . . . he heard nothing, but saw very well. Even the walls had eyes.

And then she got up and past him, not easily, but with a squeezing push of her hand; her fingers thrust him away, toppling him. In motion she had terrific strength. She bowled him over in order to get away. Kicked him aside, just to spring up. Heels, hands—she walked over him and was gone, across the room, not moving lightly but striking the asphalt tile floor with the soles of her feet, impacting so that she gained good traction—she could not afford to fall. At the door she made a mistake with the knob; she had a moment in which she could not go any further.

At once he was after her, talking all the way. "Where are you going?" No reply could be expected; he did not even wait. "You have to admit you know how I feel. I'll bet you think I stopped off and had a couple of drinks at the Western. Well, I've got news for you."

By then she had the door open. Down the cypress needle path she went, only her back visible to him, her hair, shoulders, belt, legs and heels. Showed me her heels, he thought. She got to the car, her Buick parked in the garage. Standing in the doorway he watched her back out. God, how fast she can go backward in that car . . . the long gray Buick off down the driveway, its nose, its grill and headlights facing him. Through the open gate, on to the road. Which way? Toward the sheriff's house? She's going to turn me in, he thought. I deserve it. Felony wife-beating.

The Buick rolled out of sight, leaving exhaust smoke hanging. The noise of its engine remained audible to him; he pictured it going along the narrow road, turning this way and that, both car and road turning together; she knew the road so well that she would never go off, not even in the worst fog. What a really superb driver, he thought. I take off my hat to her.

Well, she'll either come back with Sheriff Chisholm or she'll cool off.

But now he saw something he did not expect: the Buick reappeared, rolling into the driveway, narrowly missing the gate. Christ! The Buick rolled up and halted directly ahead of him.

"How come you're back?" he said, speaking as matter-of-factly as possible.

Fay said, "I don't want to leave the kids here with you."

"Hell," he said, dumbfounded.

"May I take them?" she said, facing him. "Do you mind?" Her words poured out briskly.

"Suit yourself," he said, having trouble speaking. "For how long did you mean? Just for right now?"

"I don't know," she said.

"I think we ought to be able to talk this over," he said. "We should be able to sit down about it. Let's go on inside. Okay?"

Passing by him, into the house, Fay said, "Do you mind if I try to calm the children?" She disappeared beyond the edge of the kitchen cabinets; presently he heard her calling the girls, somewhere off in the bedroom area of the house.

"You don't have to worry about any more rough stuff," he said, following after her.

"What?" she said, from within one of the bathrooms, hers which was off their bedroom and which the girls used occasionally.

"That was something I had to get out of my system," he said, blocking the doorway as she started out of the bathroom.

Fay said, "Did the girls go outside?"

"Very possibly," he said.

"Would you mind letting me past?" Her voice showed the strain she felt. And, he saw, she held her hand inside her shirt, against her chest. "I think you cracked a rib," she said, breathing through her mouth. "I can hardly get my breath." But her manner was calm. She had gotten complete control of herself; he saw that she was not afraid of him, only wary. That perfect wariness of hers . . . the quickness of her responses. But she had let him haul off and let fly—she hadn't been wary enough. So, he thought, she's not such a hot specimen after all. If she's in such darn good physical shape— if those exercises she takes in the morning are worth doing— she should have been able to block my right. Of course, he thought, she's pretty good at tennis and golf and ping pong . . . so she's okay. And she keeps her figure better than any of the other women up here . . . I'll bet she's got the best figure in the whole Marin County PTA.


While Fay found and comforted the children, he roamed about the house, looking for something to do. He carried a pasteboard carton of trash out to the incinerator and set fire to it. Then, taking a screwdriver from the workshop, he tightened up the large brass screws that held the strap to her new leather purse . . . the screws came loose from time to time, dumping one end of her purse at odd moments. Anything else? he asked himself, pausing.

In the living room the radio had stopped playing classical music and had started on some dinner jazz. So he went to find another station. And then, while he turned the dial, he began thinking about dinner. It occurred to him to go into the kitchen and see how things were going.

He found that he had interrupted her while she was making the salad. A half-opened can of anchovies lay on the sideboard, beside a head of lettuce, tomatoes, and a green pepper. On the electric range—a wall installation that he had supervised—a pot of water boiled. He turned the knob from *hi* to *sim*. Picking up a paring knife, he began to peel an avocado . . . Fay had never been good at peeling avocadoes—she was too impatient. He always did that job himself.

# 4

In the spring of 1958 my older brother Jack, who was living in Seville, California, and was then thirty-three, stole a can of chocolate-covered ants from a supermarket and was caught by the store manager and turned over to the police.

We drove down from Marin County, my husband and I, to make sure he had gotten through it all right.

The police had let him go; the store hadn't pressed charges, although they had made him sign a statement admitting that he had stolen the ants. Their idea was that he would never dare steal a can of ants from them again, since, if he were caught a second time, his signed statement would put him in the city jail. It was a horse-trading deal; he got to go home— which was all he would be thinking about, with his limited brain—and the store could count on his absence from then on—he would not even dare be seen in the store, or even rooting around the empty orange crates in the rear by the loading dock.

For several months Jack had rented a room on Oil Street near Tyler, which is in the colored district of Seville, although colored or not it is one of the few interesting parts of the town. There are little dried-up stores twenty to a block that set out on the sidewalk every morning a stack of bedsprings and galvanized iron tubs and hunting knives. Always, when we were in our teens, we used to imagine that every store was a front for something. The rent there is cheap, too, and with that loathsome little job of his at that crooked tire outfit, plus his expenses for clothes and going out with his pals, he has always had to live in such a place.

We parked in a 25¢ an hour lot and jaywalked across the street, among the yellow buses, to the rooming house. It made Charley nervous to be down in such a district; he kept peering at his trousers to see if he had walked on anything— obviously psychological, because in his work he is always up to his ass in metal filings and sparks and grease. The pavement was covered with gum wrappers and spit and dog urine and old contraceptives, and Charley got that grim disapproving Protestant expression.

"Just make sure you wash your hands after we leave," I said.

"Can you get venereal disease from lamp posts or mail boxes?" Charley asked me.

"You can if you have that sort of mind," I said.

Upstairs in the damp, dark hall we rapped on Jack's door. I had been there only once before, but I recognized his room by the great stain on the ceiling, probably from an ancient overflowed toilet.

"You suppose he thought they were a delicacy?" Charley asked me. "Or did he disapprove of a supermarket stocking ants?"

I said, "You know he's always loved animals."

From within the room we could hear stirrings, as if Jack had been in bed. The time was one-thirty in the afternoon. The door did not open, however, and presently the stirrings died down.

"It's Fay," I said, close to the door.

A pause, and then the door was unlocked.

The room was neat, as it of course would have to be if Jack were to live there. Everything was clean; all objects were stacked in order, where he could find them, and of course he had carried this to the shopping newses: he had a pile of them, opened and flattened, stacked by the window. He saved everything, especially tinfoil and string. The bed had been turned back, to air it, and he seated himself on the exposed sheets. Placing his hands on his knees he gazed up at us.

He had, because of this crisis, reverted to wearing the clothes that, as a child, he had worn around the house. Here again was the pair of brown corduroy slacks that our mother had picked out for him back in the early 'forties. And he had on a blue cotton shirt—clean, but so repeatedly washed that it had turned white. The collar was almost nothing but threads and all the buttons were off it. He had fastened the front together with paperclips.

"You poop," I said.

Roaming around, Charley said, "Why do you save all this junk?" He had come upon a table covered with small washed rocks.

"I got those because of the possibility of radioactive ores," Jack said.

That meant, that, even with his job, he still took his long walks. Sure enough, in his closet, under a heap of sweaters that had fallen from their hangers, a cardboard box of worn-out Army surplus boots had been carefully tied up with twine and marked in Jack's crabbed handwriting. Every month or so, as a high school boy, he had worn out a pair of boots, those old-fashioned high topped boots with hooks on the tops.

To me this was more serious than the stealing, and I cleared a heap of *Life* magazines from a chair and seated myself, having decided to stay long enough for a real talk with him. Charley, naturally, remained standing to keep me aware that he wanted to go. Jack made him nervous. They did not know each other at all, but while Jack paid no attention to him, Charley always seemed to imagine that something to his disadvantage was going to happen. After he had met Jack for the first time he told me straightforwardly—Charley never could keep anything to himself—that my brother was the most screwed-up person he had ever met. When I asked him why he said that, he answered that he knew god damn well that Jack did not have to act the way he did; he acted like that because he wanted to. To me the distinction was meaningless, but Charley always set great store by such matters.

The long walks had begun in junior high school, back in the 'thirties, before World War Two. We were living on a street named Garibaldi Street, and during the Spanish Civil War because of the feeling against the Italians the street name was changed to Cervantes Street. Jack soon got the notion that all the street names were going to be changed and for a while he seemed to be living among the new names—all ancient writers and poets, no doubt—but when no other street names were changed that mood passed. Anyhow it had made the world situation seem real to him for a month or so, and we thought of that as an improvement; up to then he had seemed unable to imagine either the war as an actual event or, for that matter, the real world itself in which that war was taking place. He had never been able to distinguish between what he read and what he actually experienced. To him, vividness was the criterion, and those nauseating accounts in the Sunday supplements about lost continents and jungle goddesses had always been more compelling and convincing than the daily headlines.

"Are you still working?" Charley said from behind him.

"Of course he is," I said.

But Jack said, "I temporarily gave up my job at the tire place."

"Why?" I demanded.

"I'm too busy," Jack said.

"Doing what?"

He pointed to a pile of notebooks, filled, I could see, with pages of his writing. At one time he had spent his spare time writing letters to the newspapers, and here, once more, he was involved in some long-winded crank project, probably elaborating some schemes for irrigating the Sahara Desert. Picking up the first notebook, Charley thumbed through it and then tossed it down. "It's a diary," he said.

"No," Jack said, arising. His thin, knobbly face got that cold, superior look, that travesty of the hauteur of the scholar who faces the layman. "It's a scientific account of proven facts," he said.

I said, "How are you supporting yourself?" I knew instinctively how he was supporting himself; he was once again depending on handouts from home, from our parents—who, at this late point in their lives, couldn't afford to support anyone, scarcely themselves.

"I'm okay," Jack said. But of course he would say that; as soon as money came in he spent it, usually for flashy clothes, or else lost it or lent it or invested it in some madness he heard about in a pulp magazine: giant mushrooms, perhaps, or skin-healing salve to be peddled from door to door. At least the tire job, although bordering on the crooked, had been steady.

"How much money do you have?" I demanded, keeping after him.

"I'll see," he said. He opened a dresser drawer. From it he took a cigar box. He sat down on the bed, again on the sheets, and, placing the cigar box on his lap, opened it. The cigar box was empty except for a few dozen pennies and three nickels.

"Are you trying to get another job?" I asked.

"Yes," he said.

In the past he had held the dregs of jobs; he had helped

deliver washing machines for an appliance store; he had un-
crated vegetables for a grocery store; he had swept out a
drug store; once he had even given out tools at the Alameda
Naval Air Station. During the summer he had now and then
hired himself out as a fruit picker and gotten carried, by open
truck, miles out into the country; that was his favorite job
because he got to stuff himself with fruit. And in the fall he
invariably walked to the Heinz cannery near San Jose and
filled cans with Bartlett pears.

"You know what you are?" I said. "You're the most
ignorant, inept individual on the face of the globe. In my
entire life I've never seen anyone with such rubbish in their
head. How do you manage to stay alive at all? How the hell
did you get born into my family? There were never any nuts
before you."

"Take it easy," Charley said.

"It's true," I said to him. "Good god, he probably thinks
this is the bottom of the ocean and we're living in a castle
left over from Atlantis. What year is this?" I asked Jack.
"Why did you steal those ants?" I said. "Why? Tell me."
Grabbing him I started to shake him, as I had done as a
child, a very small child, when I had first heard him spout
the nutty rubbish that filled his mind. When in exasperation—and fear—I had realized that his brain simply had a
warp to it, that in distinguishing fact from fiction he chose
fiction, and between good sense and foolishness he preferred
foolishness. He could tell the difference—but he preferred
the rubbish; he stuffed it into himself with great systemiza-
tion. Like some creep in the Middle Ages memorizing all
that absurd St. Thomas Aquinas system about the universe,
that creaky, false structure that finally collapsed—except for
little intellectual swamp-like areas, such as in my brother's
brain.

Jack said, "I needed to perform an experiment."

"What kind?" I demanded.

"There are known cases of toads staying alive in suspended animation in mud for centuries," Jack said.

I saw, then, what his mind had conceived: that the ants, being dipped in chocolate, might be preserved, embalmed, and might be brought back to life.

"Get me out of here," I said to Charley.

Opening the door I left the room and went out into the hall. I was really shaking: I couldn't stand it. Charley followed after me and then said, in a low voice, "He obviously can't take care of himself."

"That's for sure," I said. I felt that if I didn't get into some place I could have a drink I'd go out of my mind. I wished to hell we hadn't driven down from Marin County; I hadn't seen Jack in months and at this point I would have been glad never to see him again.

"Look, Fay," Charley said. "He's your flesh and blood. You can't just leave him."

"I sure can," I said.

"He ought to be up in the country," Charley said. "In the healthy air. Where he could be with animals."

Several times Charley had tried to get my brother up to the farm area around Petaluma; he wanted to get him on to one of the big dairy farms as a milker. All Jack would have to do was open a wooden door, head a cow in, push the electric gadgets on to its teats, start the vacuum working, stop the vacuum at the right moment, unhook the cow, go on to the next cow. Over and over again—the pit, as far as creative jobs go, but something that Jack could handle. It paid about a dollar and a half an hour, and the milkers got their meals and a bunkhouse to sleep in. Why not? And he'd be up where there were animals—big dirty cows crapping and swilling, crapping and swilling.

"I'm not against it," I said. We knew a number of the ranchers; we could easily get him on as a novice milker.

"Let's drive him back up with us," Charley said.

• • •

To get him up to Marin County we had to pack all his valuables, his collection of facts, his rocks, his writing and drawings, and all his junky clothes and his elegant sweaters and slacks that he put on to dazzle the punks at Reno on weekends . . . everything got put in boxes and loaded in the rear of the Buick. When he had finished—Charley did the actual work; I sat in the front seat of the car reading, and Jack disappeared for an hour to say good-bye to some of his pals—the room was almost empty, except for the shopping news piles, which I refused to let him bring.

Just like his room when he was a child, I thought. During the war, when he had been, for a few months, in the Service, we had gone in and cleared out everything and destroyed it. Naturally, when he got back—given a medical discharge because of allergies . . . he had spells of asthma—he had a terrible fit, and then a long drawn-out depression. He pined for the missing junk. And after that, instead of growing up and getting involved in something more reasonable, he had moved out and gotten a room of his own and begun all over again.

As Charley drove off towards the freeway going north, with me beside him and Jack with all his boxes in the back, I dreaded what would become of my house with my loony brother taking up residence in it, even for a few days. However, we did have the utility room which we could turn over to him. And the children kept their part of the house a mess as it was. Surely he couldn't do more than draw on the walls with crayon, grind clay into the curtains and couch cushions, spill paint on the patio concrete, leave last month's socks stuffed in the sugar shaker, sneeze in his soup, fall down while carrying out the garbage and cut his eye half out of his head on a sardine can lid. A child is a filthy amoral animal, without instincts of sense, that fouls its own nest if given a chance. Offhand I can't think of any redeeming features in a child, except that as long as it is small it can be kicked around. Charley and I lived in the front part of the house, and, in the rear, the children gradually pushed their mess forward inch by inch . . . until we and Mrs. Medini would go in and clean it all up, throw everything away, burn all the rubbish, and the process would begin again. Jack would simply add to the chaos; he would bring nothing new, only more of the same.

Of course, being physically mature, he could not be handled as we handled the children, and this frightened me. In some respects I had been frightened of him for years; always I felt that I never could tell what he might do or say next, what unnatural ideas might spill out—that he regarded lamp posts as authority figures, perhaps, and policemen as objects made out of wire. I know that, as a child, he had had the notion that various people's heads were going to fall off; he had told us about that. And I know that he believed his high school geometry teacher to be a rooster wearing a suit . . . an idea that he may have gotten from seeing an old Charley Chaplin movie. Certainly that teacher had a rooster-like way of stalking around the front of the classroom.

Suppose, for instance, he ran amok and ate the neighbors' sheep. In farm country, sheep-killing is a major crime, and a thing that kills sheep is always shot on sight. Once a farm boy had gone around breaking the necks of all the new calves for miles around . . . no one had been able to figure out why, but no doubt it was the rural equivalent for the city child's breaking windows or knifing auto tires. Vandalism in the country, though, so often involves killing, because farm property is expressed in terms of flocks of ducks and chickens, herds of dairy cows, lambs and sheep, even goats. To the right of us the Lardners, an old couple, raised goats, and every so often they killed and ate a goat, having such things as goat stew and goat soup. To people in the country, a prize sheep or cow is to be guarded against any menace; they are used to poisoning rats and shooting foxes and coons and dogs and cats who infringe, and I could just see Jack being shot, some night, while crawling under a barbed wire fence with a bloody lamb in his jaws.

So now, driving back to Drake's Landing, I was beginning to pick up morbid anxiety fantasies . . . having them for Jack, possibly, as he seemed to be rather calm and undisturbed.

But that is one aspect of country life. I have sat in the living room, listening to Bach on the hi-fi, and looked through the windows and across the field to the ranch on the hillside beyond, and seen some ghastly act taking place: some old rancher in his manure-impregnated blue jeans, his boots and hat, out with an ax knocking in the skull of a dog found nosing around his chicken-coop. Nothing to do but keep on listening to Bach and trying to read *By Love Possessed*. And of course we killed our own ducks when it came time to eat them, and the dog killed gophers and squirrels daily. And at least once a week we found a half-eaten deer head by the front door, carried there by the dog from a garbage can somewhere in the neighborhood.

Of course there was simply the problem of having a horse's ass like Jack underfoot all the time. It was easy for Charley; he spent all day down at the plant, and in the evenings he shut himself up in his study and did paperwork, and on weekends he usually went outdoors and used the roto-tiller or the chain saw. Contemplating my brother lounging around the house all day made me realize how really cooped-up you are in the country; there's no place to go and nobody to visit—you just sit home all day reading or doing housework or taking care of the kids. When did I get out of the house? On Tuesday and Thursday nights I had my sculpture class down in San Rafael. On Wednesday afternoon I had the Bluebirds over, to bake bread or weave mats. On Monday morning I drove down to San Francisco to see Doctor Andrews, my analyst. On Friday morning I drove over to Petaluma to the Purity Market to shop. And on Tuesday afternoon I had my modern dance at the hall. And that was it, except for occasionally having dinner with the Fineburgs or the Meritans or driving out on weekends to the beach. The most exciting thing that had happened in years was the hay truck losing its load on the Petaluma road and smashing Alise Hatfield's station wagon with her and her three kids inside. And the four teenagers who got beaten up at Olema by the twenty loggers. This is the country. This isn't the city.

You're lucky, up where we live, to be able to get the daily San Francisco *Chronicle;* they don't deliver it—you have to drive over to the Mayfair Market and buy it off the stands.

As we drove through San Francisco, Jack perked up and began to comment on the buildings and traffic. The city obviously stimulated him, no doubt unwholesomely. He caught sight of the tiny, scrunched-together shops along Mission and he wanted to stop. Luckily we got out of the South of Market district and on to Van Ness. Charley gazed at the various imported cars in the dealers' display windows, but Jack did not seem interested. When we got on to the Golden Gate Bridge neither of them paid attention to the incredible view of the City and the Bay and the Marin hills; both of them had no capacity to enjoy anything esthetically—for Charley things had to be financially valuable, and for Jack they had to be—what? God knows. Weird facts, like the rain of frogs. Miracles and the like. This spectacular sight was wasted on both of them, but I kept my eyes on the view as long as possible, until finally we were out of the hills, past the forts, and back among the rubbishy little suburban towns, Mill Valley, San Rafael—the pit, as far as I'm concerned. The really all-time low, with the dirt and smog, and always the County machinery tearing up the roads for a new freeway.

At a slow rate we drove through Ross and San Anselmo, fighting the commute traffic. And then, past Fairfax, we left the stores and apartments and got out on that stretch in the first pasture land, the first canyons. All at once there were cows instead of gas stations.

"How does it look to you?" Charley asked my brother.

Jack said, "It's deserted."

With bitterness, I said, "Well, who'd want to live out here with the cows."

"A cow has four stomachs," Jack said.

White's Hill impressed him, with its terrible steep and winding grade, and then, on the far side, the San Geronimo Valley made the three of us feel pleased. Charley got the Buick up to eighty-five on the straightaway, and the warm mid-day wind, the fresh-smelling country wind, blew in around us and cleaned the car of the smell of moldy paper and old laundry. The fields on both sides of us had turned brown from the sun and lack of water, but around the clusters of live oak trees, mixed in with the granite boulders, we saw grass and wild flowers.

We would have liked to have lived down here, closer to San Francisco, but land cost too much and the traffic, in summer, had a depressing element to it, the resort people heading for Lagunitas and the cabins there and the campers on their way to Samuel Taylor Park. Now we passed through Lagunitas with its one general store, and then the road curved, suddenly as always, forcing Charley to slow so radically that the nose of the Buick sank down and all four tires squealed. The warm dry sunlight disappeared and we were down deep in the redwoods, sniffing the stream, the wet needles, the cold, dark places where ferns grew in July.

Rousing himself, Jack said, "Hey, didn't we go picnicking here once?" He craned his neck at the sight of the tables and barbecue pits.

"No," I said. "That was Muir Woods. You were nine."

After we had reached the hills overlooking Olema and Tomales Bay, Jack began to recognize that he had passed entirely out of the town area and had entered the country.

He noticed the shabby, peeling old wooden windmills, the boarded-up abandoned buildings, the chickens scratching in driveways, and that indubitable sign of the country: the butane tanks mounted one behind each house. There, too, was the sign to the right of the road just before reaching the Inverness Wye: *so-and-so well driller.*

As we drove by Paper Mill Creek he saw the fishermen down in the water and he saw, for the first time in his life, a flashing white egret out on the marshes, fishing.

"You see blue heron up here," I said. "And once we saw a flock of wild swan. Eighteen of them, on an inlet near Drake's Estero."

After we had passed through Drake's Landing and had started up the narrow blacktop road, Saw Mill Road, to our place, Jack said, "It's sure quiet up here."

"Yes," Charley said. "At night you'll hear the cows bellowing."

"They sound like dinosaurs stuck in the swamp," I said.

Perched on the telephone wires, at the last bend of the road, was a falcon. I told Jack how that particular falcon spent his time standing on the wire, year in year out, catching frogs and grasshoppers. Sometimes he looked sleek, but other times his feathers had a molting, disreputable look. And not far from us the Hallinans lost goldfish from their outdoor pond to a kingfisher who stationed himself in the cypress tree nearby.

Not so many years ago elk and bear had roamed around the hills overlooking Tomales Bay, and the winter before, Charley claimed to have spotted a huge black leg at the edge of his headlights; something had gone off into the woods, and if it wasn't a bear it was a man in a bear suit. But I did not discuss this with Jack. There was no point in providing him with the local myths, because he would soon enough be concocting myths of his own; and it would not be bears or elk that meandered down into the vegetable garden after dark and ate the rhubarb—it would be Martians whose flying saucers had landed in the Inverness canyons. Now it occurred to me to remember the feverish flying saucer activity at Inverness Park; a rabid group already existed, that would no doubt draw Jack into their midst and give him the benefit of their twice-weekly explorations into hypnosis, reincarnation, Zen Buddhism, ESP, and of course UFOs.

# 5

The boy and girl, in rust-colored turtle-necked wool sweaters and jeans, rested their bikes against the pharmacy building and leaned against each other. The girl lifted a finger and brushed a speck from the boy's eye. She and the boy conferred at their leisure. Her face, in profile, with its ringlets of chestnut hair, was like the profile on an earlier coin, possibly a coin from the 'twenties or the turn of the century . . . an archaic profile, the face of allegory: mild, introspective, impersonal, gentle. The boy's hair had been cut to the shape of his head, a black cap. Both he and the girl were slender. He stood slightly taller.

Beside him, Fay watched through the windshield of the car as the boy and girl moved away together. "I have to know them," she said. "I think I'll get out and go ask them to come up to the house and have a martini." She started to open the car door. "Aren't they beautiful?" she said. "Like something out of Nietzsche." Her face had become remorseless; she would not let them get away, and he saw her keeping her eyes on them, not losing sight of them. She had them in view; she had located them. "You stay here," she said, stepping on to the ground and starting to close the car door after her; her purse, from its leather strap, swung against the car. As she started off her prescription-ground sunglasses fell from her arms, to the gravel parking lot. With haste she snatched them back up, hardly noticing if the lenses remained intact. So concerned was she with making contact with the boy and girl that she began to lope. And yet she retained her grace, the poise of her lean legs. She ran after them with consciousness of herself; she kept in mind what impression her appearance would make on them and on the other people who might be watching.

Leaning out of the car, he called after her, "Wait."

Fay paused questioningly, with impatience.

"Come back," he said in a false tone of voice, making it sound as if she were going in to shop and he had remembered some item.

Her head shook, gesturing no.

"Come on," he repeated, this time stepping out.

Without moving toward him or any farther away, she waited as he approached her. "God damn you, you mother-fucker," she said, as he got up to her. "They're going to get on their god damn bikes and pedal away."

"Let them," he said. "We don't know them." Her determined interest in them, the extent of the fascination that showed on her face, had made him suspicious. "What do you care about them?" he demanded. "They're just kids— no more than eighteen at the most. Probably up for a swim in the bay."

"I wonder if they're brother and sister," Fay said. "Or if they're married and on their honeymoon. They can't live around here. They must be just visiting. I wonder who would know them. Did you see which way they came from? From which end of town?" She watched the boy and girl pedal off up the hill of Highway One. "Maybe they're on a bicycle tour of the United States," she said, shading her eyes to see.

Having lost them, she got back into the car with him. As they drove home she conjectured.

"I can ask Pete the Postmaster," she said. "He'd know them if anybody does. Or Florence Rhodes."

"God damn you," he said, "what do you want to meet them for? You intend to screw them? Which? Both?"

"They're so pretty," Fay said. "They're like something that dropped out of the sky; I have to know them or perish." She spoke in a flat, harsh voice, with no sentimentality. "The next time I see them I'm going up to them and tell them point blank that I can't stand not to know two such fascinating people, and who the hell are they and why."

"I guess you're pretty lonely up here," he said presently, feeling indignation and melancholy. "Living up in the country where there's nothing to do and nobody worth knowing."

"I just don't intend to overlook a chance to meet somebody," Fay said. "Would you? If you were me? You know I like to have people over at dinnertime—otherwise it's nothing but child-feeding and dishwashing and mat-wiping and garbage-disposing."

He said, "You crave society."

At that, his wife laughed. "I crave it like crazy. I'm almost out of my mind for it. That's why I spend most of my time in the garden. That's why I always go running around in blue jeans."

"You Marin County society matrons," he said, half joking, half with wrath. "Sipping coffee and gossiping."

"Is that how you see me?"

"Ex-college queen," he said. "Ex-sorority girl marries well-to-do man, moves to Marin County, starts modern dance group." He saw, to their right, the white clapboard three-story hall in which the dance group met. "Culture to the farmers and milkers," he said.

"Kiss my ass," Fay said. And after that neither of them said anything; they stared ahead, ignoring each other until he had entered the driveway and was parking.

"One of the girls left the door open," Fay said in a low voice as she stepped from the car. The front door of the house stood open, and the collie's tail could be seen. Without waiting for him she walked away and into the house, leaving him by himself.

It bothers me, he thought. Her reaction to those two young people. Because—why? Shows something is lacking. She doesn't get something she should get.

True, he thought. Neither of us do. We both crave it . . . he had first noticed the boy and girl himself, had called his wife's attention to them. The soft fluffy sweaters. Warm colors. The pure skin, such freshness. What had they conversed about in such low tones? The girl stroking the boy's face, soothing and cherishing him . . . deep in their combined world, while standing before the Tomales Bay Pharmacy, in the middle of Saturday afternoon, with the sun shining down. And neither of them perspiring . . .

Barely touched by us, he thought. Not even aware. We're shadows drifting around, going nowhere.


The next day, while he was in the post office buying stamps, he saw the boy and girl again. This time he had driven down alone, leaving Fay home. He saw them, with their bikes, at the corner, apparently trying to decide on something; they had stopped on the curb.

An impulse came to him to stroll out of the post office and up to them. Lost? he would ask. Trying to find some house in particular? No street numbers; too small a town.

But he did not. He remained in the post office. And presently they pushed their bikes from the curb, into the street, and wheeled off out of sight.

At that he felt empty.

Too bad, he thought. Opportunity missed. If Fay had been here, out the door she would have gone. That's the difference

between us; I would think of it, she'd do it. Be doing it while
I was trying to figure out how to do it. Just start doing it—
she wouldn't think.

That's what I admire about her, he thought. Where she's
superior to me. Now, that time . . . when I met her. I would
just have stood there forever, staring at her, wishing I knew
her. But she started talking to me, asked about the car.
Without hesitation.

It occurred to him that if Fay hadn't started up a conversation with him that day in the grocery store, back in 1951,
they never would have met. They wouldn't be married now;
there would be no Bonnie and Elsie; no house; he wouldn't
even be living in Marin County. She makes life over, he
realized. She controls life, whereas I just sit on my can and
let it happen to me.

God, he thought. And she's certainly got firm control of
me; didn't she engineer this whole business? Get me, get the
house?

All the money I earn, he thought, goes into maintaining
that damn house and everything in it. It drains, it absorbs.
Devours me and everything I make. And who gets the benefit
from it? Not me.

Like the time she got rid of my cat. He had found the cat
hiding in a supply shed down at the plant, and for almost a
year he had fed it in the office, buying cat food for it and
giving it scraps brought back to the office from his lunch. It
had been a large fuzzy gray and white cat, a male, and in
the year it had become devoted to him, tagging around after
him, which amused both him and his employees. It never
paid attention to anyone else. One day Fay had stopped by
the office for something and had seen the cat, had noticed
its devotion to him.

"Why don't you bring it home?" she asked, scrutinizing it
as it made itself comfortable on his desk.

He answered, "It keeps me company here. When I'm
doing paperwork at night."

"Does it have a name?" She tried to stroke it, but the cat moved away from her.

"I call it Porky," he said.

"Why?"

"Because it eats everything anybody gives it," he said, feeling embarrassed, as if caught in an immodest or unmasculine thing.

"The girls would love it," Fay said. "You know how they've been wanting a cat. Bing is too big for them, and that guinea pig they got at the museum did nothing but crap all the time and hide."

"It would run away," he said. "The dog would scare it."

"No," she said firmly. "Bring it home. We'll keep it inside. I'll feed it; it'll be much happier there. You know you're only down here at night once a week at the most—look, it'll be in a warm house, which cats love, and it'll have all the bones and scraps from three meals—" Petting the cat, she added, "And I want a cat, too."

In the end she persuaded him. And yet, watching her try to stroke the cat, he felt convinced that she did not really want the cat around the house; she was actually jealous of it because he liked it and wanted to keep it away from her, down at the plant. He kept the cat separate from his life with her, and to Fay that was intolerable; she strove to draw the cat in as part of her world, dependent on her. In his mind he had a quick image of Fay weaning the cat away from him, pampering it, overfeeding it, getting it to sleep on her lap— not because she loved it but because it was important to her to think of it as belonging to her.

That night he brought the cat home in a box. The two girls were delighted and set out milk and a can of Norwegian sardines for it. The cat stayed in during the night, sleeping on the couch, apparently contented. The dog was kept locked up in a bathroom, and neither animal came in contact with the other. For a day or so Fay fed and cared for the cat, and then one night, when he got home, he found the front door open.

With apprehension he tracked down his wife. He found her out on the patio, knitting. "Why's the door open?" he demanded. "You know we're keeping the cat in for another couple of days."

"He wanted out," Fay said, her expression lost behind her huge glasses. "He cried, and the girls wanted to let him out, so we did. He's around somewhere, probably down in the cypress trees chasing squirrels."

For several hours he roamed around with a flashlight, calling the cat, trying to catch sight of it. He saw no sign of it. The cat had gone off. Fay did not seem worried; she served dinner calmly. The two girls never mentioned the cat. Their minds were on a party that some boy had invited them to on Sunday morning. With despair and fury he choked down his dinner and then arose to resume searching.

"Don't worry," Fay said, as she ate her dessert. "He's a full-grown cat and nothing'll happen to him. He'll turn up in the morning, if not here then back at the plant."

In a frenzy, he said, "You think it can hike twenty-five miles across to Petaluma?"

"Cats travel thousands of miles," Fay said.

They never saw the cat again. He put an ad in the Baywood *Press,* but no one reported having seen it. Every evening for over a week he drove slowly around the area, calling the cat and searching for it.

And all the time he had the deep, intuitive sense that she had done it on purpose. Got the cat home so that she could let it go. Had deliberately gotten rid of it because of her jealousy of it.

One evening, with wariness, he said to Fay, "You don't seem especially disturbed."

"By what?" she said, glancing up from her pottery. On the big dining room table she was busy shaping bowls from clay. She wore her blue smock, shorts and sandals, and she looked quite pretty. Resting on the edge of the table, mostly ash now, her cigarette burned away.

"By the cat disappearing," he said.

"The girls were quite upset," she said. "But I told them that a cat is more adept at taking care of itself than any other kind of pet that gets out and goes off. And up here there's gophers and rabbits—" Tossing her hair back she finished, "It probably caught the scent of game, and now it's gone wild, having a hell of a good time out there in the woods. They say a lot of cats brought up here do that, get the scent and go out after it."

He said with care, "You didn't mention that when you got me to bring it here."

To that she did not bother to reply. Her strong, effective fingers shaped the clay; he watched and noticed how much pressure she was capable of exerting on the material. The muscles along her arms rose and changed shape; the tendons stood out.

"Anyhow," Fay said at last, after he had said nothing but still remained, "you were too emotionally involved with it. It's not healthy to be that involved with an animal."

"Then you did get rid of it on purpose!" he said loudly.

"No I didn't. I'm just commenting. Maybe it's better that it ran off. This proves you were too deeply involved, or you wouldn't be carrying on so. My god, it was just a cat. You've got a wife and two children and you're carrying on about a cat." The sharp contempt in her voice made him shiver. It was her most effective tone, full of the weight of authority; it recalled to him his teachers in school, his mother, the whole pack of them.

Unable to carry it any further he turned and walked off, to pick up the evening paper.

There in the post office, recalling his lost cat, he felt a terrible loneliness and sense of deprivation. After buying his stamps he set off, back to his parked car, recognizing that

the failure on his part to make contact with the boy and girl
had linked itself in his mind with the loss of the cat. The
breakdown of relationships between living things . . . the
gulf between him and other living things. Why? he asked
himself as he got into the car.

Fuck it all, he thought with bitterness.

He drove reflectively, doing a bad job of getting the car
from the lot and on to the street. And then, just past the
Mayfair Market, he saw propped up against the loading dock
two racing bikes. Their bikes—they had gone into the Mayfair Market. Without reflection he brought the car to the
curb, leaped out, and hurried across the street and up on to
the sidewalk and through the open door and into the dark,
cool old wooden market building, among the vegetables and
displays of wine bottles and magazine racks.

Toward the back of the store the boy and girl lingered together at the shelf of canned vegetables. He hurried toward
them; he had to approach them, or have the weight of consci-
ence on him for months. Fay would never forgive him—im-
pelled toward them, he arrived to confront them as they filled
a wire basket with cans and packages and a loaf of bread.

"Hey," he said, his ears red and burning. Astonished in
a controlled manner, they turned toward him. "Listen," he
said, plucking at his belt buckle and staring down, then back
up at them. "My wife and I noticed you yesterday—or the
other day, I mean. We live up here, at Drake's Landing,
about five miles down the road around Paper Mill Creek,
past Inverness Park. My wife's up at the house dying for
company." He added, "We've got a horse if you like to ride.
How about dropping by and chewing the fat? Could you be
talked into staying for dinner?"

Wordlessly, the boy and girl exchanged glances. As he
stood there, they communicated silently between them and
came to a conclusion.

"We just recently moved in up here," the girl said in a
soft, low voice.

"You're newlyweds?" Charley asked.

They both nodded. Both of them seemed shy and reserved, but glad that he had approached them.

"It's hard to get to know people around here," he said to them, feeling immensely pleased with himself for having made the contact with them; he had done it, been successful. Fay would be filled with respect. "You have a car?" he said. "Oh that's right—you're on bikes. We noticed the bikes." He heard himself chuckle. "Well, we can toss them in the back of the car."

The boy and girl finished their shopping with much exacting deliberation. Charley stood off self-consciously to one side, smoking a cigarette and glancing around him.

Presently the three of them were walking toward the bikes, and then the car.

The boy's name was Nat Anteil. His wife's was Gwen. During the morning Nat worked for a small, modern real estate firm in Mill Valley and in the afternoon he drove back up here to Point Reyes and spent his time studying; he was in his second year of a college extension course mailed out by the University of Chicago. When he got finished, he explained he would have a BA in history.

"What are you going to do with that?" Charley asked.

With some shyness, Nat said, "Maybe go on and teach."

Gwen said, "It's more for his own edification, not to make money from. We both want to be aware of what's happening in the world."

"I'm in the iron business," Charley said. "But don't let that fool you. My wife's the one who brought culture to this area; she got all the cultural affairs going, here."

"I see," Gwen said, nodding.

"Such as the modern dance group," Charley said. "And I'm a member of the Inverness Yacht Club. We own a hi-fi—mounted right in the wall. We had the house built ourselves; we got our own architect. God, it set me back almost forty thousand dollars. Wait'll you see it; it's only four years old. We've got ten acres." As they drove he told them all about the sheep and the collie, pouring out his words faster and faster, unable to stop.

The Anteils listened raptly.

"We can play badminton out back," Charley said, as they came within sight of the cypress trees. "Wait'll you see my wife. She's the best god damn good-looking woman up here. They're all a bunch of dogs compared to her. Why hell, even after having two kids she's still a size twelve." That sounded right to him; or was it a size sixteen? "She really keeps her figure," he said, as he turned from the road into the driveway.

"What lovely big trees," Gwen said, staring out at the cypress. "Do they belong to you?" To her husband she said excitedly, "Nat—look at that collie. It's blue."

"That dog's worth five hundred bucks," Charley said, delighted at their response. He saw them straining to see the house, making out the sight of the horse as it cropped grass out in the field. "Come on," he said, opening the door for them. "She'll sure be pleased to see you." As the three of them walked toward the house he explained, in disjointed phrases, how Fay had felt about them and how badly they both had wanted to meet them.

# 6

When I saw Charley coming up the path from the car with those two delightful apparitions I could hardly believe my eyes. It was the greatest present he could have given me, and I completely adored him for it. Putting down my book I ran into my bedroom and took a look at myself in the mirror. Why at this time had that little queer down in Fairfax chosen to cut my hair on one side shorter than on the other? From my closet I grabbed out my blue-striped shirt and began buttoning it over my halter and tucking it into my shorts.

"Honey!" Charley called from the living room. "Hey, look who I talked into coming home with me!"

At the mirror I put on lipstick, blotted it, brushed my hair in back, put away my dark glasses which I had worn into the house from outside, and then I hurried into the living room.

There they stood, shyly, peeking around at the bookcases and the record shelves, like a pair of children in a historic shrine—the way I had felt when we visited the mission over in Sonoma and I found myself standing in the old chapel, with the straw sticking out of the adobe where it had broken away. I was glad that Mrs. Mendini had seen fit to do a good job scrubbing the floor and dusting; at least the house looked good, even if I was a trifle messy.

I smiled at them and they smiled back. This is historic, I thought. Like Lewis and Clarke meeting. Or Gilbert and Sullivan. "Hi," I said to them.

The girl said, "What a lovely house."

"Thank you," I said. Going toward the bar I said, "What would you like to drink?" I opened the liquor cabinet and got out the bottle of gin and vermouth. Feeling nervous— for some reason—I found myself spilling the gin as I poured it into the mixer. "I'm Fay Hume," I said. "What are your names? Are you married or are you brother and sister? I can't wait to find out; I have to know."

"This is my wife Gwen," the boy said. "My name is Nathan Anteil." They came a few steps into the kitchen and stood self-consciously, watching me fix martinis, as if they didn't want to drink but did not know how to stop me. So I went on fixing the drinks. Married, I thought.

"You look like my brother," I said to the boy. And with surprise I thought, He doesn't look like Jack at all, not a bit. Jack is horrible-looking and this boy is stunning; what's the matter with me? "Don't you think he could be my brother?" I said to Charley.

"Well," Charley said, "you're both on the lanky side." He, too, seemed ill-at-ease, but obviously pleased at having gotten them to come along with them. "I'll have some of that Danish beer," he said. To the Anteils, he said, "How about some imported dark beer?" Passing me, he opened the refrigerator door. "Try some," he said, getting the opener.

Presently we were seated in the living room, Charley and I on chairs, the Anteils on the couch. Gwen and I drank martinis; they drank beer.

"Nat's in the real estate game," Charley said.

At that, the boy got a cross expression on his face. Both he and his wife seemed to fluff up. "That's somewhat misleading," Gwen said. "Nat is getting his degree in history," she explained to me. "He just works down there so we can pay the bills."

"There's nothing wrong with real estate," Charley said with uneasiness, apparently realizing that he had offended them.

"History," I said, dazzled by our good fortune. "There's a retired history professor from the University of California living up here—he raises peaches. We'll have to introduce you to him. He and I play chess once a month. And there's an archaeologist across the bay in Point Reyes Station. Where do you live?"

"In Point Reyes," the boy said. "We're renting a little house there, on the hill above the creamery."

"And down in Olema," Charley put in, "there's a guy who used to write articles for *Harper's*. And an old guy who still does illustrations for the *Saturday Evening Post*—he's living in what used to be the Olema city hall. Picked it up for four thousand dollars."

Talking to the Anteils, I found that they came from Berkeley. The girl's parents owned a summer cabin in Inverness, and the two of them—Nat and she—had come up and stayed in the area, and had gotten to like it, naturally, as anyone does who sees it. They knew a few people in the area, mostly in Inverness, and they knew the public beaches and the park and what birds they could expect to see. But they hadn't been to any of the private beaches; they didn't know any of the big ranchers and had never even heard of Bear Valley Ranch.

"Good god," I said. "Well, we'll have to take you there. The road's barred by three padlocked gates but I can get the key; we know them and they let us drive across the ridge to their beach. It's so big it's got something like six thousand wild deer on it."

"It's a huge place," Charley said.

We talked for a while about the area, and then I told Nat about a paper I had written in college about the Roman general Stilicho.

"Oh yes," Nat said, nodding. "That's an interesting period."

We discussed Rome, he and I. Gwen wandered around the living room. I saw, now, after being closer to them for a time, that a difference between them existed, one that I hadn't noticed originally. At the start, spying them from a distance I had tended to lump them together in my mind, to find them equally attractive and desirable. But now I saw that there was with Gwen an absent-mindedness, almost a vapidness. She lacked the acuteness of her husband. And it seemed to me that much of the resemblance between them was not accidental; the girl had deliberately styled her manner of dress so that it matched his, and I saw, too, that the ideas—the intellectual material—common to the two of them originated in him. In discussions, Gwen took little or no part. She retired, like many wives.

It seemed to me that Nat relished talking to a woman who could hold her own with him on his own subject. As we talked, he became more stern; his forehead wrinkled, and his voice dropped to a low, determined pitch. Weighing his words carefully he gave me a long theory of his on the economic situation in Rome during the reign of Theodoric. I found it fascinating, but toward the end my attention began to wander.

During a pause, while he tried to recall the name of a particular Roman administrative district, I couldn't refrain from bursting in with, "You know, you're so young."

At this, his eyes opened wide and he stared at me. "Why do you say that?" he said slowly.

I said, "Well, you take all this so seriously."

Quite brusquely he said, "It's my field."

"Yes, I know," I said. "But you're so intense. How old

are you? Come on, tell me. You seem so much younger than us."

With apparent difficulty, Nat said, "I'm twenty-eight."

That surprised me. "Good god," I said, "We thought you two were only eighteen or nineteen. Another generation." His face, at that, got even darker. "It's hard to believe you're really twenty-eight," I said. "I'm thirty-one," I said. "I'm only three years older than you, but my god, it's another generation."

We talked some more about the area, and then the Anteils arose and said that they had to get back. I felt tired, now, I was sorry they had to leave, but at the same time the meeting between us and them had, in the final analysis, disappointed me. Nothing of any importance had come out of it, although god knows what I had expected. We made a tentative date to get together for dinner one evening toward the end of the week, and then I sent Charley off to drive them home.

After the three of them left the house I went into the bathroom and took a couple of Anacin. My head hurt and I decided that probably it was eyestrain. But anyhow I returned to the living room and got down from the bookshelf a book by Robert Graves that dealt with the Roman period; going outdoors on the patio I made myself comfortable on the chaise longue and began to reread the book—it had been several years since I had read anything on the Roman period, and I felt that if I was going to discuss it with Nat I should bone up on it.

How odd it was . . . we had wanted so badly to meet the Anteils; we had been drawn to them so intensely, and now that it had come about—not boredom, surely, but—not what we had expected, somehow. And yet I felt terribly tense. My entire body, all my muscles, were drawn up and tense. Leaving my book I went to the kitchen and poured myself another martini. Here I was, keyed-up and feeling irritable. The sun hurt my eyes, and that always indicated that I was getting into a foul mood. Or perhaps I was pregnant again. My legs certainly ached; all those big thigh muscles hurt, as if I had, for the last hour or so, been carrying an enormous load.

Lying down on the concrete, outdoors on the patio, I began doing a few exercises. Certainly I could still get my legs up as well as ever. My stomach felt somewhat bloated, though. So I got the trowel and began weeding in the garden, a good exercise, that squatting and weeding; the best in the world.

A day or so later, during the afternoon, I got a phone call from Mary Woulden about the Bluebird's peanut sale fund. During our discussion she mentioned that the Anteils had told about meeting Charley and me.

"Oh my god," I said, "do you know them? Why didn't you say so? We turned heaven and earth over to try to meet them—when we first laid eyes on them we swore we'd get to know them and invite them up to the house, and we finally just had to walk up to them cold and introduce ourselves and invite them up."

"They're sweet people," Mary said. "They've been coming up to Inverness for years, but now they're renting a house all year round. They were just summer people; that's why you never saw them. You know how summer people are; they spend all their time at McClure's Beach." And then she gave it to me right between the eyes. I had no warning whatsoever. "Apparently you didn't make too much of a hit with him," Mary said.

"Why?" I said, on my guard and apprehensive. I started, at once, to have hot and cold flashes. "They seemed to be enjoying themselves—we put ourselves out trying to make them comfortable. And good god, we practically picked them up off the street."

"She likes you," Mary said. "And I think he does too. What he said was, if I can remember it exactly . . . something about you striking him as being a bossy person." She added, "Actually he came out and said he didn't particularly care for you."

"Well, we argued about history," I said, feeling the back of my neck boil with heat. "Possibly he resents the idea of a woman discussing his pet subject with him."

We talked about various trifles, and then I rang off. As soon as the connection was broken I dialed the operator and got the Anteils' number. I dialed them, seated on the bed and seeing my hands shaking. In fact I was trembling all over with indignation and a variety of other emotions that I did not have time to decipher.

The boy himself answered. "Hello."

"Listen," I said, trying to keep my voice calm. It seems to me that I did keep it calm too. "Maybe I just don't understand the masculine mind, but in my book anybody who talks about another person behind his back but doesn't have the integrity to come out to their face and say what he thinks—" I had trouble winding up what I had to say. "Didn't we treat you hospitably?" I demanded, and at that point my voice broke.

"Who is this?" Anteil said.

"This is Fay Hume."

After a pause, Anteil said, "Evidently some inadvertent remarks made in conversation got carried back to you."

"Yes," I said, breathing with difficulty and trying to keep the racket from being picked up by the phone.

"Mrs. Hume," he said in a slow, somber voice, "I'm sorry you're so upset. Let me assure you that it's needless."

"It's upsetting," I said, "to have somebody go through the motions of pretending to enjoy your hospitality, and talk about you. Do you object if I try to talk to you in your terms? I took a history minor; I like to discuss Rome. I may not be competent to discuss it, but—"

"This is difficult to discuss over the phone," Anteil broke in.

"Well, what do you propose?" I said. "Frankly, I'm not particularly interested in discussing it with you; I just wanted to acquaint you with my feelings." At that point I hung up.

Almost at once I felt, acutely, that I was a hysterical nut. They shouldn't trust you with the phone, I said to myself. Getting up from the bed I paced around the bedroom. Now it'll get all over town, I realized. Fay Hume calls up some people in Point Reyes and raves like a drunk. That's what they'll say: I was drunk. Sheriff Chisholm will be by to take me away. Maybe I ought to phone him myself and eliminate the middleman.

I did not know what to do, but I had the keen insight that I had left it at a bad point, that someone had to do something. And here I was, the hostess, the woman of this quite outstanding house, placing a vast emphasis on providing people with a meal and conversation they would remember . . . a few incidents like this and I could forget considering myself hostess to anybody. What a faux pas. You're just a child, a two-year-old, I told myself. Worse than Elsie or Bonnie. Even the dog has more self-control, more diplomacy.

That night Gwen Anteil appeared at the front door. Charley and I were doing the dishes; the children had gone off to watch tv. "I'm sorry to bother you," Gwen said in her sweet but somewhat hollow fashion. "May I come in for a moment?" Her bike was propped at the edge of the porch, and she had on capri pants and a sweatshirt. Her hair was tied back and her face was flushed, probably from the bike-riding.

"Come in," Charley said. I hadn't told him about either Mary's call or mine to Anteil, so for a moment I floundered; I knew at once that Gwen's visit had to do with the business between me and her husband, and I knew this was going to be difficult. I had to get rid of Charley, so I said,

"Honey, there's something we have to discuss that doesn't concern you." Putting my hand on his shoulder I propelled him away, in the direction of his study. "You leave us alone for a while. Okay?" And before he realized what had happened, I had gotten him into his study and was shutting the door after him.

Sullenly, he said, "You god damn women and your women's subjects." But already he had started switching on his desk lamp. "Did she come alone?" he said. "If Nat shows up, send him on in." He was starting to complain some more, but I closed the door after him, and, turning to Gwen, forgot about him.

"I owe your husband an apology," I said to her.

Gwen said, "That's what I'm here about. Nat is terribly disturbed that something he said could cause you distress. You both were so nice to us the other day when we were over." She made no move to sit down but stood by the door, like a school child, reciting her set piece. "I didn't tell him I was coming over to patch it up," she said. "It's just one of those things that a third party can blow up if they want all out of proportion. Nat likes both you and your husband, and he's desperately concerned to get this out of the way." She added, "I told him I was going to visit the McRaes. I think you know them."

"Yes," I said absentmindedly. I was trying to figure out if he had sent her, or if this was her idea. If it was her idea, then he might not care so much about making amends; it might merely seem to her that in such a rural area, with so few families, no one could afford a social hiatus of this sort, especially a new couple that had just moved in and was trying to get established and accepted by the people already here. After all, their whole social life depended on healing up a rift of this sort; I could afford to drop them, but could they afford to drop the Humes? Thoughts of that kind certainly had entered this girl's mind; I could see it written all over her rather fatuous face. "I'm quite happy to stay on good terms with your husband," I said. "I think he's headstrong and too wrapped up in himself and what he thinks, but you're both marvelous people. It was just a misunderstanding." I smiled at her.

But instead of smiling back, Gwen said, "I think you should be careful not to lord it over people just because you have a big house." And without another word she stalked out of the house, got on her bike, put on her headlight, and rode off.

Good god.

I stayed in the doorway, staring after her, wondering who was crazy, she or I. Then I ran, got my purse, ran down to the Buick, hopped in, started up the motor, and drove after her. Sure enough, there she was, pedaling along the road for all she was worth. Pulling up beside her and going at the same speed as she, I leaned out and called,

"What in god's name did I do now?"

Saying nothing, merely pedaling, she kept on.

"Look," I said. "This is a small town and we all have to be on good terms. You'll find it's not like the city; you can't be so choosy. Now what did I say? I don't get it."

After a time Gwen said, "Just go back to your big house."

"You know you're welcome in my house," I said.

"Sure," she said.

"You are," I said. "Honest to god you are. What do I have to do to prove it to you? Do I have to get down on my knees and beg you to come back? Okay, if I have to I will. I beg you to come back and talk like an adult and stop acting like a child. What's the matter with you two, are you adults, a married couple, or are you a pair of children?" Now I had raised my voice. "This whole thing is too much for me," I called to her. "Why can't we be friends? I'm just crazy about you and your husband. How did all this dissension get started?"

After a long time Gwen said, "Well, maybe we're both too sensitive about looking so young."

"God!" I said. "I wish I looked as young as you. I wish to heaven I looked so young. You're both adorable; you're like something from heaven. We never saw such a beautiful couple before. I'd like to hug both of you—I wish I could adopt you or something. Please come back. Look," I said, driving as close to her bike as possible. "Let's go pick up your husband, and I'll drive you over to the Western and we'll have a seafood dinner. Have you had dinner? Or we'll go to the Drake's Arms and have dinner there. Please. Let me take you out to dinner. As a favor to me." I got my most wheedling tone.

Finally, she weakened. "You don't have to take us out to dinner."

"Have you ever been to the Drake's Arms? We'll play darts—I tell you what: I'll challenge both of you, a dollar a game. I can beat anybody except Oko himself."

In the end she gave in. I loaded her bike into the back of the car and her into the front seat beside me—she was steaming with perspiration from the exertion of biking—and picked up speed. Now I felt happy, really happy, for the first time in months. I felt I had genuinely accomplished something, breaking down the barriers and getting to these fine, handsome people who were so shy, so sensitive, so easily hurt. In my mind I swore an oath that I'd be more careful and not insult them in my usual big-footed way. Now that I had humbled—in fact humiliated—myself to recapture their friendliness, I did not want to throw it away.

And you know how you are, Fay, I said to myself. You know how your witless tongue gets you into trouble; you always say anything that comes into your mind, without any thought for the consequences.

"When you get to know me better," I told her, "you'll learn not to pay any attention to me. I'm a crude, vulgar person. I remember one day in the public library I said the word 'fuck' in front of a librarian. I could have died. I could have sunk through the floor. I never went back; I never could look at her again."

Gwen laughed slightly, I thought a little uneasily.

"I pick up language like that from Charley," I explained, and then I described his factory to her, how many men he employed, what he netted in a year. She seemed to be interested, to some extent at least.

# 7

The ride up to their house in Marin County made me carsick, due to the sharp turns through Samuel P. Taylor Park. On each turn I thought Charley was going to leave the road. Both he and Fay knew the road so well that they knew exactly how far up they could push the gas pedal on each turn. One mile an hour more and the car would have gone off into the creek. At one time he hit sixty miles an hour. Most drivers would have had to take it at twenty-five, especially those weekend drivers who putter along. And Charley used the whole road, not just his lane; he went all the way over to the shoulder on the far side. He seemed to know whether a car was coming or not, even though I could see nothing but trees. Fay did not show any signs of nervousness, beside him in the front seat; in fact she seemed to be half asleep.

But around me all my goods slid and rocked. What an odd sensation it was, to have them with me in motion, not back at the room. For all intents and purposes I had given up my room; now I was going to live with my sister and her husband, at their house—I had no actual place of my own. It was like going back to childhood, and I felt depressed and uncomfortable. However, the scenery cheered me up. And I knew, from their description, what sort of a house it was; I knew that it was very swanky, with all the latest gadgets.

To keep my spirits up I thought of the animals. At one time during high school I had worked for a veterinarian, sweeping out, cleaning the cages, helping people bring their pets in from their cars, feeding the animals boarded there, getting rid of dead animals. I had enjoyed being around the animals. And long ago, when I was about eleven, I had spent a lot of time catching insects and making analyses of them. I had taken apart those giant yellow slugs. I used to catch flies and hang them from loops of thread . . . however the weight of the fly's body was usually too slight to close the noose, so I usually had to pull down on the fly. At that point the fly's eyes would pop from his head and his head would come off.

When we arrived at the house Charley helped me carry my boxes of possessions indoors and to a room in the rear that they had decided to present me for my use. Evidently they had used it for storage; we had to carry out one armload after another of garden tools, children's discarded games and toys, even a bed that the collie dog had spent time in.

Shutting myself in the room I began putting my clothes in the closet and setting out my things, trying to give this new room an air of familiarity. With scotch tape I put up various important facts on the walls. I inserted items from my rock collection into the corners. Last of all, for a time I put my head in the bag containing my collection of milk bottle tops and breathed in the rich, sour odor of the bottle tops, a smell that had been with me since the fourth grade. That raised my spirits and I looked out of the window for the first time.

Dinner that night made me conscious of the luxury in which my sister was now living. Outdoors on the patio she had Charley broiling t-bone steak in a charcoal pit, while inside she fixed hors d'oeuvres of minced clams and cream cheese baked on English muffins, martinis, avocado salad, baked

potatoes, Italian beans from their freezer that they had originally grown themselves . . . and, for dessert, huckleberries
that they had picked the summer before somewhere out near
the Point. They had coffee; the two children and I had milk.
And the children and I had whipped cream on our huckleberries.

After dinner I carried the children around on my back,
while Fay and Charley sat in the living room having a second
martini and listening to longhair music on the hi-fi. In the
fireplace they had a fire of oak logs from the cord stacked
up near the side of the house. I don't think I have ever
enjoyed such comfort, and I threw myself into playing with
the girls, getting a great kick out of swinging them around,
tossing them high up and recatching them, hiding from them
and letting them find me. Their yells seemed to annoy Fay
and all at once she got up to go put the dishes in the automatic
dishwater.

Later I helped put the children to bed. I read a story to
them from the Oz book. It made me feel strange to be reading
one of the stories that I knew so well . . . books so much a
part of my life, and these children had not even been born
until the 'fifties. They hadn't even been alive during World
War Two.

I realized that this was the first time I had ever had anything
to do with children.

"You sure have nice kids," I said to Fay, after we had left
the children's rooms.

Fay said, "Everybody says that, so it must be true. Personally I find them a lot of work. You enjoy playing with
them, but after they've pestered you day in day out for
years—wait'll you've got up every morning at seven and fixed
breakfast for them."

Fixing breakfast was one thing my sister hated; she liked
to lie in bed late, until nine or ten, and with the girls in school
she had no choice but to get up early. Charley of course had
to be off to his factory, so he could not take the responsibility

of dressing the girls, brushing their hair, preparing their lunches, seeing that they had their books and so forth. After a week or so I found that I did not mind getting up early and setting the table, putting on water for the Cream of Wheat, making the peanut butter and jelly sandwiches and filling the thermos jugs with tomato soup, opening the drapes, frying bacon, cutting open the grapefruit, buttoning the girls' dresses, and then, after I had served breakfast to them, clearing the table, washing the dishes, taking out the garbage and trash, and finally sweeping the floor around the breakfast table. Meanwhile Charley got shaved, dressed, ate his soft boiled egg, toast and coffee, and set off for Petaluma. At nine or so Fay got up, took a shower, dressed, carried a cup of coffee and a dish of applesauce out on to the patio, ate, read the *Chronicle*—if somebody had thought to go out and get it for her—and then sat by herself smoking a cigarette.

Not only did I enjoy fixing breakfast, but I also enjoyed baby-sitting in the evenings, and that was a godsend for Fay. It meant that once again she could begin getting out and visiting people; she could get down to the Bay Area to movies and plays and classes, she could even go three times a week to her analyst in San Francisco instead of only once, and because they did not have to worry about keeping me up late, as they had had to with teenage baby-sitters, they could stay as late in the city as they wanted, going to parties or bars. And on Friday morning I went with my sister to Petaluma and carried the groceries for her, putting everything away when we got home and even burning the leftover bags and cartons in the incinerator.

In exchange for all this I got truly wonderful meals, and I got to ride the horse and play games with the kids. A metal pole had been erected outdoors for tether ball, and the children and I played tether ball almost every afternoon. I got really skilled at it.

"You know," Charley said to me once, "you missed your

vocation. You should have been a playground director or worked for the YMCA. I never saw anybody take to kids so. The noise doesn't bother you. That's what bothers me." In the evenings he always looked tired.

I said, "I think parents should spend more time with their kids."

"How can they help it?" Fay said. "Good god, the kids are underfoot all the time. Kids grow up better if adults don't interfere with them too much. They should be let alone." She was glad to have me baby-sit and play with the girls, but she did not approve of my mixing into the continual quarrels that the girls had with each other. She had always simply let them fight it out, but I soon saw that the older girl, being more advanced intellectually and much heavier physically, always won. It was not fair, and I felt required to step in.

"The only way kids can learn what's justice is if adults teach them," I said to Fay.

"What do you know about justice?" Fay said. "Here you are up here in my house freeloading. How'd you get up here anyhow?" She glared at me with that half-serious, half-joking exasperation that I was familiar with; she had this way of mixing a serious statement in with irony so that it was never possible to tell how seriously she meant what she said. "Who brought you here?" she demanded.

In my own mind I had no guilt. I was giving back plenty for what I took; I did a great deal of Fay's housework for her, and by baby-sitting I made it possible for them to save a lot of money. On an average, baby-sitting alone had run them three dollars a night, and over a period of a month this sometimes added up to sixty or seventy dollars. All these figures I recorded in my notebooks; I calculated how much I cost them and how much I saved them. The only real cost that I added to their budget was that of food. But I was not eating sixty dollars worth of food a month, so by baby-sitting alone I earned my keep. I didn't add appreciably to the heating bills, or the water, although of course I did bathe and wash, and my clothes had to be put into the automatic washer. And I went around turning off lights not in use, and lowering thermostats when people left rooms, so in my estimation—such a thing is admittedly very hard to estimate—I actually saved them money on their utility bills. And by riding the horse I prolonged his life, since, not being ridden, he was getting overly fat, which put an unnatural strain on his heart.

More than anything else, however, and something that could not be calculated in dollars and cents, I improved the atmosphere regarding the children. In me they had someone who cared about them, who enjoyed playing with them and listening to them and giving them affection—I did not consider it a duty or a chore. I took them on long walks, bought them bubble gum at the store, watched "Gunsmoke" with them on tv, cleaned up their rooms.

And that's another thing: by doing heavy household work such as scrubbing the floors I made it possible for Fay to let Mrs. Mendini, her cleaning woman, go. Consider that Mrs. Mendini's presence had always annoyed Fay; she felt that Mrs. Mendini was listening to everything anybody said, and Fay had always liked privacy. That was one of her major motives for desiring a large house isolated in the country.

One Saturday afternoon when Fay had gone into San Rafael to shop, and the two girls were over at Edith Keever's place playing with her children, Charley started talking to me out in the field by the duck pen. He had been running a new pipe to the ducks' water trough.

"Doesn't it bother you to do housework?" he asked me.

"No," I said.

"I don't think a man should do that kind of stuff," he said. Later on he said, "I don't think that the girls should see a man doing it either. It gives them the idea a man can be bossed around by a woman."

To that, I said nothing; I could think of nothing pertinent. Charley said, "She can't get me to do her god damn errands."

"I see," I said politely.

"A man has to keep his self-respect," Charley said. "Doing housework robs him of his masculinity."

I had noticed, almost as soon as I had moved in with them, how touchy Charley was with her. He seemed to resent her asking him to do anything, even helping her around the garden. One night, when she asked him to open a can or a jar for her—I didn't see it clearly, although I came in from my room to watch—he blew up, threw the jar down on the floor, and started calling her names. I noted that in my records, because I could perceive a pattern.

Once a week or so Charley would go off by himself, usually down to the Western Bar, or a bar in Olema that he liked, and get tanked up on beer. That seemed to be his system for getting his resentment of my sister out in the open; otherwise it merely simmered away down inside him, making him quarrelsome and moody. But when he had had a few drinks he could threaten her physically. I never saw him actually hit her, but I could tell by her response, when he came home from the bar, that at such times she was genuinely afraid of him. I don't think she realized why he drank, that he was releasing stored-up resentment; she thought of it more as a character defect on his part, and possibly a defect common with all men.

Each time he went off drinking she became more businesslike with him. She shafted him with quiet, rational upbraiding. Over a period of time she managed to convince him that there was something wrong with him for going out and drinking and coming home and taking a few swings at her; instead of viewing it as a simple means of working off steam she chose to consider it a symptom of some deep pervasive—even dangerous—malformation in him.

Or possibly she only pretended to think that. In any case

it was her policy to regard him as a malformed man, one who should be matched, and by talking along this line she made hay from each of his binges. The more he resisted her by going out and getting drunk and coming home and taking a swing at her, the more she built up this picture of him, and it was a picture that when not drunk he, too, had to accept. The household was pervaded by this atmosphere of a calm adult woman and a man who gave in to his animal impulses. She reported to him in great detail what her analyst, Dr. Andrews in San Francisco, said about his binges and his hostility; she used Charley's money to pay Dr. Andrews to catalog his abnormalities. And of course Charley never heard anything directly from the doctor; he had no way of keeping her from reporting what served her and holding back what did not. The doctor, too, had no way to get at the truth of what she told him; no doubt she only gave him the facts that suited her picture, so that the doctor's view of Charley was based on what she wanted him to know. By the time she had edited it both going and coming there was little of it outside her control.

Like any slob, Charley grumbled at her going to the doctor and at the same time took as holy writ whatever she reported. Any man who charged twenty dollars an hour had to be good.

Sometimes I asked myself what she was up to, if anything. I had nothing to do in the early afternoons, after I had done the lunch dishes, and I now and then sat around and watched her mold clay pots or knit or read; she had turned out to be a good-looking woman, although she had little or no bust line, and she had this big modern house, with ten acres, and all the rest of it—beyond any doubt she was unhappy. But she wanted something she lacked. After a month or so I came to the conclusion that she simply wanted Charley to be different from what he was; she had a deeply ingrained image of what a husband should be like—she was always very choosy—and although in some respects he met her requirements, in others he did not. For instance, he had enough money to build this house, and he did most of the things she wanted. And he was reasonably good-looking. But for one thing he was a slob, and there has always been this aristocratic, disapproving, judging tendency in Fay. It showed up strongly in high school when she began to work toward going to college; she took courses in literature and history and felt that the girls who took cooking courses—and the boys who took shop courses—were the riffraff of the world.

Beyond any doubt, Charley didn't care for what she regarded as the civilized things in life, such as the longhair music she listened to on the hi-fi. I grant that he was a slob. But he was a slob when she married him; he was a slob that day in the roadside grocery store when he mistook the Mozart tune for a hymn. If she knew that, then she was wrong to disapprove of him as if it was some secret trait that he had concealed from her and then sprung on her after they were married. My god, Charley had always been completely honest with her—and he had given her everything in his power. Now, instead of driving his Mercedes, he drove a Buick because she preferred the color schemes and the automatic shift. In his own area, such as with cars, he knew more than she did; she was the barbarian, the slob. But that did not help him, since she did not choose to regard those areas as important. The fact that he could lay a good pipeline to the ducks' trough did not impress her; only slobs were good at that, and so her point was proved.

And yet she accepted, even used, his language.

I suppose that she was ambivalent about him, that on the one hand she thought of him as rough and masculine, which was vital to her—he qualified as a man sexually. What she wanted was, it seems to me, paradoxical; she wanted him to be a man, but at the same time to meet her own standards, and these standards, having been set for herself, were not a man's standards. On that point—her own sex—she had some confusion, too. She hated to do housework, I think, because it made her feel like a woman, and this was intolerable to her. No wonder Charley loathed doing her chores for her; if it was degrading for her to do them, surely it was worse for him—not because of his feelings about them—at one time he might not have minded—but because of their insignificance to her. Doing housework proved that a person was a drudge, a domestic, a servant, a maid; she could not bring herself to do them, but she was willing to let her husband do them. She could not, for example, bear to go down to the store and buy her Tampax; it was the sine qua non of proof that she was a woman, and so she got him to do it.

Naturally he came home and hit her.

But I didn't mind doing the housework, because for me it was a job, not a symbol. I got my meals in return, and a warm house . . . I got something back, and it seemed just to me. Living with them I was much happier and more satisfied than I had ever been at any time in my life, before or since. I liked being with the children and the animals; I liked building fires in the fireplace—I liked the barbecued steaks. Wasn't it more degrading for me to work for Poity at his tire-regrooving place?

The oddest part was Fay's feeling that this house belonged to her and that Charley, her husband, was somebody who came in and sat down in a chair and got that chair dirty. He sweated on the furniture. But again this might not have been her actual attitude, but more a pose; she might simply have *wanted* to keep the idea current that this was primarily her house, and that in the house her laws functioned. Down underneath she may have recognized perfectly well that without Charley and his money there would have been no house—but, like the drinking, a particular theory fitted her needs and so she entertained the theory. She let him know that the house was her sphere . . . and what did that leave him? An office down at his factory to work in at night, plus the factory itself . . . and possibly the outdoors surrounding the house, the bare unimproved fields.

And this, too, Charley tended to accept, because first of

all he wasn't as quick with his tongue as she—and, in the final analysis, he imagined that since she was more intelligent and educated than he then she must, when they disagreed, be right. He considered her much the same as a book or a newspaper: he might grumble against it, denounce it, but ultimately what it said was true. He had no faith in his own ideas. Like everyone else, he too recognized himself as a grade A slob.

Take their friends, for instance. Take the Anteils. Both of them, Gwen and Nat, were obviously university people who had shared her interests in cultural and scholarly subjects. Here was a man, another man, not a woman, who showed up and sat around discussing—not business or plowing techniques—but Medieval religious sects. Fay and the Anteils could communicate, and so it became three to one, not one to one. Charley used to listen awhile and then go off to his study to do paperwork. This was true not only with the Anteils but with the Fineburgs and the Meritans and all the rest of them—artists, dress-designers, university people who had moved up to Inverness . . . all of them belonged to her, not him.

# 8

They took an hour off to fly kites. His got up off the ground and stayed, not falling but not going higher; he ran along the mushy pasture, splashing, unreeling the string, and still his kite stayed up the same height, only now the string was played out, parallel to the ground.

Off beyond the horse's barn, Fay raced like a water bug across a pond: her feet landed and rose, carrying her at enormous speed. Her kite shot straight up. When she stopped at the fence she turned, and they both saw nothing at first; the kite had gone so high that for a moment neither of them could spot it. The kite was directly above their heads, a true celestial object, launched out of the world's gravity.

The children screamed to be allowed to take the string of Fay's kite; they cursed Fay for not letting them fly it, and at the same time they marveled at her success. Admiration and anger . . . he stood gasping, holding his second-rate kite by its sagging string.

Having given her kite string to the children, Fay walked toward him, her hands in the front pockets of her jeans.

Smiling against the mid-day glare she reached him, halted and said,

"Now let's put *you* on the end of a string. And I'll fly *you*."

That filled him with wrath, terrible wrath. But at the same time he felt so winded and spent from the kiteflying that he could not express it; he could not even yell at her. All he could do was turn his back and without speaking start slowly in the direction of the house.

"What's the matter?" Fay called. "Are you mad again?"

He still said nothing. He felt depressed, a complete hopelessness. Suddenly he wished he could die; he wished he was dead.

"Can't you take a joke?" Fay said, catching up with him. "Say, you look as if you felt sick." Putting her hand up she touched his forehead, the way she did with the children. "Maybe it's the flu," she said. "Why did that upset you?"

He said, "I don't know."

"Remember," she said, going along with him, "that time you had gone into the duck pen to feed the ducks—it must have been the first time you fed them, after we had just gotten them—and I was standing outside the pen watching you, and all of a sudden I said, 'You know, I think of you as a pet duck; why don't you stay in there and I'll feed you.' Could you have been thinking of that? Did my remark about the kite make you remember that? I know that upset you at the time. It was really a dreadful thing to say; I can't imagine why I said it. You know I say every kind of thing—I have no control over my tongue." Catching hold of his arm, she dragged against him, saying, "You know nothing I say means anything. Right? Wrong? Inbetween?"

"Leave me alone," he said, jerking away.

"Don't go in," she said. "Please. At least play badminton with me for a little while . . . remember, the Anteils are coming over for dinner tonight, so if we don't play now we won't get a chance to play—and tomorrow I have to go into the city. So couldn't we play, just for a minute?"

"I'm too tired," he said. "I don't feel well."

"It'll do you good," she said. "Just for a minute." Passing him, she raced across the field, the patio, and into the house. By the time he had reached the house, there she stood, holding up the badminton rackets and the shuttles.

The two girls appeared, shouting together. "Can't we play? Where's the other paddles?" Seeing that Fay had all four rackets, they struggled to get two of them away from her.

In the end they did play. He and Bonnie took one side, with Fay and Elsie on the other. His arms felt so tired that he could barely lift his racket to swat the shuttle. Finally, in running back to get a long one, his weary legs caught together, became rigid, and he tumbled over backward. The children set up a wail and hurried to him; Fay remained where she was, looking on.

"I'm okay," he said, getting up. But his racket had snapped in half. He stood holding the pieces and trying to get his breath; his chest hurt and bones seemed to be sticking into his lungs.

"There's one more racket in the house," Fay said, from the far side of the net. "Remember, Leslie O'Neill brought it over to play, and left it. It's in the cupboard in the study."

He started into the house to get it. After a long rummaging about he found it; starting back out again he felt his head swim and his legs wobble like cheap plastic, the junk they used to make free toys, he thought. Toys they give away in cereal packages or hand out in stores . . .

Then he fell forward. As he fell he reached for the ground; he sank his hands into it and clutched it. He tore it up, stuffed it into him, ate it and drank it and breathed it in; he lost his breath, trying to breathe it in—he could not get it inside him, into his lungs. And, after that, he could not do anything.


Next he knew he lay in a big bed, his face and body shaved. His hands, his fingers on the bedsheets, looked like the pink fingers of a pig. I turned into a pig, he thought. They took my hair away and curled what was left; I've been squealing for a long time.

He tried to squeal but all that came out was a rasp.

At that, a figure appeared. His brother-in-law Jack Isidore peering down at him, wearing a cloth jacket and baggy brown pants, a knapsack on his back. His face had been scrubbed.

"You had an occlusion," Jack said.

"What's that?" he said, thinking that someone had hit him.

"You had a heart attack," Jack said, and then he went into a mass of technical details. Presently he went off. A nurse took his place, and then, at last, a doctor.

"How'm I doing?" Charley said. "Pretty robust for an old man. Lots of life in the old frame left. Right?"

"Yes, you're in good shape," the doctor said, and left.

By himself, he lay on his back thinking, waiting for someone to come. The doctor eventually returned.

"Listen," Charley said. "The reason I'm here is that my wife's responsible. This was her idea from the start. She wants the house and the plant and the only way she can get it is if I die, so she fixed it up so I'd have this heart attack and drop dead according to plan."

The doctor bent down to listen.

"And I was going to kill her," he said. "God damn her."

The doctor departed.

After a long time, evidently several days—he saw the room get dark, then light, then dark, and they shaved him and washed him with warm water and a sponge, and had him urinate, and fed him—several persons entered the room and stood off together talking. At last, beside his bed, Fay appeared.

His wife had on a blue coat and heavy skirt and leotards and her pointed Italian shoes. Her face was orangish and pale, the way it often was early in the morning. Even her eyes were orange, and her hair. Her neck had wrinkles in it, as if her head had twisted back and forth. She carried her big leather purse under her arm, and as she came to the bed he smelled the leather of the purse.

Seeing her, he began to cry. The warm water from his eyes spilled down his cheeks. Fay got Kleenex from her purse, spilling things out on to the floor, and, crouching down, roughly rubbed his face dry. She scoured his face until it burned.

"I'm sick," he said to her, wanting to reach up and fondle her.

Fay said, "The girls made you an ashtray and I had it fired down at the kiln." Her voice sounded like the rasp that was his, as if she had been smoking too much again. She did not try to clear her throat as she usually did. "Can I get you anything? Bring you your toothbrush and pajamas? They didn't let me until I asked you. I have mail for you." On his chest, near his right hand, she laid a stack of mail. "Everyone's writing, even your aunt in Washington, D.C. The dog is all right, the children miss you but they're not feeling frightened or anything, the horse is all right, one of the sheep got out and we had to get Tom Sibley to get it with his pickup truck." She turned her head this way and that to stare at him.

"How's the plant doing?" he said.

"They all send their regards. It's doing fine."

Later on, in the next week or so, he was considered well enough to be allowed to sit up and drink milk through a bent glass tube. Propped up on pillows he took in the sun. They put him in a cart and wheeled him around, raised and lowered him. Different people, his family, men from the plant, friends, Fay and the children, people from the area, came to see him.

One day as he lay out in the solarium, getting sun through the double windows, Nathan Anteil and Gwen Anteil came to see him, bringing a bottle of aftershave. He read the label on the bottle. It came from England.

"Thanks," he said.

"Anything else we can bring you?" Nat Anteil asked.

"No," he said. "Maybe the back issues of the Sunday *Chronicle*."

"Okay," Nat said.

"Has the place gone to pot? The house?"

"The weeds need to be roto-tilled," Nat said. "That's about all."

Gwen said, "Nat was going to ask you if you wanted him to do it."

"Fay can operate the roto-tiller," he answered. For a time he thought about it, the weeds, the gallon bottle of white gas, how long it had been since the roto-tiller had been started up. "She can't work the carburetor," he said. "Maybe you could get it started up for her. It's hard to get the mix right, when it's been sitting."

"The doctors say you're doing fine," Gwen said. "You have to stay here a while longer and recuperate, that's all."

"Okay," he said.

"They're building your strength back up," Gwen said. "It shouldn't be long. They're really good here; they've got a really good reputation here at the U.C. Hospital."

He nodded.

"It's cold down here in San Francisco," Nat said. "The fog. But the wind isn't so much as back up at Point Reyes."

He said, "How does Fay seem to be holding up under this?"

"She's been very strong," Gwen said.

"She's a very strong woman," Nat said.

"The drive down here from Point Reyes is pretty bad," Gwen said. "With the children in the car especially."

"Yes," he said. "It's about eighty miles round trip."

Nat said, "She's come down every day."

He nodded.

"Even when she knew she couldn't see you," Gwen said, "she still made the drive, with the kids in the back of the car."

"How about the house?" he said. "Can she manage okay in such a big house?"

Gwen said, "She told me that she's been a little uneasy alone at night, in such a big house. She had a couple of bad dreams. But she keeps the dog around. She has the kids come into her bedroom and sleep with her. At first she started locking all the doors, but Dr. Andrews said that once she got started on that there'd be no end of it, so she managed to throw off her fears, and now she doesn't lock any of the doors; she leaves them all unlocked."

He said, "There's ten doors leading into that house."

"Ten," Gwen said. "Is that so."

"Three into the living room," Charley said. "One into the family room. Three into her bedroom. That's seven right there. Two in the kids' rooms. That's nine. So there's more than ten. Two into the hall, one from each side of the house."

"That's eleven so far," Gwen said.

"One into the utility room," Charley said.

"Twelve."

"None into the study," Charley said. "I guess it's twelve. At least twelve. There's always one of them hanging open, letting out heat."

"Fay's brother has been giving her a lot of help," Gwen said. "He's been doing all the shopping and housecleaning for her, running all kinds of errands for her."

"That's right," Charley said. "I forgot about him completely. He's there, if anything happens." It had been in his mind that Fay and the children were the only ones there, alone in the house, now, without a man. The Anteils had overlooked him, too. None of them considered it the same as there being a man in the house, and apparently Fay felt the same way. But anyhow Jack did the chores for her, so she did not have the burden of work around the house, along with her worry.

"There's no financial problems that you've heard her mention, is there?" he asked. "There shouldn't be. She has the

joint checking account, and I have insurance that ought to
be paying off around now."

"She never mentioned any problem if there is one," Gwen
said. "She seems to have money."

"She's always down at the Mayfair cashing a check," Nat
said, with a smile.

"She'll manage to get it spent," Charley said.

"Yes, she seems to be doing okay," Nat said.

"I hope she remembers the bills," Charley said.

Gwen said, "She has a whole box of bills; I saw it on the
desk in the study. She was going over them, trying to decide
which ones to pay."

"I usually do that," Charley said. "Tell her to pay the
utility bills. That's the rule. Always pay them first."

"Well, there's no problem, is there?" Nat said. "She has
the ready capital to pay all of them, doesn't she?"

"Probably does," Charley said. "Unless this god damn
hospitalization is running too much."

"She could always borrow from the bank," Gwen said.

"Yes," Charley said. "But she shouldn't have to. We have
plenty of money. Unless she fouls it up."

"She's quite resourceful," Nat said. "Anyhow, she always
gives the impression; I assume she is."

"She is," Charley said. "She's good in a crisis. That's when
she's the best. One time we were out on Tomales Bay in a
sailboat and we couldn't pump. The pump was busted. Water
was coming in. She steered the boat while I bailed by hand.
She never got scared. But actually we might have gone
down."

"You told us about that," Gwen said, nodding.

"She can always get somebody to help her," Charley said.
"If she breaks down on the road she always gets somebody
to stop."

"A lot of women are like that," Nat said. "They have to
be. It's almost impossible for a woman to change a tire."

"She wouldn't change a tire," Charley said. "She'd rustle

up somebody to change it for her. Do you think she'd change a tire? Are you kidding?"

Nat said, "She sure is a good driver."

"She's a fine driver," he said. "She likes to drive." He added, "She's good at anything she likes to do. But if she doesn't like to do it she doesn't do it; she gets somebody else to do it. I never saw her do anything she didn't want to do. That's her philosophy. You must know that; you're always talking philosophy with her."

"She's made the drive down here," Gwen said. "There's nothing pleasurable about that."

"Sure she's made the drive," Charley said. "You know what she never has done and never will do? Think of another person beside herself. Everybody's just somebody to do things for her."

"Oh, I wouldn't say that," Gwen said.

"Don't tell me about my wife," he said. "I know my wife; I've been married to her for seven years. Everybody in the world's a servant. That's what they are, servants. I'm a servant. Her brother is a servant. She'll get you to wait on her. She'll sit there and have you doing things for her."

The doctor came in and said that the Anteils had to go. Or perhaps it was the nurse. He saw a white figure approach; he heard them talking. Then the Anteils said a rapid good-bye and were gone.

Alone, he lay in bed, thinking.


Several times in the next few days Fay visited him, with and without the children, and Jack, and friends.

The next time that the Anteils came back only Nat came. He explained that Gwen had to go to the dentist in San Francisco, and that she had let him off here at the U.C. Hospital.

"Where is this hospital?" Charley said. "What part of San Francisco is this?"

Nat said, "Out around Parnassus and Fourth. Getting toward the beach. We're up high, overlooking the Panhandle of Golden Gate Park. It's a stiff walk around here."

"I see," Charley said. "I could see houses, but I couldn't figure out what part of the city it was. I don't know San Francisco very well. The green I saw must be the park."

"The beginning of the park," Nat said.

After a time Charley said, "Listen, has she got started getting you to do things?"

With deliberation, Nat said, "I'm not sure what you mean. Both Gwen and I are glad to do anything we can, not for her as such but for you, both of you. For the family."

"Don't let her get you to do things," he said.

Nat said, "It's natural to do things, anyhow it's natural to do certain kinds of things. Of course, there's a limit. We both recognize, Gwen and I, that she's impulsive. She's frank; she speaks right out."

"She's got the mind of a child," he said. "She wants something so she goes after it. She won't take no."

Nat said nothing to that.

"Does it bother you?" Charley said. "My saying that? Good God, I don't want you trotting around doing errands for her. I don't want to see her rob you of your self-respect. No man should do a woman's errands for her."

"Okay," Nat said in a low voice.

"Sorry if this upsets you," Charley said.

"No, it's okay."

"I just want to warn you. She's an exciting person and people are drawn to her. I'm not saying anything against her. I love her. If I had to I'd marry her again." No, he thought. If I could I'd kill her. If I could get out of this bed I'd kill her. He said aloud, "God damn her."

"It's okay," Nat said, to make him stop.

"No," he said, "it's not okay. That bitch. That devouring bitch. She ate me up. When I get back there I'm going to take her apart piece by piece. God, you know your original reaction to her. I heard. You told Betty Heinz that Fay was a bossy, demanding woman and you didn't like her."

"I told Mary Woulden that I had difficulty dealing with her because she was so intense," Nat said. "And I said she was bossy. We patched it up."

"Yes," Charley said. "She was sore. She can't stand that."

"We haven't had any difficulty carrying on a relationship with your wife. We've had a very equitable relationship with her. We're not terribly close to her, but we enjoy her company; we enjoy the children and the house—we like to be over there."

Charley said nothing.

"To some extent I know what you mean," Nat said presently.

"Anyhow it doesn't matter," Charley said. "Because when I get out of here, I'm going to kill her. I don't care who knows it. I don't care if Sheriff Chisholm knows it. She can swear out a warrant. Did she tell you I hit her one time?"

Nat nodded.

"She can swear out a warrant for felony wife-beating," he said. "It's all the same to me. She can get that twenty-dollars-an-hour psychoanalyst to swear in court that it's all in my mind, that I'm eaten up with hostility, that I resent her because she has taste and refinement. I don't care. I don't give a good god damn about anything. I don't even care about my kids. I don't care if I never see either of them again. I don't expect to see that house again; I can tell you that. I'll probably see them, the kids; she'll bring them here."

"Yes," Nat said. "She's been bringing them down regularly."

"I'll never get out of this hospital," Charley said. "I know that."

"Sure you will," Nat said.

"Tell her I know it," he said, "and I don't care. Tell her

it's all the same; I don't give a god damn. She can have the house. She can remarry anybody she likes. She can do anything she wants with it."

"You'll feel better later," Nat said, patting him on the arm.

"No," he said. "I won't feel better."

# 9

In the evening, Nathan Anteil sat at the kitchen table of their one-bedroom home, studying. He had shut the door to the living room to diminish the sound of the tv set; Gwen was watching Playhouse 90. The oven, propped open, let heat out to warm the kitchen. Beside him he had put a cup of coffee where he could get at it, but he had become too involved in his studying and the coffee had cooled.

Dimly, he noticed that Gwen had opened the door and come into the kitchen. "What is it?" he said finally, laying down his ball-point pen.

Gwen said, "It's Fay Hume on the phone."

He had not even been aware that the phone had rung. "What's she want?" he said. When they had seen her last he had taken pains to tell her that he would be tied up all week studying; he had an exam, to be taken down at the San Rafael public library.

"She's got her bank statement and she can't get it reconciled with her stubs," Gwen said.

"So she wants one of us to come over and help her."

"Yes," Gwen said.

"Tell her we can't."

"I'll go," Gwen said. "I told her you were studying."

"She knows that." Picking up his pen he resumed taking notes.

"Yes," Gwen said, "she said you mentioned it. She thought maybe I could come over. She really can't do that kind of thing—you know she hasn't got any head for finances."

"Can't her brother do it?"

"That goof," Gwen said.

"You go do it," he said. But he knew that his wife could not because she was no better at reconciling a checkbook than Fay Hume was, possibly even a little worse. "Go on," he said, with annoyance. "You know I can't."

Dithering, Gwen said, "She says she'll drive over and pick you up. I really think you ought to go . . . it'll only take you half an hour—you know that. And she'll fix you a steak sandwich; she promised. Please. I think you should."

"Why?"

Gwen said, "Well, she's all alone there in the evenings, and she gets nervous; you know how nervous she gets with him in the hospital. Probably it's just an excuse to get somebody over to talk to; she really needs company. She's going down to that analyst three times a week, now; did you know that?"

"I know," he said. He continued to write. But Gwen did not go out of the room. "Is she still on the phone?" he demanded. "Is she waiting?"

"Yes," Gwen said.

"Okay," he said. "If she'll pick me up and drive me back."

"Of course she will," Gwen said. "She'll be so pleased. And it'll only take you fifteen minutes; you're so good with math." She left the room, and he heard her, in the living room, telling Fay Hume that he would be glad to help her.

He thought, If it's just a pretext so she can have company, then why can't Gwen go? Because, he realized, even though she does want company—and in a sense, it is a pretext—she also does want somebody to balance her checkbook. She wants both. Very efficient. Both things done at once.

Putting away his pen, he went to get his coat from the closet.

"You do object, don't you?" Gwen said, as he stood by the front door, waiting to see the headlights of Fay's Buick flash at the corner.

"I'm busy," he said.

"But oftentimes even when you're busy you don't mind stopping and doing things."

"No," he repeated. "I'm just involved and I don't like to be disturbed." But she was right. There was more to it.

The Buick's horn brought him from the house and on to the porch. As he started down the front steps, Fay leaned out and called,

"You're very sweet—I know you're studying. But this won't take a minute." She held the door open for him as he got into the seat beside her. Starting up the car, she continued, "Actually I guess I could have done it myself; there's one check in particular—evidently I forgot to mark a stub. It's a check for one hundred dollars that I cashed at the Purity in Petaluma."

"I see," he said. He did not particularly feel like talking; looking out the window he watched the dark trees and bushes go by. She did drive very well; the car sailed around the curves.

"Are you still thinking about your studying?"

"Somewhat."

"I'll get you right back as soon as I can," she said. "I swear I won't keep you very long; I hesitated a long time before I called—as a matter of fact, I almost didn't call. I hate to bother you when you're studying." She did not mention Gwen and he was aware of that. No doubt she had known that Gwen was out of the question.

He thought, I shouldn't be doing this.

One afternoon, over at her place, he had happened to notice an opened bill lying on the coffee table in the living room. The bill was from a clothing store in San Rafael, for children's dresses. The amount would have paid his and Gwen's bills for the entire month, all of them. And this was for the girls' clothing alone.

His income, from his part-time job, and Gwen's income from her two-day-a-week job in San Anselmo, added up to about two hundred dollars a month. It was barely enough for them to squeeze by on. To the Humes, two hundred dollars amounted to nothing; her psychiatrist bill, he knew, often came to more than that a month. And their heating bill—even a utility bill, he thought. One utility. The money would keep us alive. And she wants me to go over her check stubs for the month. I have to scrutinize every check. See all that money, all that waste. Things they don't need . . .

One night, when he and Gwen had eaten dinner at the Humes' he had stood by watching while Fay handed the dog a t-bone steak which she had unfrozen, along with the others, but which had not fitted on to the grill of the barbecue pit. He had asked her, trying to keep his feelings out of sight, why she simply didn't put the uncooked, uneaten steak into the refrigerator and have it in the following day or so. Fay had stared at him and said,

"I can't stand leftovers. Little remains in the bottoms of cups. I always throw what's left from dinner to the dog. If he won't eat it then it goes down the disposal."

He had seen her put smoked oysters and artichoke hearts down the disposal; the dog did not care for either.

Aloud to her now he said, "You should keep a stub for every check you write, regardless."

"Oh I know," she said. "Sometimes I'm overdrawn at the bank by two or three hundred dollars. But they always put through my checks; they never send them back. They know me. They know I'm good for it. God, if they ever sent back one of my checks I'd never speak to them again; I'd raise such a ruckus there that they'd never get over it."

"If you don't have funds," he said, "they ought to send the check back."

"Why?" she said.

"Because it's not good," he said.

"Oh, it is good," she said. "Don't you know that? What do you mean, not good? Don't you think I'm good for it?"

He gave up and relapsed into silence.

"Why so quiet?" she said.

"They put them through for you," he said, "but if I'm overdrawn they don't put them through. They send them back."

"Do you know why?" Fay said.

"Why?"

She said, "Because they never heard of you."

Turning toward her, he stared at her. But there was no malice on her face, only the cautious alertness for the road. "Well," he said with hard irony, "that's the price you pay for being a nonentity. For not being a big person in the community."

"Do you know what I've done for this community?" Fay said. "I've done more for this community than anyone else; when they were trying to get rid of the Principal over at the grammar school I went down to San Rafael and got my attorney and paid him to look up the laws and see how Mr. Pars, the Principal, could be kept on in spite of the school board; we found six or seven ways."

"Good for you," he said.

"You bet good for me," Fay said. "And I got the petition up and circulated it for putting in the street lights; when we moved in up here there wasn't a single street light in Drake's Landing. It's unincorporated. And we did a lot to get the old firehouse torn down and the new one built."

"Incredible," he said.

"Why do you say that?" She shot him a brief glance.

He said, "You've practically made this area over single-handedly."

"It sounds as if you resent it."

"I resent your making so much out of it."

To that, she said nothing; she seemed to shrink back. But then, when she had turned the Buick into the cypress-lined driveway of their house, she said, "You know, you didn't have to come over. I know how you feel about me; you think I'm heedless and demanding and indifferent to other people's welfare. But I've done more for other people's welfare than anybody else around here. What have you done for this area, since you moved in?" She said it all calmly, but he saw that she was upset. "Well?" she said.

I think he's right, he thought. Charley is right about her. At least to some extent. She does have a childish quality, a sort of brashness.

Then why am I here? he asked himself.

Can't I say no to her?

"You want to go back?" Fay said. Stopping the car she put the automatic transmission into reverse, and, with a squeal of tires, backed out of the driveway, swinging the car wildly into a turn as it reached the road. The front end missed the mailbox on its post by inches; he automatically tensed himself, waiting for the sound of metal against wood.

"I'll drive you back," she said, shifting into forward range and starting back down the road. "I'm not going to make you do something you don't want to do. The decision's yours."

He said, feeling as if he were talking to an angry child, "I don't mind helping you with your bills."

At that, to his surprise, she said, "I didn't ask you to come over to help me with the bills. The hell with the bills." Her voice rose. "What do I care about the bills? That's none of my business. It's up to him to pay them, the god damn bills.

Fuck the bills. I wanted you to come over because I'm lonely. Good god—" Her voice grated. "Charley's been in the hospital for over a month and I'm going crazy sitting around the house; I'm about ready to go out of my mind. Cooped up with the kids driving me nuts! And that nutty motherfucking brother of mine. That fruit."

She sounded so mad, so fed up and exasperated, that he was amused. The strident clamorousness of her . . . it did not go with her appearance, her leanness, her slight, almost underdeveloped body. Now she had begun to cough: deep, hoarse coughs, as if a man were sitting beside him coughing, a man's cough.

"I've been smoking three packs of L & Ms a day," she informed him. "Good god, I never smoked so much in my entire life! No wonder I can't gain any weight. God." She said it with stunned amazement. "What do I pay that hick psychiatrist three hundred dollars a month for? That asshole . . ."

"Calm down," he said to her. "Drive back to your place; we'll get the bills done, and then we'll have a drink or a cup of coffee and then I have to get back to my studies."

"Why didn't you bring your books over, you asshole?" she said.

"I thought I was coming over to work."

"God," she said, "Good god. I never heard anything so ridiculous in my entire life. My goodness." She seemed utterly floored. "I went to so much trouble to find something that wouldn't bring that—1926-looking wife of yours along. It doesn't bother you if I talk about your wife, does it?" Slowing the car, driving with one hand, she turned toward him, saying, "You know you've stimulated me ever since I first laid eyes on you. Don't you? My God, I've as much as told you half a dozen times. Remember that night I asked you to wrestle with me? What did you think I wanted to wrestle with you for? I was sure your wife caught on. And my god, all you did was throw me on the floor and walk off and leave me. Did you know I had a black and blue mark on my ass for a week afterward?"

To that, he said nothing; his head was swimming.

"God," she said, more composedly, now. "I've never been so attracted to a man. I was attracted to both of you, you in your big old wool sweaters . . . where did you ever get those sweaters?" Without pausing she said, "Why do you ride a bike? Didn't you have a bike as a child? Didn't your family give you a bike?"

He said, "There's nothing wrong with a grown person riding a bike."

"Can I ride it sometime?"

"Sure," he said. "Of course you can."

"Is it hard?"

He said. "You haven't ever ridden a bike?"

"No," she said.

"This one has a gearshift," he said. "It's English."

Now she did not seem to be listening to him; she drove in a preoccupied manner, her face somber. "Listen," she said after a while. "Are you going to go running home to your wife and tell her about me propositioning you?"

He said, "Are you propositioning me?"

"No," she said. "Of course not. You propositioned me. Don't you remember?" She said it with absolute conviction. "Isn't that why you came over? Good god, I wouldn't dare let you in the house. That's why I'm driving you back." They had gotten almost to his house, now, and he realized abruptly that she really intended to drop him off. "I'm not letting you into my place," she told him. "Not without your wife. If you want to come over you bring her along."

With anger he said loudly, "You're a nut. A real nut."

"What?" she said, falteringly.

"Don't you pay any attention to anything you say?"

That seemed to crush her. "Don't pick on me," she said. "Don't you get picky. Why do you pick on me?" Her tone reminded him of the younger child's tone, the whining, self-pitying tone. Perhaps she was calculatedly imitating her child's tone; he had an intuition to that effect. It was both a satire and a theft. She used it and satirized it simultaneously, waiting to see how he reacted.

"I think you're a real kick," he said. And he did. She intrigued him, her flashing moods; he could not tell at any moment which way she would jump. She seemed to have an infinite supply of energy. She went on and on, without fatigue.

"You don't take me seriously at all," she said, and then she smiled at him, a mechanical, even formal smile. "Well, thanks for wanting to help me." They had come to his house and she was stopping the car. She evidently was quite angry at him, quite cold. "I really am furious with you," she said in a dead, level voice. "I really am. I'll never forgive you for your treatment of me. The hell with you." She leaned over and grabbed at the car door. "So long."

"So long!" he said, stepping out.

The door slammed; the car roared off. In a daze, he started up the steps to his own porch.


The next day he telephoned her, not from home but from his real estate office. "Hi, Fay," he said. "I hope I didn't catch you when you're busy."

"No," she said. "I'm not busy." On the phone her voice had a thin, brisk quality, as if he were talking to a woman accustomed to doing a great deal of her business transactions on the phone. "Who is this? Not that fink Nathan Anteil?"

He thought, And this is a thirty-two-year-old woman. He said, "Fay, you use the worst language of any woman I've ever known."

"Stick it up your ass!" she said animatedly. "Did you phone me to pick on me some more, or what? Yes, why did you phone me? Just a second." He heard her throw down

the phone and then go shut a door. Back again, she said
deafeningly in his ear, "I've been sitting here going over what
happened last night. Evidently, I don't understand the masculine mind. What got into you? For that matter, what got
into me?"

Today, she seemed to be in a sportive mood, taking nothing very seriously. She seemed to be in, for her, a relatively
good mood. "Why don't I come over for a while tonight,"
he said, feeling himself become tense. "For a little while."

"All right," she said. "Want me to pick you up?"

"No," he said. He had an old Studebaker that he used to
get into Mill Valley to his job. "I'll get over there on my
own power."

"You're not bringing that wife, are you? Whatever her
name is. Say, just what is her name again, anyhow?"

"I'll see you," he said. He hung up.

Her tone had been stark and overly loud, once she had
realized who it was and why he had called. She knows, he
thought. We both know.

What do we know?

He thought, We know that something is up; we are doing
something. It does not involve my wife or her husband.

What is it? He asked himself. What do I have in mind?
How far do I want to go? How far does Fay Hume want to
go?

Perhaps, he thought, neither of us knows.

Then he asked himself why he was doing it. I have a really
wonderful wife, he thought. And I like Charley Hume. And,
he thought, Fay is married and she has two children.

Why, then?

Because I want to, he decided.

Much later in the day, as he was driving back to north
west Marin County, he thought, And because she wants to.

# 10

In order to visit Charley in the University of California Hospital at Fourth and Parnassus, in San Francisco, I had to take the 6:20 Greyhound bus from Inverness. That got me to San Francisco at 8:00 in the morning. I generally went to the San Francisco public library, where I read the new magazines, picked out books that Charley might like, and did research. Now that he had had his heart attack, I did research on the circulatory system, copying scientific information into notebooks, and, when possible, checking out the actual reference books on articles to take to him to read.

When he saw me coming into his room, with my knapsack filled with library books and technical magazines, he almost always said, "Well, Isidore, what's the latest on my heart?"

I gave him what information I had been able to pick up from hospital personnel on his condition and how soon he might expect to get out and back to the house. He seemed to appreciate this detailed account; without me he got the usual clichés about his condition, so to an extent he was dependent on me.

After I had given him the scientific information I got out

the notebook that I used for information concerning the situation back at Drake's Landing.

"Let's hear the latest on the old homestead," he almost always said.

On this particular occasion, I referred to my notebook to get my facts in order, and then I said, "Your wife is beginning to become involved with Nathan Anteil in extramarital relationships."

I had intended to go on, but Charley stopped me. "What do you mean?" he said.

"For the last four days," I said, checking my facts, "Nathan Anteil has come over in the evening without his wife. And he and Fay have talked in such a way as to suggest a romance between them."

I did not enjoy giving him this information, but I had set out to keep him apprised of the situation at home; I had made it part of my job, in exchange for what I received in the way of food and lodgings. Along with my other chores bringing him information was my duty, and it had to be scrupulously done, with regard only for accuracy and completeness.

"They sat together on Thursday night drinking martinis until two a.m.," I informed him.

"Well," he said presently. "Go on."

"At one point—they were seated together on the couch—he put his arm around her and kissed her. On the mouth."

Charley said nothing. But obviously he was listening. So I continued.

"Nathan didn't actually come out and say that he loved your wife—"

Charley interrupted, "I don't give a damn."

"How do you mean?" I said. "You mean you don't give a damn about that particular piece of information or—"

He interrupted, "I don't give a damn about the whole subject." He was silent for a long time and then he said, "What else happened at the old homestead during the week?

And don't give me any more on that topic, about him or her. Tell me about the ducks."

"The ducks," I said, glancing at my notes. "The ducks laid a total of thirty eggs since my last report. The Pekins laid the most of that, with the Rouens laying the least."

He said nothing.

"What else would you like to know?" I asked. "How much egg-gro they consumed?" I had it both by weight and by volume.

"Okay," he said. "Tell me about that."

I felt keenly that his failure to take an interest in such an important topic as his wife's relationship with Nathan Anteil was due to my inability to relate it properly. Obviously I had failed to do justice to it; I had not given him a convincing picture. He had been present, he would have reacted, but all he had to go on were the barren statements that I presented him. A newspaper or a magazine, when it wants to stir an emotional reaction in its readers, does an expert job of presenting a topic; it does not merely list facts in chronological order, as was my tendency.

Then and there I saw the limitation of my systematic method. As a means of recording significant data it was unexcelled, but as a means of conveying that data to another person, it had no merit. Up to now, my recording and preservation of significant facts had been for my own use . . . but now I was gathering facts for the use of another person, in this case a man who had little or no scientific education. Looking back, I recalled that in the past a great number of facts that had impressed me had been conveyed in highly dramatized articles, such as those in the *American Weekly,* and other facts had been conveyed in fictional forms, such as in the stories I read in *Thrilling Wonder* and *Astonishing.*

Obviously I had a thing or two to learn. I left the hospital feeling very chagrined, and, for the first time in years, basically questioning myself and my methods.

• • •

A day or so later, while spending the afternoon alone in the house, I heard the doorbell chime. I had been folding the laundry that had come out of the clothes drier. Leaving the heaps of clothes on the table I went to open the door, thinking that possibly Fay was back from town and wanted me to carry something in from the car.

When I opened the door I found myself facing a woman that I had never seen before.

"Hello," she said.

"Hello," I said.

The woman was quite small, with a huge black pony tail of such heavy hair that I thought she must be a foreigner. Her face had a dark quality, like an Italian's, but her nose had the bony prominence of an American Indian's. She had quite a strong chin and large brown eyes that stared at me so hard and fixedly that I became nervous. After saying hello she said nothing at all but smiled. She had sharp teeth, like a savage's, and that also made me uneasy. She wore a green shirt, like a man's, out at the waist, and shorts, and gold sandals, and she carried a purse and a manila envelope and a pair of sunglasses. I saw parked in the driveway a new Ford station wagon painted bright red. In some respects the woman seemed to be breathtakingly beautiful, but at the same time I was aware that something was wrong with her proportions. Her head was slightly too large for her shoulders—although it may have been an illusion due to her heavy black hair—and her chest was somewhat concave, actually hollow, not like a woman's chest at all. And her hips were too small in proportion to her shoulders, and then, in order, her legs were too short for her hips, and her feet too small for her legs. So she resembled an inverted pyramid.

It came to me that although this woman was in her thirties, she had the figure of a somewhat underweight but very good-looking fourteen-year-old girl. Her body had not matured, only her face. She had not developed beyond a certain point, and this top-heavy effect was not an illusion. If you noticed only her face she seemed absolutely ravishingly beautiful, but if your gaze took in all of her, then you were conscious that there was something wrong with her, something fundamentally out of proportion.

Her voice had a rasping, husky quality, very low-pitched. Like her eyes it had a strong and intense authority to it, and I found myself unable to break away from her gaze. Although she had never seen me before—laid eyes on me, as they say—she acted as if she had expected to see me, as if I was familiar to her. Her smile had a sly certitude to it. After a moment she started forward and I stood aside; she came on into the house, gliding with very small steps and making no sound at all. Apparently she had been there before because she went without hesitation into the living room and put her purse down on one of the tables there, the same table on which Fay always put her purse. Then she turned to look back at me and said,

"Have you been having any pains in your head lately? Around your temples?" She put up her hand and traced a line across her forehead from eye to eye. "I have. Do you know what it is?" She came gliding forward and stopped a short distance away. "That's the crown of thorns," she said. "We all have to wear it before the world can end and a new world take its place. I'm wearing it now. I've been wearing it since last Friday, when I ascended the cross and was crucified and then spent a night in the tomb." Smiling at me, and keeping her large brown eyes fixed on me, she continued, "I slept the whole night outdoors in the cold and never even knew it. My husband and children didn't know I was missing; it was as if no time had passed. I had been transfigured into eternity. The whole house vibrated—I saw it vibrate, my god, as if it was going to fly up into the sky like a spaceship."

"I see," I said, unable to take my eyes away from hers.

"Over the house," she continued, "there was a huge blue

light hanging, like crackling electric fire. I laid on the ground and that fire consumed me, from that spaceship. The whole house became a spaceship ready to go into space."

I couldn't help nodding.

In the same tone of voice she went on, "I'm Mrs. Hambro. Claudia Hambro. I live over in Inverness Park. You're Fay's brother, aren't you?"

"Yes," I said. "Fay isn't here; she went into town."

"I know," Mrs. Hambro said. "I knew that when I woke up this morning." She walked over to the window, looked out at the sheep, who were going by the fence. Then she turned and seated herself in a chair, crossing her bare legs and setting her purse on her lap; she opened her purse, got out a package of cigarettes, and lit up. "Why did you come here?" she said. "To Drake's Landing. Do you know the reason?"

I shook my head.

"It's the force that's pulling us all together," she said. "Throughout the world. There's groups forming everywhere. The message is the same: suffer and die to save the world. Christ was not suffering for our sins, he was suffering to show us the way. We all have to suffer. We all have to ascend the cross to gain eternal life, each in his own way." She blew smoke from her nostrils up at me. "Christ was from another planet. From a more evolved race. Earth is the most backward planet in the universe. At night I can lie awake—sometimes it really scares me—and listen to them talking. The other night they began to open my head. They cut a flap open this way and one that way." With her hand she traced lines across her head. "And I heard this terrible noise; it was the loudest noise I have ever heard. It absolutely deafened me. You know what it was? It was Aaron's rod coming down; it appeared in the air before me. Since then I haven't been able to look at the sun. The cosmic ray intensity is too great; it's burning our minds out. By the end of May it'll reach its ultimate and the world will come to an end, according to scientists. The poles are about to switch positions. Did you know that? San Francisco is getting closer to Los Angeles."

"Yes," I said. I remembered having read that in the newspaper.

"The most evolved beings of all live in the sun," Mrs. Hambro went on. "They've been entering my head every night now. I'm an initiate. Soon I'll know the whole mystery. It's very exciting." All at once she laughed, showing me her sharp-pointed teeth. "Do you think I'm out of my mind? Are you going to call the loony bin?"

"No," I said.

She said, "I've suffered, but it's worth it. None of us can hide from it; it's destiny. You've been hiding all your life, haven't you? But destiny brought you here. Look at this." Putting her cigarette down on the edge of the coffee table she opened her manila envelope and brought out a folded-up paper; she unrolled it, and I saw an intricate pencil sketch of an old Chinaman. "That's our guru," she said. "We've never seen him, but Barbara Mulchy drew that under hypnotic suggestion when we asked to see He Who's Leading us. No one has been able to read the inscription. It predates any known language." She pointed to some Chinese-looking writing at the bottom of the picture. "He drew you up here to Drake's Landing," she said. "He's been guiding you all your life."

In many respects what she said was difficult to accept. But certainly it was true that I had felt that I did not understand the real purpose of my life. And certainly I had been brought to Drake's Landing not of my own free will . . .

"Our group has made several scientifically-authenticated sightings," Mrs. Hambro continued. "We've established contact with these evolved superior beings who are in control of the universe and who are directing the cosmic radiation here in an effort to save us from our own anti-christ. I saw the anti-christ last night. That's why I'm here. I knew then that I had to contact you and get you into our group. We've had eleven or twelve people contact us in the last week or so, due to various articles printed in newspapers, some of them facetious in tone." From this manila envelope she got a newspaper clipping and passed it to me.

The clipping read:

### LOCAL SAUCER GROUP SAYS SUPERIOR BEINGS CONTROLLING MAN, LEADING US TO WORLD WAR III

Inverness Park. World War Three will begin before the end of May, and not to destroy man but to save him, according to Mrs. Edward Hambro of Inverness Park, Marin County. The flying saucer group of which she is the spokesman declares that several psychic contacts have been made with the "superior beings who are in control of our lives," and who "are leading us to material destruction for the purpose of spiritual salvation," Mrs. Hambro's words. The group meets once a week to report sightings of UFOs, unidentified flying objects. There are twelve members of the group, from Inverness Park and surrounding towns of north west Marin County. They meet in Mrs. Hambro's home. "Scientists know that the world is about to explode," Mrs. Hambro declared. "Either from a build-up of internal pressures, or from man-made atomic radiation. In any case, man must prepare for the end of the world."

I handed the clipping back to Mrs. Hambro and she returned it to her envelope. "That was in the San Rafael *Journal*," she said. "It also appeared in Petaluma newspapers and Sacramento newspapers. They didn't give a fair impression of what I said."

"I see," I said, feeling odd and weak. The strength of her gaze made my head hum. I have never met another person to this day who affected me as much as Claudia Hambro. The sunlight, when it reached her eyes, didn't reflect in the usual way but was broken up into splinters. That fascinated me. Sitting across from her, not very far from her, I saw a portion of the room reflected in her eyes, and it was not the same; it became bits instead of a single plane of reality. As she talked I kept watching that fragmented light. And never once, in all the time that she talked, did she blink.

"Have you had queer sensations recently, like silk being drawn across your stomach?" she asked me. "Or heard loud whistles, or people talking? I hear them saying, 'Don't wake Claudia. It's not time for her to awake.' "

"I have had some sensations," I said. For the past month I had a terrible tight feeling around my head, as if my forehead were about to burst. And my nose had been so constricted that I had been almost unable to breathe. Fay had said it was the usual sinus inflammation that people felt so near the ocean, with the strong winds, plus the pollen from all the flowers and trees, but I had never been convinced.

"Are they getting stronger?" Mrs. Hambro asked.

"Yes," I said.

"Will you be over Friday afternoon?" she said. "To the group? When it meets?"

I nodded.

At that, she arose and put out her cigarette. "If Fay wants to come," she said, "she's welcome. Tell her she's always welcome." Without another word she left.

Completely overwhelmed, I remained seated where I was.


That evening, when Fay found out that Claudia Hambro had come by, she had a terrible fit.

"That woman's a nut!" she cried. She was in the bathroom washing her hair at the bowl; I was holding the spray for her and she was rubbing the shampoo out. The girls had gone to their rooms to watch tv. "She's really out of her mind. My god, she had shock treatment a couple of years ago and she tried to kill herself once. She believes Martians are in touch with us—she has that nutty group that meets over in Inverness Park—they hypnotize people. Her father's one of the most arch-reactionaries in Marin County, one of the big dairy ranchers out on the Point that's responsible for our having the worst high school in the fourteen western states."

I said, "She asked me to come over on Friday and take part in a meeting of their group."

"Of course she did," Fay said. "She tracks down everybody who moves up here. I'll bet she told you it was 'destiny that brought you up here.' Right?"

I nodded.

"They think they're pawns in the hands of superior beings," she said, "when actually they're pawns in the hands of their own subconsciouses, which have run amok. She ought to be in an institution." Grabbing a towel she pushed rudely past me, and out of the bathroom, down the hall to the living room. Following after her I found her kneeling down in front of the fireplace, drying her hair. "I suppose they're harmless," she said. "Maybe it's better for their systemized schizophrenia to take the form of delusions about superior beings than to go into overt paranoia of a persecution type and imagine people are trying to kill them."

Hearing Fay say all this, I had to admit that there was a good deal of truth in it. A lot of what Mrs. Hambro had said hadn't rung right to me; it did have the sound of mental derangement.

But on the other hand, every prophet and saint had been called "insane" by his times. Naturally a prophet would appear insane, because he would hear and see and understand things that no one else could. They would be stoned and derided during their lifetimes, exactly as Christ had been. I could see what Fay meant, but also I could see not a little logic in what Claudia Hambro said.

"Are you going?" Fay said.

"Maybe so," I said, feeling embarrassed to admit it.

"I knew this would happen," was all she would say. For the rest of the evening she refused to say another word to me; in fact it wasn't until the next morning, when she wanted me to go down to the Mayfair and shop for her, that she said anything to me.

"Her whole family's that way," Fay said. At the closet she was putting on her suede leather jacket. "Her sister, her father, her aunt—it's in their blood. Listen, insanity is an infection. Look how it's infected this whole area, all around Tomales Bay, here. A whole group of people being influenced by that nut. When I first met her three years ago I thought, My god, what an attractive woman. She really is beautiful. She looks like some jungle princess or something. But she impressed me as cold. She has no emotions. She has no capacity to feel normal human emotions. Here she's got six kids and yet she hates kids; she has no love for them or for Ed. And she's always pregnant. She's nuts. It's the two-year-old mind that controls the world."

I said nothing.

"She looks like some successful Marin County upper middle class suburban housewife that gives barbecue parties," Fay said. "And instead she's a grade A nut."

Opening the front door she started out.

"I'm going down to San Francisco," she said. "And visit Charley. You be sure and be here when the girls get home. You know how scared they are to get home and find nobody here."

"Right," I said. Since their father's heart attack, both children had had a lot of anxiety during the night, had dreams for instance, and spells of unmanageability. And Elsie had begun to wet her bed again. Both girls now asked for a bottle each night before going to bed. That probably had a good deal to do with the bed wetting.

I knew that in actuality she was not going down to San Francisco to see Charley but was going to meet Nat Anteil, probably somewhere between Point Reyes and Mill Valley, possibly in Fairfax, and have lunch with him. They had been having trouble meeting each other, since his wife Gwen had become suspicious of the time they spent together and had insisted on accompanying him over in the evenings. Since his wife no longer permitted him to visit Fay by himself, he and Fay were up against it.

And in a small town where everybody knows everybody, it is very hard, if not impossible, to have a secret relationship. If you go into a bar with somebody else's wife, you are recognized by everyone who is there, and the next day it's written up in the Baywood *Press*. If you stop to buy gas, Earl Fankis, who owns the Standard Station, recognizes your car and you. If you go into the post office, you are recognized because the postmaster knows everyone in the area; it's his job. The barber notices you as you walk by his window. The man in the feed store sits at his desk watching the street all day long. All the clerks at the Mayfair Market know everyone, since everyone charges there. So Fay and Nat had to meet outside the area if they were going to meet at all. And if their relationship became a matter of public knowledge, it was not my fault.

However, they had done fairly well in keeping it under cover. When I was downtown shopping, I didn't hear anybody discussing it, either at the Mayfair or the post office or the drug store. Several people asked me how Charley was. So they had been discreet. After all, even Nat's wife was ignorant. All she knew for sure was that he and Fay had been together at Fay's house several times, and no doubt Nat had told her that I was present, and possibly the two girls. Possibly he and Fay had even concocted a story to explain it—Fay had a set of the Britannica, for instance, and the big Webster's dictionary, and Nat could always say that he was over using her various reference books. And she had already given the pretext that she needed help with her checkbook. And everybody in north west Marin County knew that Fay called up everyone and asked them for favors; she made use of everybody she met, and the sign of Nat Anteil driving over to her house or being driven over might stir no comment, as such, because he simply became another person ensnared, doing her work for her while she sat out on the patio and smoked and read the *New Yorker*.

The real fact was that for all her energetic bouncing around, her scaling cliffs and gardening and badminton playing, my sister had always been lazy. If she could she would sleep until noon. Her idea of work is to spend two evenings a week—four hours—shaping clay pots, something that the Bluebirds did in the afternoon with about as much effort— and to them it was considered fun. The house had six or seven statues that Fay had made, and to me they looked like nothing on earth. Building a trf tuner, in my high school days, I used to spend whole days, ten hours without interruption. I never saw Fay spend more than an hour at any one thing; after that she became bored, stopped, did something else. For instance, she could not bear to iron clothes. It was too tedious for her. She wanted me to try my hand, but I simply couldn't get the hang of it, and so it had to be taken down to San Rafael to a laundry there. Her idea of work, of creative work, was derived from the progressive nursery schools that she had gone to as a child in the 'thirties. She had never had to work, as I had done and still do.

But I did not object to doing her work for her, as Charley did and, to some extent, Nat did. I could not be sure how Nat felt, or if he understood that in addition to her having an emotional relationship with him she was also employing him as she employed everyone else around her. In fact, she employed her children. She had persuaded them that it was their job to fix their breakfasts on Saturday and Sunday morning, and until I came she simply refused to cook breakfast for them on the weekends, no matter how hungry they got. Usually they had fixed themselves cocoa and jelly sandwiches and gone off to watch tv until afternoon. I put an end to that, of course, preparing for them an even heartier breakfast than I did on weekdays. It seemed to me that on Sundays especially they should have a really important breakfast, and so I fixed waffles for them, with bacon; sometimes nut waf-

fles, or strawberry waffles—in other words, something that
constituted a genuine Sunday breakfast. Charley, too, before
his heart attack, appreciated this. Fay, however, complained
that I was fixing so much food that she was becoming fat.
She actually became irritable when she appeared at the
breakfast table and found that instead of grape juice and
toast and coffee and applesauce I had prepared bacon and
eggs or hash and eggs and cereal and rolls. It made her angry
because she wanted to eat it, and having no capacity to deny
herself anything, she sooner or later ate what I had fixed her,
her lower lip stuck out with petulance throughout the meal.

One morning when I got up as usual before anyone else—
about seven o'clock—and walked from my bedroom into the
kitchen to open the drapes and put on water for Fay's coffee
and generally begin fixing breakfast, I saw that the door to
the study had been shut and locked from the other side. I
knew that it had been locked, just to see it, because unless
the lock is thrown the door hangs open slightly. Somebody
had to be in there, and I suspected that it was Nat Anteil.
Sure enough, about seven-thirty when the girls had gotten
up and Fay was combing her hair, Nat appeared from the
front part of the house.

"Hi," he said to us.

The girls stared at him, and then Elsie said, "Where did
you come from? Did you sleep here last night?"

Nat said, "No, I just walked in the front door. Nobody
heard me." He seated himself at the breakfast table and said,
"Could I have some breakfast?"

"Of course," Fay said, showing no surprise at seeing him.
Why should she? But she did not even go through the motions
of pretending, of asking him why he had come over so
early . . . after all, nobody comes calling at seven-thirty in
the morning.

I put out an extra plate and silverware and cup for him,
and presently there he was eating with us, having his grapefruit and cereal and toast and bacon and eggs. He had quite

an appetite, as always; he really enjoyed the food that he got to eat, the food that Charley Hume sick in the hospital provided.

As soon as I had cleared the table and done the dishes I went off into my room and sat down on my bed to record, in my notebook, the fact that Nathan Anteil had spent the night.

Later in the morning, after Nat had departed and I was busy sweeping the patio, Fay approached me. "Did it bother you," she said, "fixing breakfast for him?"

"No," I said.

With ill-concealed agitation, she hung around me as I worked. Suddenly she burst out in her impatient manner, "You're no doubt conscious that he spent the night in the study. He was working on a paper last night and he couldn't make it home he was so tired, so I said, you can sleep in the study. It's perfectly all right, but when you go down to visit Charley don't say anything to him; it might get him all upset for nothing."

I nodded as I worked.

"Okay?" she said.

"It's none of my business," I said. "It's not my house."

"True," she said. "But you're such a horse's ass there's no telling what you might do."

To that, I said nothing. But as I worked I was busy constructing in my head, a more vivid method of presenting the true facts to Charley. A dramatization, such as you see on tv when they are showing the effects of, say, Anacin or aspirin. Something to really drive the message home to him.

# 11

In Nat Anteil's mind a suspicion had appeared, and he could do nothing to get rid of it. It seemed to him that Fay Hume had gotten herself involved with him because her husband was dying and she wanted to be sure that, when he did die, she would have another man to take his place.

But, he thought, what's so bad about that? Is it unnatural for a woman who has two children to take care of, plus a big house, plus all those animals and all that land, to want a man to take the responsibility off her shoulders?

It was the deliberateness of it that bothered him. She had seen him, selected him, and set about getting him despite the fact that he was married and had a life already planned for himself. It did not matter to her that he wanted to get his degree and support himself and his wife in the modest fashion that he now engaged in; she saw him only as a support to her life. Or at least that was his suspicion. He could not pin her down; she appeared genuinely emotionally involved with him, possibly even against her will. After all, she was taking a terrible risk, jeopardizing her house and home, her whole life, by her meetings with him.

He thought, When it comes down to it, I don't fully understand her. I have no way of knowing how deliberately she acts, how conscious she is of the consequences of her actions. On the surface she seems impatient, childish, wanting something in the immediate present, with no concern for the future. She plays for the short haul. Admittedly, she saw me and Gwen and wanted to meet us; there's never been any doubt of that. And she herself admits that she's selfish, that she's used to having her own way. That if she's denied something she has a tantrum. Her having an affair with me—when she's a social pillar of the community, owns such a large and important home, here, knows everyone, has two children in school—proves how shortsighted she is. Is this the action of a woman thinking about long-term consequences?

And yet, he thought, I consider myself a mature and responsible person, and I'm involved with her. I have a wife, a family, a career to think about, yet I'm jeopardizing everything in this involvement; I'm throwing away the future— possibly—for something in the present.

Can we know our own motives?

He thought, Actually a human being is an unfolding biological organism that's every so often gripped by instinctive forces. He can't perceive the purpose of those forces, what their goal is. All he's conscious of is the stress they put on him, the pressure. They force him to do something. But why . . . he can't tell that at the time. Perhaps later. Someday I may look back and see exactly why I got involved with Fay Hume, and why she risked everything to get involved with me.

Anyhow, he thought, I have this conviction that whatever the reason, it's some deeply serious, deeply responsible, calculated matter, and not the caprice of the moment. She knows what she's doing, better than I.

And, he thought, she's using me; she's the prime mover in this, has always been, and I'm nothing but her instrument. So what does that make me? Where does that put me? Is my life to be turned to the serving of another person, a woman who is determined to keep her family on a sound operating basis and doesn't mind breaking up somebody else's marriage, future, dreams, so that she can accomplish it?

But if she's not conscious of this, if she's acting instinctively, can I hold her morally responsible?

Am I thinking like the college boy that I am?

For days now he had tormented himself with such notions. And he seemed to be getting himself deeper into the circular swamp of pure reasoning. It was his philosophy class all over again, where debate led not to solution or insight but to further and further debate. Words begat words. Thoughts begat a feverish preoccupation with thinking, with logic as such.

Who would know? Fay? Her brother? Charley?

Surely if anybody knows, it would be Charley Hume, lying there in his hospital bed.

Or, Nat thought, maybe he never worked it out either. From what Fay had said, apparently Charley had been ambivalent toward her, sometimes loving her with hopeless devotion, sometimes feeling so trapped, so victimized and degraded, so turned into a thing, that he had bounced one thing after another off her head. Charley, lying in the hospital, knew more than he ever had; he had a dim intuition—at times—that his wife had used him to build a grand new house for her own purposes, that she used her children, too, and everyone else, but then that intuition faded out and he was left with his frantic love for her. Wasn't this a historic pattern between men and women? Women got the upper hand indirectly, through cunning.

And the trouble is, he realized, once you get started thinking along these lines, once you start looking for indications that you are being used, you can find evidence everywhere. Paranoia. If she asks you to drive her to Petaluma to pick up a hundred pound sack of duck feed, which she obviously can't lift herself, is that a sign that you are no longer a man, a human being, but merely a machine capable of picking up a hundred pounds and thrusting it into the back of the car?

Doesn't everybody pick their friends because they're useful to them? Doesn't a man marry a woman who flatters him, does things for him such as cooking, buying him clothes? Isn't that natural? Is love natural when it binds together people who otherwise would be of no practical value to each other?

On and on he reasoned.


One Sunday afternoon he and Fay drove out to the Point, to the McClures' ranch. This area might someday become a state park, this wild moor-like plateau that dropped off at the ocean's edge, one of the most desolate parts of the United States, with weather unlike that of any other part of California. For now however it belonged to the various branches of the McClure family and was used, like most of the land of the Point, for the raising of top-grade dairy herds. The McClures had already donated a stretch of coast to the state and this had been made into a public beach. But the state wanted the rest of their ranch. The McClures loved the area, loved their ranch, and the fight over the land had gone on for some time, with the issue still in doubt. Almost everyone in the area wanted to see the McClures keep their ranch.

At the moment it required a friendship with somebody in the McClure family to get permission to cross the ranch to the coast. The road through the ranch—perhaps twelve miles in length—consisted of crushed red gravel, deeply rutted from winter rains. A car that slipped into a rut or into the pasture became mired. And there were no phones by which to call the AAA.

As they drove, bouncing along, the car sliding from side to side, Nat became more and more conscious of their isolation out here. If anything happened to them they could get no help. On each side of the road semi-wild cattle roamed. He saw no telegraph poles, no wires or signs of electricity. Only the rocky, rolling grass hills. Somewhere ahead was the ocean and the end of the road. He had never been out here. Fay of course had, several times, driven out here to collect abalone. The road did not seem to bother her; at the wheel she drove confidently, chattering with him about various matters.

"The trouble with owning a VW or any sports car up here," she told him, "is that if you hit a deer, you get flipped. You're dead. Or a cow. Some of those cows weigh as much as a VW."

To him that seemed an exaggeration. But he said nothing. The ride made him carsick and he felt like a child again, being driven by his mother.

In some respects that epitomized his problem with her. She had an attitude toward men like that of a mother toward children; she took it for granted that men were frailer, shorter-lived, less good at solving problems than women. A myth of the times, he realized. All consumer goods are aimed at a female market . . . women hold the purse-strings and the manufacturers know that. On tv dramas, women are shown as the responsible ones, with men being foolish Dagwood Bumsteads . . .

I went to so much trouble, he thought, to break away from my family—in particular my mother—and get off on my own, to be economically independent, to establish my own family. And now I'm mixed up with a powerful, demanding, calculating woman who wouldn't bat an eye at putting me back in that old situation again. In fact it would seem perfectly natural to her.

Whenever they went out somewhere in public together, Fay always took a long look in advance at his choice of clothes. She made it her business to see if she approved. "Don't you think you should put on a tie?" she would say. It never occurred to him to pass judgment on what she wore, to tell her for example that he thought shorts and a halter should not be worn into a supermarket, or that a suede leather coat, chartreuse slacks, dark glasses, and sandals constituted a grotesque outfit, not worthy of being worn anywhere. If she wore clothes that clashed, he simply accepted it as part of her; he took it as a postulate of her existence.

The rutted rock trails along which they drove ended at a cypress grove on the edge of the ocean cliffs. In the center of the grove he saw a small old farmhouse, well-kept, with a garden and palm tree in front of it, and side buildings that looked much older than any he had seen in California except for the Spanish adobe buildings which of course were now all historical monuments. The farmhouse and side buildings—unlike other farm buildings he had seen—were painted a dark color. The garden, too, had a brown quality, and the palm tree had the thick, hairy quality usual with trees of its kind. The buildings seemed deserted, so completely so that he wondered if anyone had been there in the last month. But everything had remained in good order. Here, so far away from cars and people, no one came to do any damage. Even marauders were absent, this far out.

"Some of these buildings are a hundred years old," Fay told him as she drove the car from the road—it ended at a closed gate—and on to a small grassy field. At a barbed wire fence she stopped and shut off the motor. "We walk from here," she said.

They carried the fishing equipment and their lunches from the car to the fence. Fay lifted one wire and slipped easily between it and the one below, but he found it necessary to use the gate; he did not feel as slim as she. Beyond the fence they followed a trail across a pasture and then they began to climb down a sandy slope overgrown with iceplant. Now he heard the ocean breakers. The wind became stronger. Under his feet the sand crumbled and gave; he had to lie down and take hold of the tangles of iceplant. Ahead of him, Fay skipped and tumbled, caught herself and continued on

without a pause, telling him constantly how she and Charley
and the girls and assorted friends of theirs had come here to
this beach; how much trouble they had had getting down,
what they had caught, what the dangers were, who had been
scared and who not . . . he groped along after, thinking that
women could be divided into two distinct classes; those who
were good climbers and then all the others lumped together.
A woman who climbed well was not like the rest of them.
Probably the difference pervaded every part of their physical
and mental apparatus; at this moment it seemed crucial to
him, a genuine revelation.

Now Fay had come to some rocky projections. Past her
he saw what appeared to be a sheer drop, and then the tops
of rocks far below, and the surf. Crouching down, Fay descended step by step to a ledge, and there, among the piles
of sand and rock that had slid down, she took hold of a rope
attached to a metal stake driven into the rock.

"From now on," she called back, "it's by rope."

Good Christ, he thought.

"The girls can do it," she called.

"I'll tell you honestly," he said, halting with his feet
planted far apart, balancing himself with care, "I'm not sure
I can."

"I'll carry everything down," Fay said. "Throw the packs
and the fishing poles down to me."

With care, he lowered things to her. Strapping the packs
to her back, she disappeared, clinging to the rope. After a
time she reappeared, this time far below, standing on the
beach and gazing nearly straight up at him, a small figure
among the rocks. "Okay," she shouted, cupping her hands
to her mouth.

Cursing with fright, he half-slid, half-stepped down the
rock projections to the rope. He found the rope badly corroded, and that did not improve his morale. But for the first
time he discovered that the cliff was not sheer; it had easy
footholds, and the rope was merely for safety. Even without

it, in an emergency, a person could get down, foot by foot, to the beach. Fay, when he got there, had meanwhile gone off and was seeking a deep pool in which to fish; she did not even bother to watch him descend.

Later, with their poles propped up against rocks, they fished in a pool which the withdrawing tide had left. Several crabs wandered about in the water, and he saw a many-legged starfish, a type he had never before seen. Twelve legs . . . and bright orange.

"That's a sea-slug," Fay said, pointing to a nondescript blob.

They used mussels as bait. According to Fay it was possible to catch ocean trout. But they saw no fish in their pool and neither he nor she expected much luck. In any case it was exciting, here on this deserted beach at the base of the cliff, accessible only by rope . . . no beer cans, no orange peels, only cockle shells and abalone shells, and the black, slippery rocks in which both cockles and abalone could be found.

He said, "Let me ask you something."

"Okay," she said sleepily. Leaning back against the rock she had gone almost to sleep. She had on a cotton shirt and water-stained canvas trousers and an old, torn pair of tennis shoes.

"Where is this relationship of ours going?"

"Time will tell," Fay said.

"Where do you want it to go?"

She opened one eye and studied him. "Aren't you happy? My good god—you get fed glorious meals, you get to use my car, my credit card, I bought you a decent suit that isn't two years out of style with *my* money—you get to screw me. Don't you?"

That word had always bothered him, since he had first heard her use it. Now of course she would never stop; she had noticed his reaction to it.

"What more do you want?" she said.

He said, "But what do you want out of it?"

"I get a nice man," she said. "A very pretty man. You know that. You're the prettiest man I ever saw in my entire life; as soon as I saw you that day I wanted to take you to my bed and screw you. Didn't I tell you that?"

With patience, he said, "Let's look at the possibilities. First of all, your husband will either recover or he won't. That means he'll either be coming back from the hospital or he won't. Do you realize I don't know how you feel toward him? Whether you'd prefer him to come back, and if he did come back—"

She interrupted, "You know, we could lie down on the sand and screw."

"God damn you," he said.

"Why?" she said. "Because I'm using the same words as you? What do you call it? You do it, whatever you call it. You do screw me; you have screwed me . . . five times. Listen," she said, all at once becoming serious. "The last time when I was washing my diaphragm afterward—did I tell you?"

"No," he said, with apprehension.

"It was eaten away. Corroded. Are you sure your sperm doesn't have some sort of sulfuric acid in it? My good god, it was totally ruined—I had to drive down to Fairfax and get another, and I had to be measured again—she told me I always should be measured when I get a new diaphragm. I didn't know that. I've replaced my diaphragm six or seven times without being measured. She told me the one I've been using is much too small. It's a good thing it did wear out."

After a pause he tried to resume his own topic. "I want to know if you're interested in me on a permanent basis."

"What if I said no?" she said.

"Well," he said, "I'm just curious."

"Does it matter? Why do you have to have these great answers? My good god."

"Remember, I've got a wife," he said, with growing outrage. "It's important to me to know where you and I stand."

"You mean, 'are my intentions honorable'?"

"Yes," he said finally.

Fay said, "I'm in love with you. You know how you affect me; nobody ever affected me that way in my entire life. But— you mean, you're thinking about marriage, aren't you? Could you support me? I have a house budget of twelve thousand a year . . . did you know that?"

"Yes," he said.

"You couldn't support me and the two girls on your salary."

He said, "Presumably there'd be some kind of settlement."

"I own half the house," she said. "Community property. My equity is worth about fifteen thousand. And I've got property that Charley gave me as a gift . . . stock in the Ford motor company. I get in about one hundred a month from that. And I've got one hundred and fifty more coming in from an apartment building in Tampa, Florida. So I get in two-fifty a month, and that's all I have, except that I'd get the Buick; it's mine."

"Would you consider splitting up from Charley?" he said. "If he recovers?"

"Well," she said, "the girls like you. They're afraid of Charley because they've seen him hit me. You'd never hit me. Would you? I really can't stand that; I almost left him a couple of times. I god damn near drove over and got Sheriff Chisholm and had a felony wife-beating warrant sworn out . . . maybe I should have." She paused, deep in thought. "I really should get the house. It's actually mine. He should give me that."

"It's a nice house," he said. He thought to himself what it would be like. They would live partly—perhaps mostly— on Fay's money, and in Fay's house. The children would be Fay's. The car, too. Of course, he would eat well . . . assuming that the settlement with Charley went in her favor. But suppose Charley hired lawyers and got after her with a charge of adultery? Suppose they got after her with an unfit mother charge. Possibly she would wind up with no settlement at all, no alimony, no child-support.

"You wouldn't have to support the kids," she said. "I know he'd always see to their welfare."

He nodded.

"How would you feel about using my money?" she said.

"How would you feel?" he said.

"It wouldn't bother me. Money is money, nothing more. It would be money I got from him."

He said, "Suppose something went wrong and you didn't get it. You wound up with no money, with only my means of support."

"You could stop your studying," she said. "Go to work fulltime. Couldn't you earn enough in the real estate game to support us? I know a man, a San Francisco man, who earns about fourteen thousand a year in real estate. Men make fortunes in real estate." She went on, then, to tell him of all the deals, all the quick riches and comfortable livings that she had heard among realtors and land speculators. Her apartment building in Tampa, for instance. It had cost them almost nothing. Charley was very good at picking up property cheap . . . their ten acres here in Marin County hadn't set them back much, and at one time they had options on all sorts of acreage around Marin County, including some very choice land.

"I think," he said, "I'd be a lot better off ultimately if I went on and got my degree."

"Oh balls," she said. "My god, I've got a BA and I couldn't earn a nickel with it; I tried. I wasn't qualified for any high-paying jobs, any professional jobs, and when I applied for the usual stuff they give to business school graduates—typing and shorthand stuff, office stuff—they were suspicious of me because I had a degree. They told me I 'wouldn't be happy.' That was before I was married, of course. I'd rather be dead than work in an office, now that I've had a chance to live a really happy life. I love it up here in the country; this is such a beautiful area. I wouldn't go back to the city for anything in the world. It would kill me."

He thought, The message is clear. She wouldn't make any attempt to put me through school. She wouldn't permit any drop in her standard of living. She wouldn't even be willing to leave Marin County or her house; she would want—expect—to go on exactly as she is, but with me instead of Charley as her husband.

In fact, she would get everything she's gotten from Charley, but without Charley. He's the only part she doesn't care for. She'd like to have me in his place. But everything else the same.

We wouldn't have a combined life, a mutual life. I'd simply be fitted into a slot from which Charley got jerked out. I'd enter her life and occupy a certain area.

But, he thought, would it be so terrible a life?

The house was far more of a house than any he could hope to buy or build or rent or own by himself, with his limited wage-earning capacity. And she was certainly an exceptional person. She made a superb companion to a man; she swore, she climbed, she played games—she was willing to try anything. She had a real sense of adventure, of exploration.

One day they had gone together up to the oyster beds to buy a quart of fresh oysters. When she had seen the oyster boat, and the rakes, she had immediately wanted to go out and be with the men gathering the oysters; she asked what time the boat left—it was a barge, carrying two or three men, plus their equipment—and if she could go along. All of them, the Mexican oyster-opener, the tough-looking owner, and himself—they had all been impressed by this slim woman who had no compunction, no anxiety.

So much fun to be with, he thought. She finds so much in each situation. As they drove along she spotted so many things that he missed . . . she lived so much more fully. Of course, she lived only in the present. And she had no ability to reflect. Or, for that matter, to read thoroughly or to contemplate. She had a limited span of attention, like a child. But, unlike a child—very unlike a child—she had the ability to pursue a goal over a long period of time . . . and once again he found himself wondering, how long a period? Years? All her life? Does she ever give up, when she wants something?

He had the intuition that she never did give up, that when she appeared to yield, she was only biding her time.

And we're all things that she wants or doesn't want, he thought. I happen to be a thing she wants; she wants me as her husband.

Aren't I lucky? Isn't it possible that a man could have a fuller, happier life being used by an exciting woman like this, rather than living out his own drab, limited life? Isn't this the trend in our society, the new role for men to play? Is it necessary that I pursue the goals I set for myself, by myself? Can't I accede and permit another person, a more vital, active person to set goals for me?

What's so wrong with that?

And yet he did feel it was wrong. Even in small matters . . . when, for instance, at the dinner table she served him salad, which he did not like, because she believed that he should eat salad. She did not serve him what he wanted; even in this she treated him as a child and served him what he ought to eat.

"Potatoes have vitamins and minerals in them," Elsie had informed him. And both girls, playfully, called him a "nice big boy." The biggest boy—the only boy—that ate dinner with them. Not actually a Daddy at all. Not like the man in the hospital.

I wonder if I'll wind up hitting her, he thought. He had never in his life hit a woman; and yet, he already sensed that Fay was the kind of woman who forced a man into hitting her. Who left him no alternative. No doubt she failed to see this; it would not be to her advantage to see this . . .

And his heart attack, he thought. When the time comes

that I've given her what she wants, when she gets tired of me, or afraid of me, and wants to get rid of me, will I have a heart attack, too?

To some extent he felt afraid of her.

If she could get me to go this far, he thought, risk losing my wife, have an affair with her, then surely she could get me to go the rest of the way. Why not? Divorce Gwen and marry her. Assuming of course that Charley had been disposed of more permanently. And if I didn't want to go through with it, if, at any time, I tried to shake loose.

I wouldn't have much luck, he thought.

Let's face it—it's probably too late now. I couldn't break loose from her now.

But why not? All I'd have to do is simply stop seeing her. Am I so weak that I couldn't go through with it?

Somewhere, he decided, Fay would find some means of drawing him back if she wished to. Some evening she would call up and say something, ask for something, and he would not be able to refuse; that is, he would not *want* to refuse.

Such a peculiar person, he thought. So complex. On the one hand she seems so agile, so athletic, and yet I've seen her appear so awkward that it embarrassed me. She gives the impression of a hard, worldly adroitness, and in some situations she's like an adolescent: rigid with ancient, middle class attitudes, unable to think for herself, falling back on the old verities . . . a victim of her family teaching, shocked by what shocks people, wanting what people usually want. She wants a home, a husband, and her idea of a husband is a man who earns a certain amount of money, helps around the garden, does the dishes . . . the idea of a good husband that's found in cartoons in *This Week* magazine; a viewpoint from the most ordinary stratum, that great ubiquitous world of bourgeois family life, transmitted from generation to generation. Despite her wild language.

Just a little housewife—she had called herself that, one day, while she was taking off her clothes to go to bed with him. One afternoon, while her brother was off somewhere, in Petaluma, shopping. He had laughed to hear her call herself that.

Why am I so drawn to her? he wondered. Physical attractiveness? In the past he had never been drawn to thin women, and admittedly she was thin; sometimes she appeared even scrawny. Was it, perhaps, those middle class values? It seemed to him that there was, in her, something sturdy and sensible. Possibly I admire those values, he thought. I feel she'd make a good wife because she does believe as she does, because she is so middle class. This is the very unrevolutionary, conservative matter. Marriage is a conservative matter.

On some deep level I trust her, he decided. That is, I trust the training that has been inscribed on her, the heritage. Things that she did not invent and does not greatly control. Yet, she grasps that underneath all her flamboyance she's quite an ordinary person—in the finest possible sense. She is not attractive because she is unusual and exciting but because she has found something exciting in the ordinary—that is, in herself.

To her, he said, "You're a square. Aren't you?"

Fay said, "Didn't you know that? Good god, what did you think I was? A Beatnik?"

"Why are you interested in me?" he demanded.

"Because you're good husband material," Fay said. "I'm being very shrewd; there's nothing romantic in this."

That left him without a retort. Leaning back, balancing herself against the rock, she closed her eyes and enjoyed the sun, the racket of the surf, while he worried. They spent the remainder of the afternoon that way.

# 12

On Friday, in spite of my sister cursing me out in her usual terms, I walked up the road to Inverness Park to Claudia Hambro's house and attended the meeting of the group.

The house had been built in one of the canyons, halfway up the side, on one of the twisting roads too narrow for cars to pass. The outside of the house had a damp appearance, as if the wood, in spite of paint, had absorbed moisture from the ground and trees. Most of the houses built in the canyons never dried off. Ferns grew on all sides of the Hambro house, some of them so tall and so densely packed in against the sides of the house that they seemed to be consuming the house. Actually the house was big: three stories, with a railed porch running along one side of it. But the foliage caused it to blend back into the canyon wall and become indistinct. I saw several cars parked in front of it, on the shoulder of the road, and that was how I knew where to go.

Mrs. Hambro met me at the front door. She wore Chinese silk trousers and slippers, and her hair, this time, had been tied back in a black, shiny rope, like a pigtail; it hung all the way down to her waist. Her fingernails, I noticed, had been lacquered silver and were long and sharp. She had on quite a bit of makeup; her eyes seemed extra dark and enlarged, and her lips so red to be almost brown.

Two glass doors, propped back with books, let me into the living room, which had walls and ceiling of black wood, with bookcases everywhere, and chairs and couches, with a fireplace at one end over which the Hambros had hung a Chinese tapestry showing the branch of a tree and a mountain in the distance. Six or seven people sat about on the chairs. As I walked around I noticed a tape recorder and a number of spools of tape, plus quite a few copies of *Fate* magazine, a magazine devoted to unusual scientific facts.

The people in the room seemed tense, and considering why we had come I could not blame them. Mrs. Hambro introduced me to them. One man, elderly, with rustic-looking clothes, worked at the hardware store in Point Reyes. A second man, she told me, was a carpenter from Inverness. The last man was almost as young as I, a blond-haired man wearing slacks and loafers, his hair cut short. According to Mrs. Hambro he owned a small dairy farm up the coast on the other side of the bay near Marshall. The other people were women. One, huge and well-dressed, in her middle fifties, was the wife of the man who owned the coffee shop in Inverness Park. Another was the wife of a technician from the RCA transmitter out on the Point. Another was the wife of a garage mechanic at Point Reyes Station.

After I had seated myself, a middle-aged couple entered. Mrs. Hambro told us that they had just moved to Inverness; the man was a landscape painter and his wife did dress alterations. They had come up to north west Marin County for reasons of health. That evidently completed the group; Mrs. Hambro closed the glass doors after the couple and seated herself in our midst.

The meeting began. The shades were pulled down and then Mrs. Hambro had the large well-dressed woman—

whose name was Mrs. Bruce—lie down on the couch. Mrs. Hambro then hypnotized her and had her recall a number of past lives, for the purpose of establishing contact with an inner personality, that only rarely came out, which had the ability to receive information dealing with the evolved beings that control our lives. It was explained to me and the couple who had arrived after me that through this inner personality of Mrs. Bruce the group had been able to gather exact information on the plans that the beings had for the disposition of the Earth and its inhabitants.

After an interval of sighing and murmuring, Mrs. Bruce said that the evolved beings had definitely decided to put an end to the Earth, and that only those who had established contact with the genuine forces of the universe would be saved. They would be taken off Earth in a flying saucer a day or so before the conflagration. After that, Mrs. Bruce passed into a deep sleep, during which she snored. Finally Mrs. Hambro had her wake up by counting to ten and clapping her hands.

All of us were, naturally, quite keyed-up by this news. If I had any doubts before, the actual sight—witnessed by myself—of this inner personality of Mrs. Bruce responding to direct transmissions from the superior evolved beings on other planets made up my mind. After all, I now had empirical verifications, the best scientific evidence in the world.

The problem before the group was now to decipher the exact date at which the world would be brought to an end. Mrs. Hambro made up twelve slips of paper each with the name of a month of the year, plus thirty-one slips each with a date between one and thirty-one. These she put in two piles on the table. Then she put Mrs. Bruce back into a trance and inquired who should be sent as an instrument of initiate knowledge to select the slips.

Mrs. Bruce stated that the person who should go had just come into the group this day, and that he came alone. Ob-

viously they meant me. When she had awakened Mrs. Bruce,
Mrs. Hambro told me to shut my eyes and go to the table
and take a slip from each pile.

With everyone watching, I walked to the table and selected
two slips. The first said April. The second said twenty-third.
So the world, according to the superior evolved beings that
control the universe, would end on April twenty-third.

It made me feel strange to realize that I had been picked
to select and announce the date on which the world would
end. But all along, as I acknowledged, these superior forces
had been controlling me; they had brought me from Seville
to Drake's Landing, no doubt for this purpose. So in a sense
there was nothing odd about my going to the table and picking out the dates. Actually, we were quite calm at this point.
Everyone in the room had his feelings under control. We
had coffee and sat in semi-silence, meditating about it.

There was some discussion as to whether we should notify
the San Rafael *Journal* and the Baywood *Press*. In the end
we decided that there was no point in making a public statement, since those to be saved by the superior evolved
beings—which we referred to as the SEBs—would be no-
tified by direct mental telepathy.

In a sort of stunned haze, we adjourned the meeting and
left Mrs. Hambro's house, tiptoeing out like the members
of a congregation leaving church. One of the group, the man
who worked at the hardware store, gave me a ride home and
dropped me off in front of the house. I never did catch his
name, and on the drive we were both too occupied with our
thoughts to talk.

When I got into the house I found Fay dusting in the living
room. I had expected her to ask about the meeting, but she
paid no attention to me; by the hectic pace at which she
dusted I realized that she was deep in some problem of her
own and wasn't interested in me or what I had to say.

"The hospital called," she said finally. "They want me to

come down; they have something they want to tell me about Charley."

"Bad news?" I said, thinking that whatever news it was it could scarcely compare with what I had to tell her. And yet, even knowing as I did that we had a only month left, I found myself concerned with the news about Charley. "What did they say?" I demanded, following her into her bedroom.

"Oh," she said vaguely. "I don't know. They want to discuss whether he can be brought home."

"You want me to go down with you?" I said.

Fay said, "I don't feel like driving. I called the Anteils and they're going to drive me down. In the state I'm in I couldn't handle the car." She disappeared into the bathroom, shutting and locking the door after her. I heard water running; she was taking a shower and changing her clothes.

"It sounds like the news isn't too bad," I said, when she reappeared. "If they're talking about bringing him home—"

"Be quiet," she said, in the tone of voice that she used with the girls. "I want to think." And then, halting, she eyed me and said, "You didn't say anything to Charley about Nathan being over here, did you?"

"No," I said.

"God damn you," she said, still eyeing me. "I'll bet you did. I know you did."

"It's my job to report scientific facts," I said. "What is there about him coming over here that makes it wrong for me to tell Charley about it? After all, this is his house. He has a right to know who comes here."

Glaring at me, she tapped herself on the chest and said loudly, "This is *my* house. This is *my* business."

Seeing the expression on her face, the worry and animosity, I felt upset. Not knowing what to say I went off by myself and played with the dog. The next I knew, the Anteils' Studebaker had appeared in the driveway, and I saw Nathan Anteil and his wife inside, with Nathan at the wheel. He honked, and Fay came out, in her suit and coat and high heels, and got into the car.

As the car started to back out, Fay rolled down the window on her side and called to me, "You be sure you're here when the girls get home. And if I'm not home by five, start fixing dinner. Better get a steak out of the freezer and start it thawing. And there's some potatoes." Then the car drove off.

Much to my dissatisfaction I hadn't had a chance to tell her about the meeting and what we had decided, that I personally had been chosen by the SEBs to pick the date for the end of the world. Feeling cheated, I returned to the house and seated myself in the living room to read last night's newspaper. And also I felt irritable and guilty at Fay's accusation; of course I had told Charley, through the pressure of duty, but nevertheless it bothered me to have her so angry with me. Even if she was in the wrong it was not a pleasant situation. I hardly enjoy having somebody angry with me.

During Fay's absence I spent time in the study, using the typewriter to get down on paper the new and more vivid presentation of facts which I felt Charley should have before him. After all, human choice is impossible without knowledge, and accurate choice is only possible where knowledge is complete and scientifically organized. That's what separates us from the brutes.

For reference—as a prototype, a model—I got out some of my few remaining *Thrilling Wonder Stories* magazines and selected stories that had especially impressed me. After studying them I was able to perceive the methods by which the authors had dramatized their points. So I set to work with the magazines open on the desk beside me.

If Charley would be coming home soon it was imperative for me to get my fictionalized account before him almost at once. He would need it as a basis on which to act in reference to the situation.

When Fay returned home that night she said that possibly within a week Charley would be home. Fortunately I had made good progess on my work during the day, and I felt sure I would complete it. As it turned out, I got the account done the following day, and on Friday I took the bus down to San Francisco, carrying the account with me rolled up and fastened with a rubber band.

After spending a short time in the public library going over the new magazines, I took a bus to the U.C. Hospital. I found Charley out on the sundeck, in a wheelchair, wearing a bathrobe.

"Hi," I said.

He glanced at me. Immediately his eyes made out the rolled-up tube of paper that I carried, and I saw that he understood—at least in a general way—what it was I had for him. He started to speak, then changed his mind.

"It won't be long now," I said. "Before you're back home."

He nodded slightly.

Pulling a chair up I sat down across from him.

"Don't read me that thing," he said.

I said, "These are the dramatized facts."

"Get out of here," he said.

That upset and confused me. I sat fooling with the rubber band, feeling like a fool. I had done all this work, and for what? Finally I said, "The difference between us and the animals is that we can use words. Isn't that right?"

With obvious reluctance he nodded.

"We expand our environment," I said. "We learn through the written word. We'd never even know about far-distant places such as Siam if we couldn't read." I went on, amplifying this idea; he listened but said nothing. After I had finished, he still said nothing. I waited and then I unrolled the rubber band from the tube, flattened the sheets of paper, and very carefully began to read.

After I had come to the end I sat waiting for his reaction.

"How'd you ever put together a thing like that?" he said, in a tone of voice suggesting that he was virtually ready to burst out laughing. His whole face seemed twisted out of shape and his eyes shone as if at the same time he was mad as hell. I saw that his hands were shaking. "It sounds like something out of an old pulp magazine," he said. "Where'd you get those phrases like 'breasts like mounds of whipped cream' and 'red-tipped cones of pure ecstasy'?"

I couldn't have been more embarrassed. Putting away the sheets of paper I mumbled, "I was simply trying to vivify it."

He stared at me with that same mixture of expressions on his face. Now he had begun to flush, and his breathing became more rapid. For a moment I thought he was going to sneeze. But then he laughed. I felt my own face flush with humiliation. Charley laughed harder and harder.

"Read me that one part again," he said finally in a choked voice. "That about 'I saw her gown open to the waist and fastened by only a single jewel at her navel.' And he again went into paroxysms of laughter.

His reaction horrified me. I had no inkling that he would respond in this manner, and it totally unnerved me; I found myself twitching and muttering, unable to speak.

"Also that part that goes—" He tried to remember; I saw his lips moving. "About 'as I kissed her hot, sweet lips I pushed her backward toward the couch. Her body yielded—' "

I interrupted, "It's not fair to harp on individual phrases. It's the overall work that's important. I tried to be absolutely accurate in this account. This is vital information that you ought to have at your disposal so you'll be able to act. Isn't that so? You need information to act."

"Act," he said. "What do you mean?"

"When you get back home," I said, seeing nothing complex about it.

"Listen," Charley said. "This is all in your mind. You're out of your head. You're a psycho. Anybody who'd write a thing like that about his sister is a psycho; let's face it. Don't you know that? Haven't you ever faced the fact that you're a warped, stunted, asshole type?"

An orderly or a nurse—or someone—came along the corridor. Charley raised his voice and yelled at them.

"Get this asshole out of here! He's driving me nuts!"

I voluntarily got up and left. I was glad to get out of there. All the way home on the bus I was shaking with anger and disbelief; it was one of the worst days in my life, and I knew I'd never forget it as long as I lived.

As the bus was passing through Samuel P. Taylor Park, the idea came to me to appeal to a disinterested person. To put this whole situation, my efforts and Charley's response— the whole business, before them and let them impartially judge if I hadn't done what was absolutely right.

First I thought of writing a letter to either the San Rafael *Journal* or to the Baywood *Press*. I even went so far as to begin composing, in my head, such a letter.

But then I thought of a better solution. Unrolling my presentation, I carefully went over it, editing out some of the phrases that Charley had called my attention to. Then I rolled it up again and wrote Claudia Hambro's name and address on it.

When the bus reached Inverness Park, I got off and walked up the road to Mrs. Hambro's house. Without making any noise that would disturb anyone in the house, I slipped the pages of the presentation under the door. Then I left.

After I had gotten almost all the way to Inverness—walking took much more time than using the bus—I suddenly realized that I hadn't put my own name on the presentation. For a moment I halted and toyed with the idea of going back. But then I realized that Mrs. Hambro would know who it

was from; there would be a telepathic communication between her and me, as soon as she saw the presentation. And,
in the presentation itself, there were Fay's name and Nat
Anteil's name, of course. So she would have no trouble discovering who had left it.

Cheered up, I reached the house with rapid steps. I had
actually opened the front door and started inside before I
remembered, all at once, that in a month the world was
coming to an end, on a date that I had decided, and that all
these people, Charley and Fay and Nat Anteil and Gwen—
all of them would be dead anyhow. And so in a sense it did
not matter. It did not matter whether I got the facts to Charley or not. It did not matter what Charley did as a result of
knowing those facts. Nothing any of them did mattered. They
were just so much radioactive dust, the whole bunch of them.
Just handfuls of black, radioactive, ashy dust.

That realization, that picture of them, stayed in my mind
vividly for days after that. I could not get it out of my mind,
even if I wanted to; several times I tried to think of something
else, but that picture came right back.

# 13

One afternoon, when Nat Anteil drove over to the Hume home, the two girls greeted him excitedly as he parked his car.

"One of the sheep had a lamb!" Bonnie shouted, as he got out of the car. "She had a lamb just a couple of minutes ago!"

"We saw it through the window!" Elsie shouted at him. "The Bluebirds saw it; we were baking bread and we saw four black feet and I said, Look there's a lamb, and it was. Mommy said it's a female lamb, it's a girl lamb. They're out in back on the patio looking at it." The girls skipped and raced along beside him as he went through the house and opened the back door on to the patio.

In an iron and canvas patio chair Fay sat in her yellow shorts and sandals and halter, sipping a martini. "One of the ewes gave birth," she said, over her shoulder. "While the Bluebirds were still here."

"The children told me," he said.

She continued to gaze out over the field, past the fence and the badminton net. After a moment he made out the sight of the ewe. She lay on her side, like a great bag of gray and black. He could not see the lamb. The only motion was an occasional twitch of one of the ewe's ears.

"That means they're agitated," Fay said. "When they twitch their ears. It's a sign of distress in sheep."

Presently the ewe struggled to her feet and he saw a tiny black spot on the grass. It was the lamb. The ewe nudged it, first with her nose and then with one of her hoofs. The lamb arose, shaking, and the ewe nosed it toward her sacks of milk.

"It's already nursed," Fay said. "I shut the dog in the bathroom, so if you go in there don't let it out. Last year that god damn dog killed all the lambs. She found them when they were just born. They evidently still had the blood on them, and she apparently thought they were just meat."

"I see," he said. He sat down on a wicker chair to watch with her. The two girls, after hanging around a while, went off on their tricycles.

Fay said, "It looks to me like she's going to have another. See how fat she still is."

"Don't you think it's just the milk?" he said.

"No," she said.

Later, at sunset, while he was bringing the girls' tricycles indoors, he saw the ewe lying on her side, again. This time the rear part of her shuddered rhythmically, and he realized that Fay had been right. He went indoors to the kitchen. At the stove Fay was mixing a salad.

"You were right," he said. "She's in labor."

Fay said, "It'll be born dead. If there's more than an hour lapse between births the second one is always dead." She left her salad and went to get her coat.

"Maybe not," he said, knowing nothing about sheep but wanting to say something to cheer her.

Taking the lantern—the sky had become dark and stars were appearing—they walked out across the pasture, to the ewe. Now she had gotten up and was cropping grass. Her lamb lay nearby, its head up.

"I'll call the vet," Fay said.

She telephoned the vet and talked with him for a long time. Nat wandered about the house, glancing out now and then at the field. Now he could see only the outline of the eucalyptus trees far off, along the highway.

Appearing from her bedroom, Fay said, "He says to call him back in an hour if nothing happens. He said possibly we could get her to walk around; that might speed up the birth. But he agrees that if it's this long there isn't much chance."

They had dinner. And then, before clearing the table, they again put on their coats, got the lantern, and went out on to the field.

The light flashed first on one ewe, then another. "No," Fay said, continuing to walk. "Flash it over there," she said, pointing.

In the light he saw the ewe standing up, trailing behind her a web of black. The web, sagging like a cloth hammock, led to a pool of wet black in the grass. To him it looked like refuse, something voided. But Fay, walking toward it, said in a flat empty voice, "It's a dead lamb. A big lamb." Bending down she said, "A perfect lamb. Looks like a male. It must have just been born." With both hands she began to strip the bloody, wet web from it. Mucus trails covered the lamb's face. "A male," she said, turning the lamb over.

"Too bad," he said, feeling no emotion, only a physical reaction, a revulsion to the blood and mucus web. Not wanting to touch the thing he hung back, now feeling guilt.

Fay reached into the dead lamb's mouth and opened its jaws. The she began pressing its rib-cage, again and again. "It's still warm," she said. "Usually I come out and find their stiff bodies. This one was too big. It took five hours. He was cut off too long." Now she had lifted the lamb by its hind legs and was slapping it. "You do this with baby puppies," she said. "No," she said. "It's hopeless. Too bad. A perfect big buck lamb. Isn't that strange? It gets so far, five months growing, and then it dies. What a shame." She continued to massage it and clean its face and slap at it. The ewe, with her surviving lamb, had gone farther off. "They know when it's dead," Fay said. "Sometimes they'll nuzzle it for an hour, trying to get it on its feet. She knows this one is dead. She isn't trying to get it up." Now she stood up. "Look at my hands," she said. "Blood all over them."

He said, "You want me to put it in the garbage can?"

"It'll have to be buried," she said.

Now he did not feel so squeamish. He picked it up by its hind feet. How heavy it was. Carrying it before him, he walked back toward the house. Fay came a step or two behind, flashing the light for him.

"Probably she could only have nursed one anyhow," she said. "We've brought them in when they were too weak to get up, and washed them and dried them and fed them Karo syrup and water and sent them back out. We never got a buck lamb. They're so fragile. There's always a good chance a buck lamb will die—they're too big to get out."

Using the pitchfork and shovel he dug a hole near the cypress trees, where the soil was moist.

"Anyhow," he said, "you still have the other one."

She said nothing.

"It was impressive," he said, "to see you go and start removing that stuff from it without hesitation." Like a farm woman, he thought. And in her shorts and sandals and blue cord coat. No fluttering or squeamishness . . . she had gotten that firm quality that he thought so much of. The quality that he knew existed in her, one of her best. It would come out, of course, in a situation like this. It had never occurred to her to hang back.

She said, "I should have breathed in its mouth. But I couldn't bear to. With all that mucus. I guess I better phone the vet back and tell him what happened." Leaving the lantern propped up for him, she went off into the house.

After he had finished burying the lamb, he washed his hands at an outdoor tap and entered the house after her. The girls had gone off to their rooms to watch tv. On the dining room table the dinner dishes remained where they had been, and he picked up some and carried them to the sink. He wondered where Jack was. Probably in his room; her brother had stayed out of sight, by himself, whenever he came over to be with Fay. He did not even eat with them.

"I'll do that," Fay said, appearing. "Leave them." She lit a cigarette. "Let's sit for a while in the living room."

"Where's your brother?" he said, as they seated themselves.

"At Claudia Hambro's. A meeting of the group. Special emergency session." She smoked meditatively.

"Are you depressed?" he said.

Beside him, she stirred about. "A little. More just thinking."

"The business about the lamb would depress anybody," he said.

"It isn't the lamb," Fay said. "It was seeing you getting ready to do the dishes. You shouldn't do that."

"Why not?" he said.

"A man shouldn't do things like dishes."

He said, "I thought you wanted me to do them." He knew how she detested the dishes; she always got someone to do them for her, if not her brother then himself.

"I never wanted you to do them," Fay said. She stubbed out her cigarette. "You should have said no." Getting restlessly to her feet she began to pace. "Mind if I pace?" she said, with a quick, mechanical smile, almost a grimace.

Perturbed, he said, "You ask me, but you want me to refuse. You want me to say no to you."

"You shouldn't let me get you to do things. It's wrong— the man should be the stronger one. He should exert his authority. The man is the ultimate authority in a marriage.

The woman follows his lead . . . how's she supposed to know what's right and wrong if he doesn't tell her? I expect you to tell me. I depend on you."

He said, "And by doing things for you, things you asked for, I've let you down."

"You've let yourself down," she corrected. "So I suppose yes, you've let me down. The best way to help me is to be yourself and do what you know is right. I'll respect you more if you assert your moral authority. The children need that."

He said, "It's wrong for the children to see a man doing the dishes?"

"Doing anything the woman tells him. They should see him telling the woman what to do. That's the principle I see in you—a deep moral authority. That's what you bring to this house. We all need that."

"And by that 'deep moral authority,' " he said, having difficulty breathing, "you mean my taking a firm stand and opposing you. Well?" he said. "Suppose I do oppose you? What will you do?"

"Respect you," she said.

"No," he said. "You won't like it. Don't you see the paradox? If I do what you say—"

She broke in, "That's right. Shift the responsibility to me."

"What?" he said.

Fay said, "I'm at fault."

He stared at her, not following her fluctuation of mood. "No," he said finally. "This is something we're involved in mutually. That's what we should strive for, a mutual sense of responsibility and authority. Not one of us manipulating the other."

Fay said, "You manipulate me. You try to change me."

"When?" he demanded.

"Right now. You're trying to change me now."

"I only want you to see the contradiction in what you want."

"I see," she said. "I see that you resent me."

Nat said, "You want to fight, don't you?"

"I'm just tired of your covert hostility," she said. "I wish you'd be honest. I wish you'd express your hostility directly instead of in these devious ways, these pious pedagogic ways."

For a time he was silent.

"You can go," she said. "Any time. You don't have to stick around here. Why should you? This isn't your home anyhow. This is my home. This is my house, my food, my money. What are you doing over here anyhow? How'd you get in here?"

He could not believe he was hearing what he seemed to hear.

"You know you dislike me," Fay said. "You've hinted at it in a thousand different ways. You feel I don't take responsibility; you feel I'm demanding and self-centered and childish, always wanting my own way, that I'm not mature, that I don't really love you—I just want to use you. Isn't that right?"

Finally he said, "To—some extent."

"Why can't you stand up to me?" she said.

"I—didn't get involved with you to 'stand up to you,' " he said. "I love you."

To that, she had nothing to say.

Nat said, "I don't understand. What's all this about?" Getting to his feet he came toward her; he wanted to put his arms around her and kiss her. "Why are you in this state?"

"Oh," she said, resting her head against his shoulder, "it's something Doctor Andrews said today." She put her arms around him. "He said that whenever I talk about you I don't really depict anything. As if I never really see you. As if nobody's really real to me. It was so much like something you said—maybe it's true. God, if I thought for one moment it was true—" Drawing away, she gazed up at him. "Suppose it's true, what Charley's always said about me, and I never accepted. That I've degraded him and used him and absorbed him to get what I want. I was so spoiled as a child . . . I always got what I wanted. And if I didn't I had tantrums. And he had to get drunk and come home and hit me; it was the only way he could fight back." She stared at him starkly. "And I made him sick. And—possibly I want him to die because I'm through with him; I don't have any further need for him. And I deliberately involved you with me, broke up your marriage—without any concern at all for Gwen, or even for you, so that I could get you because you're good husband material and I need a new husband, now that I've used up the old one. And if you do stay with me, I'll treat you the same way as I treated him. It'll be the same thing over again; you'll be running my errands for me, and doing my chores for me—I'll degrade you, and then you won't have any other resource but to get drunk and hit me." She ceased talking, then, and stood, gazing past him absently.

"I'll never hit you," he said, stroking her dry, short hair.

"Charley never hit anybody before me," she said.

"The thing is," he said, "that you and I can talk. We can discuss this. We verbalize in the same way. He doesn't."

She nodded.

"We can express our resentments. The way you're doing now. We can deal with them directly."

"Let's face it," Fay said. "I'm clumsy and vulgar. Why do you want me?"

He said, "Because you're an intelligent, brave woman." Stroking her, he said, "You remind me of a pioneer woman." He was thinking of her with the lamb, now.

"You don't think I'll make you into a domestic servant?" Pulling away from him she went to get a log and kindling for the fire. "That's what I want, an army of men; decorators to paint things, paint the house, gardens, electricians, men to cut my hair, remodel the kitchen—add a new room on the house when I want a room to work in, to work on my clay in. Would you build me a room to work in? Where I can have a wheel?"

"Sure," he said, smiling.

"Suppose I ruined you," she said. "Made you give up any hope of going on to school. Put a financial responsibility on you that tied you up for the rest of your life . . . supporting me and the girls, and I'd want to have more children, as soon as possible. Incidently, did I tell you about my diaphragm?"

"Yes," he said.

She went on, "Force you to stay in the real estate business when you actually want to—" She hesitated. "Go on into a profession. Whatever it is." Her eyes twinkling, she said, "What did you say you wanted to be?"

"Maybe a lawyer," he said.

"Oh god, then you could sue me," she said.

"I want to marry you," he said. "I want to divorce Gwen and marry you."

"What'll we do with Charley?"

"Can't you ask him for a divorce?" he said, feeling the tension everywhere in him.

Fay said, "It's wrong. I know it's bourgeois of me—it shows what a bourgeois nogoodnick I am. I just feel divorce is wrong; a marriage is for life."

"Well," he said, feeling futile, "then that's that."

"I guess that's misplaced loyalty," she said. "But I can't help it. When I married him I married him for better or worse; I took those words seriously."

He said, "So the only way you could leave him would be if he died."

"If he died," she said, "I'd have to remarry. For the girls' sake. They need a father; it's the father who establishes the authority in the home. He relates the family to the outer world, to society. The mother does nothing but keep everyone fed and clothed and warm."

After a pause, with some trepidation, he said, "Why don't you ask him?"

"Ask him what?"

"Which he'd prefer," he said, feeling that he was making a mistake to say it, but, at the same time, wanting to say it to her. "Being dead or being divorced."

At that, she got the fierce, cold look that he had seen only once or twice before. But when she spoke her voice was completely under control, as calm as he had ever heard it. It had, in fact, a deeply rational tone to it, as if she were speaking out of the depths of her wisdom and experience, from the most educated part of her. Not from emotion at all, but from the most widely-accepted, the most incontrovertible knowledge. "Well," she said, "it's a lot to ask a man, to take on the responsibility for the children, especially another man's children. I don't blame you. You have a relatively easy life, as it is. In the long run I doubt if you could sustain this family. I'd really have to be married to a man who could support me. Let's face it. You haven't got the capability to do that." She smiled at him, the brief, aloof smile that he had come to recognize. Almost a gracious smile.

There was nothing much more for him to say. Going to the closet he got his coat.

"Are you walking out on me?" she said.

Nat said, "I don't see any point in staying."

"Better you should walk out now," she said. "It's probably better for you, too, in the long run. Anyhow it's easier. Isn't it?"

"No," he said. "It isn't."

"Oh, it is," she contradicted. "It's the easiest thing in the world. All you have to do is put on your coat and go back home to Gwen." She followed after him, to the door. Her face had a white, throbbing quality. "Won't you kiss me good-bye?" she said.

He kissed her. "I'll see you," he said.

"Say hello to Gwen," she said. "Maybe we could all get together for dinner some evening. Charley should be back from the hospital in another week or so."

"Okay," he said. Hardly believing that it was happening, he shut the door after him and walked across the gravel and cypress needles to his car. The light remained on until he had backed from the driveway. Then, as soon as his car reached the road, the light went out.

In a daze, he drove home.

Suppose I hadn't started to clear the dinner dishes, he thought. Would it not have happened? It would have, he decided. Sooner or later. Our mutual hostilities and doubts would have summed up and clashed; it was only a question of time. It was inevitable.

But he still could not believe it, and now, as he drove, he began to be afraid of how he would feel when he did believe it. How it would affect him when it began to become real.

When he drove up in front of his own house he saw a strange car parked there. Getting out, he walked up the steps and into the house.

In the kitchen, Gwen sat at the table with a glass of wine in front of her. Across from her sat a man he had never seen before, a blond-haired young man wearing glasses. Both of them glanced up with dismay. But almost at once Gwen regained her composure.

"Home early," she said in a brittle, hostile voice. "I thought you were probably going to stay longer."

"Who's this?" Nat said, indicating the young man. His heart labored inside him. "I don't feel like coming home and finding a strange car parked in front of the house."

"Oh," Gwen said, in the same voice; its venom, its vast amount of loathing for him, staggered him. He had never heard her speak with such sarcasm, such giving to each syllable a sense of cruelty, the articulation of cruelty toward him, cruelty toward everything. As if, at this moment in their relationship, she could feel nothing but this. Nothing else remained. It was her total feeling. "I'm sorry," she said. "I thought you and Fay would be together for the rest of the evening. Maybe the rest of the night."

The young man started to get to his feet.

"Don't leave," Gwen said, shifting her attention to him, but still using the same tone. "Why should you leave?" To Nat, she said, "We're right in the middle of working something out. Why don't you go away and come back some other time?"

"Working what out?" he said.

"An understanding," she said. "Between the two of us. This is Robert Altrocchi. He lives down the road. Where the birds are. He raises parakeets and sells them to the dime stores in San Francisco."

Nat said nothing.

"Do you mind?" Gwen said. "If we go on?" She made a motion of dismissal toward him. "Go drive off," she said.

To the young man, Nat said, "Get out of here."

Arising with elaborate slowness, Altrocchi pushed away his wine glass and said, "I was going. I have to get to work." At the doorway he halted and said to Gwen, "I'll see you at the usual time, then?"

Ignoring Nat, she said, "Yes. Call me or I'll call you." Now she had gotten into her voice—no doubt with great care—a tone of affection. "Good night, Bob."

"Good night," Altrocchi said. Presently they heard the front door close, and then the man's car drive off.

"How's Fay?" Gwen said, still seated at the table. She sipped her wine, eying him above the glass.

"Fine," he said.

"It's okay for you to be with her," Gwen said in a wavering voice,"but not okay for me."

"I don't want to come home and find a strange car here," he said. "I never brought Fay here," he said. "It's wrong to bring somebody here. That's unfair. You can go out and see anybody you want, but don't bring them here. It's my house, too."

"We can't go to his house," Gwen said, raising her voice. "He's married and they have a six-month-old child."

Hearing that, he felt crushing melancholy and hopelessness. So this was the consequence of his relationship with Fay. Not only had his own marriage been marred, ruined, but somebody's else's, a man he had never seen before in his life, a man with a new baby.

"If it's okay for you—" Gwen began.

"I gave you the example," he interrupted.

She said nothing.

"You're paying me back," he said. "This is my payment. Some guy I never saw. His wife and child have to suffer so you can get back at me. I want to marry Fay. I'm serious. You're not. Are you? You know you aren't."

Gwen said nothing.

"This is terrible," he said. "This is the worst thing I ever heard. How could you do a thing like this?"

On his wife's face the expression of suffering and determination increased. Everything he said only made her feel more strongly.

"One of us has to get out," he said.

"Okay," she said. "You get out."

"I will," he said. Going into the bedroom he sat down on the bed. "I don't feel like it right now," he said. "Later."

"No," Gwen said. "Now."

"Go to hell," he said, feeling perspiration stand out on his forehead. "Shut up," he said weakly. "Don't talk to me any more, or I can't be responsible."

Gwen said, "Don't threaten me." But she stopped talking to him and went off by herself into the living room. He heard her seat herself on the couch.

The house was silent.

Good god, he thought. We're through. My marriage is over. Where am I? What's happened?

While he sat there, Gwen reappeared. "I'll go," she said. "So you won't have to be away from her. I'll go to Sacramento and stay with my family. Can I take the car?"

"If you take the car," he said, "how can I get to work?" His heart beat so fast and so hard that it was a great effort to speak; it cost him all his energy and after each word he had to rest.

"Then drive me to Sacramento and come back," she said.

"Okay," he said.

"Let me see what I have to take," she said. "I won't try to take everything tonight. I'll come back tomorrow. Maybe I won't go to Sacramento tonight. It's too far. It would take all night to get there. I'll stay in a motel. There's one in Point Reyes, right here."

"No," he said. "I'll take you to Sacramento."

She studied him and then, without a word, she went into the other room again. At first he heard nothing, and then he realized that she was beginning to get things together. He heard the sound of a suitcase being dragged from the closet.

"I've decided you're right," he said, staying where he was. "I can't drive you to Sacramento tonight. Wait until tomorrow—sleep here, and we'll talk about it tomorrow."

Gwen said from the other room, "I'm not sleeping with you tonight. You go over to her house and sleep, if you want me to stay here."

"You can sleep on the couch," he said. "Or I will."

"Why don't you go back there?" Gwen appeared in the doorway. "Why did you come back so early?"

He said, "We had a fight." He did not look at her but he could feel her eyes on him. "Nothing important. There was a lamb born dead and it upset her. It was horrible; it looked like a thing made out of wet tar." He began, then, to tell her about it. For a moment she listened, and then she disappeared. She had gone off and resumed her packing. Feeling rage, he leaped up from the bed and followed after her. "Don't you want to hear?" he demanded.

"I have enough to think about," Gwen said.

"You could listen to this," he said, standing in the center of the room while she packed. "Why don't you listen? It seems a hell of a thing to me, one hell of a thing, that you won't even listen. It really makes me feel bad."

"I'm sorry about the dead lamb," Gwen said. "But I don't see what it matters. I let you go and stay with her, and I never said anything; I let you do what you wanted, and when people came by and wondered where you were I said you were down in Mill Valley working late; I never told anybody about you and her."

"Thanks," he said.

"I don't know what you're going to do when he gets back from the hospital," Gwen said. "What are you going to do? Won't he find out? Somebody'll tell him—you know nobody can keep things a secret in these little towns. Everybody knows everybody."

"If you leave," he said, "then there won't be any doubt of it. No doubt at all."

"You want me to stay," she said, "to save you from being killed or whatever he's going to do when he gets home?"

"He won't do anything," he said. "He's a sick man. He'll be in bed for months, recuperating. He almost died. He could still die. It wouldn't take much."

Bitterly, Gwen said, "Maybe the shock of finding out will be enough. Then you'll have clear sailing."

"I love her," he said. "I want to marry her. This is all something I feel proud of. I know that sounds incredible—"

"No," Gwen said. "It doesn't sound incredible. You're drawn to her because you see the children, and I know you want children, but we couldn't have them because of your school. Is she going to put you through school? This way you can have both—you can go to school and at the same time have a big nice house and kids and everything else you want. T-bone steaks for dinner. Right?"

"I want a stable home and family," he said.

"You know what I think will become of you if you marry her?"

He could not keep himself from saying, "What do you think?"

"You'll be a handy man and domestic servant, keeping that place going. Keeping her house going. You'll balance her budget, turn down the thermostats to save money on the heating bill—"

"No," he interrupted. "Because it's off. I'm not seeing her again. We broke up."

"Why?"

He said, "Because of what you said just now. I don't want to wind up a domestic sevant, doing her dishes for her." As he said it he felt the full weight of his disloyalty fall on him. His treason to Fay, not to his wife; it was Fay that now held his loyalty, his sense of being morally obligated. Standing there in his own living room, with his own wife, telling his wife that he was through with Fay, he knew that he was not through with her, not if he could help it. The pull was too strong. He yearned for her. He yearned to be back in that house with her. The rest was talk.

"I don't believe it," Gwen said. "You'll never have the strength to break off with her. She's got you completely tied up. She always gets her way; she's got the mind of a two-year-old child—she wants what she sees and she gets it because she rides rough shod over everybody else."

"She recognizes that," he said. "That's why she goes down to Doctor Andrews. She's struggling with it."

Gwen laughed. "Oh?" she said. "You're optimistic? Then why are you breaking up with her?"

To that, he could give no answer.

"I don't see how you could get involved with a woman like that," Gwen said. "Do you want to be bossed the rest of your life? Do you crave to be back in a child-parent relationship?"

"I'm tired of hearing about it," he said.

"I'm not surprised that you're tired of hearing about it," Gwen said. "What I wonder is will you ever be tired of living it."

Going outside, he sat in the car and waited while she packed.

# 14

In his hospital bed, Charley Hume looked up with surprise to see Nathan Anteil entering the room.

"Hello, Charley," Nathan said.

"I'll be darned," Charley Hume said. He lay back again.

Nat said, "I brought you a couple of magazines to read." He laid a copy of *Life* and *True* on the table beside the bed. "They say you're going to be coming home in a couple of days."

"Right," Charley said. "I'm about ready for the big moment." He lay watching Nathan. "Nice to see you," he said. "What brings you down here to San Francisco?"

"Just thought I'd drop by," Nat said. "It occurred to me that I've only been down to visit you one or two times, and then with someone else. You're looking good. You know that?"

Charley said, "I'll be on a diet. Isn't that a hell of a thing? A real lousy one. To keep my weight down." He reached out and picked up the magazines, noticing as he did so that he had read the *Life*. His brother-in-law had brought it from the library on his last trip. But nevertheless he went through the motions of glancing over it. "How's everything been going?" he said finally.

"Fine," Nat said.

"World treating you okay?"

"No reason to complain," Nat said.

"Listen, boy," Charley said. He took the bull by the horns, then. "I know about you and my wife."

Across from him he saw Nathan's face speckled with shock. "Is that so?" Nathan said. He pressed his hands together, clasping and intertwining . . . the flesh became white as he pressed. He did not look at Charley for a moment, and then he raised his head, saying, "That's why I'm here. I wanted to come and tell you, face to face."

"Hell no," Charley said. "That's not why you're here; you came down here to find out what I'm going to do when I get back up there. I'll tell you what I'm going to do. When I get back—" He lowered his voice and peered past Nathan, to see if anyone were passing the open door to the hall. "Want to close that door?" he said.

Getting up, Nathan went and shut the door and returned.

Charley said, "When I get back up to Drake's Landing I'm going to kill that woman."

After a long pause Nathan licked his lip and said, "Why? Because of me?"

"Hell no," Charley said. "Because she's a bitch. I made up my mind as soon as I came to, after my heart attack. One of us has to kill the other. Didn't you know that? Didn't she tell you? She knows it. Christ, we can't both live in that house, and the only way one of us is going to leave is leave dead. I'll never leave any other way. Neither will she. It has nothing to do with you. On my word of honor."

Nathan said nothing. He stared down at the floor.

"She got me in here," Charley said. "She made me have this heart attack. I don't feel like having another one. The next one'll be the end of me."

Nat said, "I don't think you'll really kill her. You *feel* like killing her. But that's different."

"I'll be doing you the greatest favor anybody ever did you," Charley said. "Don't fight it. You'll thank me someday, for freeing you from her. You don't have the guts to break away on your own. I know that, just to look at you. God almighty, you're sitting there practically begging me to do it. You want me to do it—because you know god damn well if I don't you'll be mixed up with this mess—with her—the rest of your life, and you'll never get any peace." He paused, then, to rest. Talking so hard made him feel winded and tired.

"I don't think you'll do it," Nat repeated.

Charley said nothing.

"She has fundamentally sound traits," Nat said.

"My fucking back," Charley said. "Don't kid yourself. She never lifted a finger in her life except to increase her hold over somebody so she could use them later on."

Nathan said, "I think I can deal with her. I have no illusions about her."

"You have one illusion," Charley said. "No you have two. The first is that you'd win out over her. The second is that you'll ever have a chance to find out. You better make hay with her during the next few days, because that's all there's going to be. She knows. If she doesn't, she's dumber than I think she is."

Nathan said, "Suppose we break up. Suppose I stop seeing her."

"That doesn't make any difference. This has got nothing to do with you. I like you; I have nothing against you. What do I care if she wants to go roll in the hay with you? She doesn't mean anything to me. She's just a lousy shit of a woman that I happen to be married to that I've got a lot against, and with this heart now I know sooner or later I'm going to fall over dead, so I can't wait forever, I put it off too long as it is. I should have done it years ago, but I kept putting it off. I darn near lost my chance ever to do it." He paused to get his breath.

"I don't believe you would have got this idea in your mind," Nathan said, "this idea about murdering her, except for this situation between her and me."

"You calling me a liar?" Charley said.

Gesturing, Nathan said, "I know it's because of me."

"Then you know wrong. Believe me. I wouldn't lie to you. Why should I lie to you?"

Nathan said, "If you kill her, I'll go to my grave considering myself responsible."

At that, Charley had to laugh. "You? What do you think you are in this? When did you get mixed up in this? I'll tell you. About ten minutes ago. Ten seconds! My fucking busted back." He lapsed into silence, then.

"I'll always know it was because of my getting mixed up with her," Nathan repeated. "You're simply so outraged about this that you've lost control of your own mental processes. You don't really know what your motive is."

"I know what my motive is," Charley said.

At that moment a nurse, smiling apologetically, entered the room, looked around on the table for something, smiled at them both, and departed, leaving the door open. Nathan got up and closed it.

"Well I'll tell you," he said slowly, as he returned. "If you do try to do something to her, I'll stand up for her."

"Like standing up for Christ?" Charley said.

Nathan said, "I'll do what I can to stop you."

"Now I've heard everything," Charley said. "Man, I've really heard it. A snot-nosed punk, a college kid, comes in here and tells me he's going to take me on in a situation having to do between me and my wife. Why, you god damn punk nothing kid, what business is this of yours? Who the hell do you think you are? If I wasn't lying here recuperating so I could get back up to Drake's Landing I'd get up out of here and kick your balls down the hall and down the stairs to the main floor."

Nathan said, "It's too god damn bad, but as far as I'm concerned you're an irrational, compulsive—" He groped for words. "Anyhow," he said, "I feel sure I can handle you when the time comes. The type of man who beats up a woman is a pretty soft pile of shit when it comes down to it, in my books." Arising, he started out of the room.

"She's really got you hooked," Charley said.

At the door, Nathan said, "I'll see you."

"Boy, she really has." He tried to whistle, to show his incredulity, but his lips were too stiff. "Listen, I'll tell you what she is. I've read books. You're not the only one who can talk and discuss intellectual matters. I've seen you guys sitting around discussing Picasso and Freud. Listen to this. She's a psychopath. You know that? Fay's a psychopath. Think about that."

Nathan said nothing.

"You know what a psychopath is?" Charley demanded.

"Sure," Nathan said.

"No, you don't because if you did you'd recognize her right off. The reason I know is that I talked to Doctor Andrews and he told me." Actually, that was a lie. But he was too mad to keep to the truth. He had come across the term in an article in *This Week* magazine, several years ago, and the description had sufficiently fitted Fay to awaken his interest. "I don't have to take a mail-order college course to know that. What is it she does that's the key? She always wants her own way." He pointed a finger at Nathan. "And she can't wait, can she? She's like a child; she always wants her own way and she can't wait. Isn't that a psychopath? And she don't care about nobody else. That's a psychopath. It is. I'm not kidding you." He nodded with triumph, panting. "The world's something for her to drain dry, and people—"

He laughed. "That proves it. The way she treats people. Look it up."

"I admit she has certain character disturbances," Nathan said.

"You know why she's set her cap for you? By the way, you don't think for a minute that getting hooked up with her was *your* idea, do you?"

Nathan shrugged, still standing by the door.

"She needs you," Charley said, "because she knew if this heart attack didn't kill me I'd come back and kill her, and she wants some man to step in and protect her. Exactly what you're doing." But even to him it sounded contrived and lame. "That's why," he said, but his tone lacked conviction, and he knew that he could not convince Nathan. For a moment he had had him going, but now he had lost him. "That's one of the reasons," he said, amending his statement. "There are others. She also figures she'll need a husband when I'm dead. That's a big reason, too. You two can sit around and talk, yak, yak, yak it up the rest of your lives. I can see you two sitting there at the dining room table." He saw so clearly in his mind's eye the table, the big windows overlooking the patio, the field . . . he saw the sheep, the horse—his horse— and the dog. The dog wagging her tail for Nathan exactly as she wagged it for him, greeting him in the same way. He saw Nathan hanging his coat in the closet where *his* coats hung— had hung. He saw him washing his face and hands in his bathroom, using his towel; he saw him looking into the oven to see what was for dinner. He saw him playing with the kids, playing airplanes—carrying them around at arms' length—

He saw him with his children, his dog, his wife, seated in his easy chair, listening to the hi-fi. He saw him throughout the house, using it, enjoying it, being at home in it, living in it as her husband, as the children's father. "But you're not their father," he said aloud. And all at once he didn't give a god damn about getting back at Fay; he wanted nothing else but to be home, sitting in his living room, holding on to his life; he did not even want to ride the horse or play with the dog or lie in bed screwing his wife—the hell with that; all he asked was to be home sitting down watching them through the windows. Watching them, for instance, flying their kites, like on that last day. Fay running across the field with those long legs of hers, running so lightly, skimming across the ground faster and faster . . .

He realized that Nathan was talking. What was he saying? Something about realizing that he wasn't their father. He tried to listen, but he couldn't; he felt too woozy and tired to listen. So he sat staring down at the foot of the bed, while Nathan talked.

If I could just get back, he thought. Nothing else. Just back. With my Elsie. Driving my pick-up truck. Doing the shopping, laying pipe for the ducks' water trough—anything. Scrubbing the bathtubs and sinks and toilets, carrying out the garbage . . . I don't give a good god damn what it is. Please.

Fuck it all, he thought. It's all gone. I'll never get back; I know that. I'll never see that house again, never in a million years. And this other guy, this snot-nose, will walk in and take it all, and have it the rest of his life.

I ought to kill them all, he thought. Her and him, and that warped creep of a brother, him and his lurid pulp story that he whipped together to get sadistic pleasure out of reading to me. That nut. A family of nuts. A world of them. Like the flying saucer nuts over in Inverness Park. The pack of them at work as a team, like the Eisenhower-Dulles team.

God damn it, he thought. I will get back there, and when I do I'll get them. Even if I don't get back there—I'll still get them. I'll get them anyhow.

"Listen," he said. "You know who I am? I'm the one person in the world—the only one—who can save you from that fucking woman. Isn't that right? You know it. Right? Right?"

Nathan said nothing.

"Nobody else can do it," Charley said. "You can't, your wife can't, Doctor Sebastian that old fuddy minister can't, her nutty brother can't, the Fineburgs can't—nobody in Marin County or Contra Costa County or Sonoma County can except me, because it would take killing her, and by god you know I'll do that. So you better pray for me; you better go home and sit in your parlor and watch tv and wait and pray for me to get home and live long enough, because you're the one who's going to benefit; you'll benefit and nobody else will. And ten years from now—hell, ten days!—you'll be so god damn glad. You really will be. And something in your mind tells you that. It's your subconscious. So go home. Don't mix in where it doesn't concern you. When she phones you up, don't answer the phone. When she drives up in front of your house and toots her horn, stay indoors. Ignore her. For one week." He shouted the words. "One week, and you'll be okay! And then you can go on and get your degree and become whatever it is you want to be—otherwise you know what'll become of you?"

Nathan said nothing.

"I don't have to tell you," Charley said, and in him it was the greatest sense of triumph and joy that he had felt in all this, in everything that had happened. It was almost a mystical sense. He did not have to say, because the expression on Nathan's face showed that he already knew. "Do you know what that means?" Charley yelled at him. "That means I was right. If I wasn't right, you wouldn't know. It's not in my mind. It's the truth. We both know it. We know about her, both of us, you and me. So that proves it; it's true. Right?"

Nathan said nothing.

For the first time, Charley thought, I can see it clearly and know she really is that way; it isn't in my mind. She really is a grade A number one bitch, because I can read this boy's face, and he can read mine, and it's in both of us.

Thank god, he thought. I can know for sure.

"Right?" he repeated.

Nathan said, "I went into this recognizing her defects. When I first met her I wasn't pleased by her. I saw all these qualities."

"In a pig's ass," Charley said. "You fell for her the moment you laid eyes on her."

"No," Nathan said, glancing up. And Charley saw that he had been mistaken. I lost him again, he thought. Damn it.

"So you had an inkling," he said. But he had said the wrong thing, and he could not get it back. "It just shows that underneath you realize I'm right."

Nathan said, "I'll see you." He opened the door, left the room, shut the door behind him.

After a time Charley thought, Maybe he'll go through with it. Stick by her. The stupid son of a bitch.

I am sick, he thought. It's true. What can I do if he decides to take me on? Before my heart attack I could have handled him with one hand; I could have split his skull. But now I'm too weak. In fact between the two of them, with her keen mind, her alertness, and his physical attributes, they'll have me. Between them they're a match for me, the way I am now. The jerks.

The trouble with me, he thought, is I'm a stupid man. I can't talk good enough, not like they can. I fucked it up.

# 15

While in my bedroom sewing a rip in Elsie's blue skirt I heard the doorbell and then Bing barking. I went on sewing, expecting Jack to go to the door, but finally I realized that he had shut himself up in his room and wasn't hearing the doorbell, so I put down my sewing and hurried through the house to the door.

On the porch stood Maud Mayberry, from Inverness Park, a large florid woman whose husband works down at the mill near Olema. I knew her from the PTA.

"Come in," I said. "I'm sorry I didn't hear you right away."

We sat down at the dining room table and had coffee; I sewed on Elsie's skirt while Mrs. Mayberry chatted about various events around north west Marin.

"Have you heard about the saucer group?" she said presently. "Claudia Hambro's bunch?"

"Who cares about those nuts," I said.

"They're predicting the end of the world," Mrs. Mayberry said.

At that I put down my sewing. "Well, I have to hand it to Claudia Hambro," I said. "I take off my hat to her. Just when I get to thinking that my own life is a mess and I'm an idiot and can't handle the simplest situation, then I hear about something like this. They're psychotic; they really are. They ought to have medical attention."

Mrs. Mayberry went on to tell me details. She had gotten them second hand, but she seemed to think they were accurate. In fact, they had come from the wife of the young minister living in Point Reyes Station. The saucer group evidently expected to be whisked away to outer space just before the calamity. It was the most far-out crap I have ever heard in my entire life; it really was.

"They ought to cart that Claudia Hambro away," I said. "She's spreading this contagion like the plague. Next thing, everybody in north west Marin County will be going up on Noren's Acres and waiting for the saucer. I mean, this is going to get written up in the newspapers. This is what you read about. This happens once in a decade. I never thought it would happen with people I actually know. My good god— Claudia Hambro's little girl was over here only the other day, with the Bluebirds. My good god." I shook my head; it was really the end. And this was what my brother had gotten mixed up in.

"Your brother's in the group, isn't he?" Mrs. Mayberry said.

"Yes," I said.

"But you're far from sympathetic."

I said, "My brother's as nutty as the rest of them, and I don't care who hears me say it. I just wish I hadn't brought him up here. Hadn't let Charley persuade me to bring him up here."

Mrs. Mayberry said, "Do you know about the story your brother wrote for the group?"

"What story?" I said.

"Well, according to what Mrs. Baron said—that's who I get it from—he did some automatic writing under hypnosis, or under the telepathic influence of their spiritual leader . . .

who lives, as I understand it, down in San Anselmo. Anyhow, he brought this story to the group, and they've been reading it and passing it around, trying to get at the symbolistic meaning beneath it."

"Christ," I said, fascinated.

Mrs. Maybery said, "I'm surprised you hadn't heard about it. They had a couple of special meetings about it."

"How would I hear about it?" I said. "When do I get out? My good god, I have to go down to SF three days a week, and now that my husband's in the hospital—"

"It's about you and that young man who just recently moved up here," Mrs. Mayberry said. "Nathan Anteil, who rented the old Mondavi place."

At that, I felt cold all over. "What do you mean, about me and Mr. Anteil?" I said.

"Well, they haven't showed it to anyone outside the group. That's all Mrs. Baron knew."

I said, "Have you heard anything about me and Mr. Anteil from other sources?"

"No," Mrs. Mayberry said. "Like what?"

"That fucking Claudia Hambro," I said, and then, seeing the expression on Mrs. Mayberry's face, I said, "Excuse me." I threw down my sewing; I was so mad and upset I could hardly see. Going to my purse I got out my cigarettes, lit one, and then threw it into the fireplace. "Excuse me," I said. "I have to go out."

Running into the bedroom I changed from my jeans to a skirt and blouse; I combed my hair, put on lipstick, got my purse and car keys, and started out of the house. There, at the dining table, sat that big horse's ass, Mrs. Mayberry, staring at me as if I were a freak.

"I have to go out for a while," I told her. "Good-bye." I ran down the path and jumped into the Buick. A minute later I was driving up the road, as fast as possible, toward Inverness Park.

• • •

I found Claudia out in her cactus garden, weeding. "Listen," I said, "I think if you had any social responsibility you would have telephoned me as soon as you got your hands on that thing he wrote. Jack wrote." I was out of breath from running up her flagstone path from the car. "Can I have it, please?"

Claudia stood up, holding her trowel. "You mean that story?"

"Right," I said.

"It's being read," she said. "We passed it around the group. I don't know who has it."

"Have you read it?" she said. "What does it say about me and Nat Anteil?"

Claudia said, "It's in the form usual with telepathical writing. You can read it. I'll put your name down and when it gets back to me I'll bring it over to you." She had amazing calmness; I have to give her credit for that. She kept really poised.

"I'll sue you," I said. "I'll take you to court."

"That's right," Claudia said. "You have that big attorney down in San Rafael. You know, Mrs. Hume, in a month from now none of us will remember or even care about all this. It'll be all washed away." She smiled her dazzling, beautiful smile. Probably there wasn't another woman as physically beautiful as Claudia in Northern California. And she certainly wasn't intimidated. She didn't bat an eye, and I know I've never been so angry and upset in my entire life. I really felt that in a couple of moments with me she had gotten the upper hand. It was that magnetic personality of hers, that assurance. She really is a powerful woman. No wonder she had control of that group. Anyhow, I have never been good at dealing with women. All I could do was keep my temper and speak as rationally as possible.

"I'd appreciate having that thing back," I said. "Possibly you could contact the different members of your group and find out who has it and then I'll drive over and get it back from them. I frankly don't see what's so difficult or impossible about that. If you'll give me the names of your group I'll call them now."

Claudia said, "It'll come back. In due time."

I went away feeling like a child that had been reprimanded by its teacher. Good god, I thought. That woman completely takes over; there's nothing I can do. I know she has no right to be circulating that god damn thing, and she knows it, too, but she made it sound as if I was asking for something completely outrageous. How did she do it? Now I felt more depressed than angry; I didn't even feel scared. I just felt how incompetent and idiotic I was, how unable to handle my affairs.

Looking back on it I saw that I should have been able to march up to her and simply demand that thing, not threaten or yell but just hold out my hand, say nothing at all.

As soon as I had gotten back in my car I made up my mind to get Nathan and get him to get the damn thing back for me.

After all, it involved him, too.

I drove over to his place and parked and honked the horn. No one appeared on the porch, so I shut off the motor and got out and went up the stairs. Nobody answered my knock, so I opened the door, looked in and called. Still no one. The motherfucker, I thought. I returned to the car and began driving around purposelessly, with no more idea of what to do than a year-old baby.

After half an hour I drove back to my own house; the time was two-thirty and the girls would be getting home. Mrs. Mayberry had left, thank god. I took a look into Jack's room, but he wasn't there; he probably had been eavesdropping on me and Mrs. Mayberry and had had the good sense to get out of the house.

Going into the kitchen I poured myself a drink.

This is really the pit, I thought. It's all over town, and not

only that, it's being circulated by the screwiest, craziest, nuttiest bunch of simps in the entire North American continent.
Of all the people to get hold of the god damn thing. What
do you suppose it says anyhow? I wondered. What did the
asshole say? I called my attorney, Sam Cohen. After I had
told him the situation he advised me to sit tight and wait
until I had actually seen the document or whatever it's called.
I thanked him and went and made myself another drink.
Then I called Doctor Andrews. The receptionist said I
couldn't hope to get through to him until four; he had a
patient until then, and for me to call back. By now the girls
had come home. I hung up and went outside, on to the patio,
and watched the Rouen drake chasing the Muscovy around
the pen. First he chased her up on to the feed can, and then
she flew to the far end, on to the water trough. He ran after
her and she then flew back.

At four-ten I was able to get hold of Doctor Andrews. He
told me to take one of the Sparines he had given me and to
wait until I actually saw the god damn story.

"By then even the farms out on the Point'll know about
me and Nathan," I said.

In his usual fat-assed way he mumbled about keeping cool
and taking a long-term view.

"That's what I'm doing, you hick analyst," I told him.
"You slob. My reputation in this town is going to be ruined.
You never lived in a small town; it's easy enough for you to
say, living in San Francisco. You can screw anybody you
want and nobody gives a damn. Up here they're voting on
you in the PTA before you have your pants zipped back up.
My god, I have the Bluebirds, and the dance group—they'll
stop sending their kids, and I won't be able to get my mail
delivered, or the electricity—they won't sell me food at the
Mayfair; I'll have to drive to Petaluma every time I want a
loaf of bread—I won't even be able to buy gas for my car!"

Andrews told me I was getting worked up inordinately.
Finally I told him to go to hell and hung up.

Anyhow, I thought, that's what analysts are for, to have steam blown off at them.

In a sense he's right. I am getting too excited.

At six o'clock, while the girls and I were eating dinner— Jack was still hiding out somewhere—the front door opened and Nat Anteil walked into the house.

"Where have you been?" I said, leaping up. "I've been trying to get hold of you all day." And then I saw by the look on his face that he knew. "Can't we sue them?" I said. "For defamation of character or something?"

Nat said, "I don't know what you're talking about."

"Wait," I said. I led him out of the dining room and into the study; closing the door so the girls couldn't hear I said, "What is it?"

He said, "I was down in San Francisco, talking to your husband. Evidently Jack told him about us; anyhow he knows."

"Jack told everybody," I said. "He wrote it up and gave it to Claudia Hambro."

"Charley and I had a long talk," Nat said, but I interrupted him before he could go into one of his two-hour speeches.

"You have to go over to Claudia's and get it back," I told him. "Tell her you'll give her a hundred bucks for it; that ought to get it out of her." Going to the desk I got my checkbook out and sat down on the bed to write out a check. "Okay?" I said. "I'll leave it up to you. It's entirely in your hands; it's your responsibility."

Nat said, "I'll go do what I can." He stood holding the check, however, not doing a damn thing.

"Go on," I said. "Go get it. Or is this another of those degrading domestic errands that so offends you?"

"Your husband said that when he gets back up here he's going to kill you."

I said, "Oh, the hell he is. I'll kill him. I'll buy a gun and shoot him. Go get that thing from Claudia, will you? Don't worry about Charley; he'll probably fall dead of a heart attack on the way home. He's been saying that for years. He came home one day when I sent him to buy me Tampax and practically killed me on the spot. It's the kind of solution that comes into the mind of a man like that; it's predictable, and when you've been married to him—"

By this time Nat had started out of the study, holding the check in his hand.

"You're going to do it?" I said, following him. "Get it back? For me? For us?"

"Okay," he said, in a weary voice, "I'll try."

"Work your sexy charm on her," I said. "Do you know her? Have you ever met her? Go home and get that marvelous rust-colored skiing sweater you had on that day I first met you—god, have you got an experience in store, meeting Claudia Hambro." I followed him outdoors, to his car. "She's the most sensationally beautiful woman I've ever seen in my entire life. She looks like a jungle princess, with that mane of hair and those filed teeth."

I told him how to find her house, and he drove off without saying anything further.

Feeling much more cheerful, I returned to the house. The girls were fooling around at the dinner table, sliding mounds of spinach back and forth at each other. I gave them a couple of swats with my hand and then reseated myself and lit a cigarette.

I'm smoking too much, I thought. I'll have to get Nat to help me cut down. He'd probably force me to stop entirely, once I gave him an inch. He probably thinks it's too expensive anyway.

Later on, since Jack had not put in an appearance, I cleared the table and got the girls to do the dishes. Seated in the living room in front of the fireplace, I began meditating about what Nat had said, the business about Charley.

Like hell he'll kill me, I thought. But maybe he will. I'll have to get the sheriff or something. Get somebody to come over and stick around.

I thought of calling Doctor Andrews at his home and asking him about Charley. In the past he had been able to predict what Charley was going to do; it was part of his field to know those things. How the hell could I tell? Maybe the heart attack had scared him so much he might actually do it.

The front door opened. For a moment I thought it was Nat, back with the document, but instead it was Jack, wearing his old army raincoat and hiking boots. Jumping up, I said, "God damn it, I don't mind you telling Charley, but why the hell did you have to tell the Inverness Park flying saucer group?"

He glanced down sheepishly and grinned in that idiotic way.

"What did you say in that nutty piece of writing?" I demanded. "Do you have a copy of it? Yes? No? Do you remember? You probably don't even remember what it said, you—" I couldn't think of any words to fit him. "Get out of here," I said. "Get out of my house. Go on, get your stuff and go. Pile it in the car and I'll drive you down to San Francisco. I mean it." By his reaction I saw that he didn't believe I was serious. "I wouldn't have you around here," I told him. "You lunatic."

In his creaky voice he said, "I have an open invitation from the Hambros to stay with them."

"Then go stay with them!" I shouted. "And get that woman to pick up your crap; tell her to come drive you and it over there." I grabbed up something—it felt like one of the children's toys—and threw it at him. I was so furious at him I was virtually out of my mind; if he could stay at the Hambros' we'd never get him out of town—he could stay there and give all the inside dope on us, write one telepathical paper after another, supply junk for an endless number of meetings. "And don't expect me to drive you over," I yelled, running past him to open the door. "You get over there on your own power. And get all your crap out of here tonight."

Still grinning his idiotic grin he sidled past me and out.

Without a word—after all, what could he say?—he shambled off down the driveway to the road and disappeared into the darkness beyond the cypress tress. I slammed the front door, and then I hurried through the house, to his room, and began gathering up all his crap.

At first I tried to lug it out front, to the driveway. But after a few trips I gave up. Why should I carry his stuff for him? Kill myself over a lot of rubbish—

Getting madder and madder, I threw it all together into the cardboard carton we had intended to use as a cage for the girls' guinea pig. Taking hold of one end, I dragged it out the back of his room, on to the field and over to the incinerator. And then I did something that at the time I knew was wrong. Getting the gallon jug of white gas which we used with the roto-tiller, I poured gas onto the carton, and, with my cigarette lighter, ignited it. In ten minutes the whole thing was nothing but glowing embers. Except for his collection of rocks, the whole thing had been burned up, and I for one was relieved. Now that I had done it I ceased feeling regret; I was glad.

Later in the evening I heard a car out front. Presently Jack opened the front door. "Where's my stuff?" he said. "I only see a little out front."

I had seated myself in the big easy chair, facing him. "I burned it all," I said. "I threw it in the incinerator, the whole god damn mess."

He stared at me with that asinine expression on his face, that giggle. "You did?" he said.

"Why aren't you leaving?" I said. "What's keeping you here?"

After fidgeting around, he wandered out, leaving the front door open. I saw him gather the junk that I had put out front into Claudia's car. And then Claudia backed down the driveway to the road.

Wow, I thought. Well, that's that.

I got the bottle of bourbon from the cupboard in the

kitchen and carried it and a glass and the tray of ice cubes into the living room and put them down beside the big chair. For a time I sat drinking and feeling better and better. At least I had gotten my asshole brother out of the house, and that was something. I could get Nathan to help me in a lot of ways that Jack had helped. The girls would miss him, but again Nat would take his place.

And then I began thinking about Nat and Claudia Hambro, and I stopped feeling better and felt worse. Was he over at their house? Was everybody over there, my brother and Nat both? House guests of the Hambros?

No doubt Claudia Hambro was ten times as attractive as I. And Nat had never seen her before. Her magnetic personality—her ability to influence people; look at how she had gotten the upper hand with me, and Nat was far weaker a person than I. Not only that, it had always been evident that he was the kind of man that a woman can easily deal with. I saw that from the start. If an ordinary-looking woman like me, with only average intelligence and charm, could get such a reaction from him, what would Claudia get?

Thinking that, I began to drink as never before. After a while I lost count. All I could think of was Nat and Claudia Hambro, and then it all became mixed in with Charley coming back and killing me, possibly killing the girls . . . I saw Charley coming in the front door with the jar of smoked oysters for me again, and I found myself getting up out of my chair and going toward him, reaching for the oysters and being so glad that he had brought me a present.

He really will kill me, I realized. This time when he comes in the door he won't hit me; he'll kill me.

I got up from the chair and told the girls to put themselves to bed. Then I went into the utility room, bumping into the washer and drier as I did so, and got the little ax that I used to cut up kindling. Going into my bedroom I locked the door and all windows and sat there on the bed with the ax on my lap.

I was still sitting there when I heard a man come in the front door. Is that him? I thought. Is that Charley or Jack or Nat? He couldn't get out of the hospital tonight; he's not supposed to get out until the day after tomorrow. And Jack hasn't got a car. Didn't I hear a car? Going to the window I tried to see on to the driveway, but a cypress tree blocked my view.

"Fay?" a man's voice called from somewhere in the house.

"I'm in here," I said.

Presently the man came to the door. "You in there, Fay?" he said.

"Yes," I said.

He tried the door and discovered that it was locked. "It's me," he said. "Nat Anteil."

I got up, then, and unlocked the door.

When he saw the ax he said, "What's wrong?" As he took it out of my hands he saw the empty bourbon bottle; I had carried it into the bedroom with me and finished it. "Good god," he said, putting his arms around me.

"Don't you hug me," I said. "Go hug Claudia Hambro." With all my strength I shoved him away. "How was she?" I said. "A real good lay?"

He took me by the shoulder and half-led, half-pushed me into the kitchen. There, he seated me at the table and put on the kettle of water.

"Go to hell," I said. "I don't want any coffee. Caffeine gives me nocturnal palpitations."

"Then I'll fix you some Sanka," he said, getting down the jar of instant Sanka.

"That nothing coffee," I said. But I let him fix me a cup of it anyhow.

# 16

At one in the afternoon his wife was to pick him up at the front entrance of the hospital and drive him home. But the night before, he telephoned Bill Jaffers, the shop foreman at his plant in Petaluma, and told him to come by the hospital with a pick-up truck at nine in the morning. He explained to Jaffers that his wife was too nervous to take the responsibility of driving him home.

So at eight-thirty he got out of his hospital bed, put on his clothes—his tie and white shirt and suit and shined black oxfords—made sure he had all his possessions in his suitcase, paid his bill at the business office of the hospital, and then sat outside on the steps waiting for Jaffers. The day was cool and bright, with no fog.

Finally the plant's pick-up truck appeared and parked. Jaffers, a big dark-haired man in his early thirties, stepped out and up to Charly Hume.

"Hey, you're looking almost well," he said. He began picking up the pile of possessions stacked beside Charley and putting them into the bed of the truck.

"I feel okay," Charley said, standing up. He felt weak and

sick to his stomach, and he waited for Jaffers to help him into the cab.

Soon they were driving through downtown San Francisco, toward the Golden Gate Bridge. As always, traffic was heavy.

"Take your time," he told Jaffers. As he figured it Fay would leave the house about eleven. He did not want to get there before she left, so that gave them two hours. "Don't go tear-assing around curves like you do when you're on company time, wearing out rubber that doesn't cost you anything to replace." He felt despondent and leaned against the door to gaze out at the cars and houses and streets. "Anyhow, I have to stop along the way and buy some things," he said.

"What do you have to get?" Jaffers said.

"None of your business," Charley said. "I'll get it."

Sometime later they parked in the shopping district of one of the suburban Marin towns. Leaving Jaffers he got out of the truck and walked down the street and around the corner to a large hardware store that he knew. There he bought a .22 revolver and two cartons of bullets. At home he had a number of guns, both rifles and pistols, but beyond any doubt Fay would have gotten them hidden. He had the clerk wrap the revolver and ammunition in such a way that no one could tell what it might be, and then he paid cash and left the store. Presently he was back in the truck, with the parcel on his lap.

As they drove on, Jaffers said, "Bet that's for your wife."

"You're not kidding," Charley said.

"That's quite some wife you have," Jaffers said.

Charley said, "You're not just-a-whistling Dixie."

In Fairfax they stopped at a drive-in and had something to eat. Jaffers ate two hamburgers and a vanilla milkshake, but he himself had only a bowl of soup.

As they drove up the Sir Francis Drake highway, through the park, Jaffers said, "This is sure beautiful country. We used to come up here all the time, up around Inverness, and fish. We used to catch salmon and bass." He went on to describe the fishing equipment that he liked. Charley half-listened. "So the way I feel about spinners," Jaffers concluded, "is that it's fine for, say, surf fishing, but for stream fishing I don't see the use. And Jesus, the good ones can cost you ninety-five bucks, just for the spinner alone."

"That's for sure," Charley murmured.

The time, when they reached Drake's Landing, was eleven-ten. She must have left, he decided. But as the truck reached the cypress lane that preceded his house he saw, between the trees, the flash of sunlight on the hood of the Buick. God damn her, he thought. She had not left.

"Go on by," he said to Jaffers.

"What do you mean?" Jaffers said, slowing the truck and starting to turn into the driveway.

With ferocity, he said, "Keep going, you fink. Keep driving. Don't go in the driveway."

Bewildered, Jaffers brought the truck back on to the road and kept on. Peering back, Charley saw the front door of the house standing open. Evidently she was almost ready to leave.

"I don't get it," Jaffers said. He had apparently put together the sight of the Buick in the driveway and Charley's desire to go on and not stop. "Doesn't she know I picked you up? Christ's sake, don't you want to stop her before she leaves?"

"You mind your business or you're fired," Charley said. "You want to be out of a job? So help me god, I'll fire you; I'll write you out two weeks' notice right now."

"Okay," Jaffers said. "But it's a hell of a thing to let her drive all the way down to Frisco and all the way back for nothing." He became moodily silent, continuing to drive.

"Park here," Charley said, when they reached the top of a rise. "Get over on the shoulder. No, turn the truck around."

They parked in such a way that he could see down the

road as far as Inverness Park. When the Buick left the driveway he would see it take off.

"Can I smoke?" Jaffers said.

"Sure," he said.

Fifteen minutes later the Buick appeared on the road and shot off in the direction of Highway One.

"There she goes," he said. "Okay," he said, "let's get back. I feel tired. Come on, let's go."

This time they found the driveway empty. Jaffers parked the truck and began carrying Charley's possessions into the house. I hope she didn't forget anything, Charley thought. Doesn't turn around and come back. He got out of the cab, and, with Jaffers supporting him, walked up the path and into the house. There, in the living room, he lowered himself onto the couch.

"Thanks," he said to Jaffers. "Now you can take off."

"You want to go to bed, don't you?" Jaffers said, lingering.

"No," he said, "I don't want to go to bed. If I wanted to I'd go to bed; I'd be in bed now. I want to sit here. You can leave."

After hanging around a little longer, Jaffers at last left. Seated on the couch, Charley heard the truck back out of the driveway and go off down the road.

Beyond doubt, he had all the time in the world. She would not get to the U.C. Hospital until one, and then it would take her two more hours to get back. So he had until three o'clock. He did not have to hurry. He could rest and recover his strength; he could even take a nap.

Lifting his feet up on to the couch he lay back with his head on a pillow. Then he turned on his side to look out the window at the pasture.

There, as big as life, stood his horse, cropping weeds. And, beyond the horse, he saw one of the sheep. Near the sheep lay a small dark shape that occasionally stirred. My god, he thought. A lamb. That ewe's had a lamb. He tried to make out the other sheep, to see if they had had their lambs, too.

But he could see only this one. It looked to be Alice, the oldest of the three. That's a fine old ewe, he thought to himself, watching her. Almost eight years old, and wise as hell. Smarter than some humans.

He watched another ewe approach her, and her lamb amble toward it. The other ewe butted the lamb back to its own mother, and that gave him a charge. You'd think a blow like that would break it in half, he thought. But it doesn't. She has to butt it; needs her own milk for her own lambs.

Big wise old black-faced sheep . . . he recalled the girls feeding Alice by hand, the great tranquil, intelligent face as the ewe bent to push its muzzle against their flat palms. Don't curl your fingers, he told them. Like when you feed the horse . . . don't stick up anything for her to nip off. They really have strength in those jaws . . . grind the grass, like rotary blades. Bone roto-tillers, and good for a hell of a lot longer than that monkey ward's piece of tin.

He thought suddenly, Of course, when she gets to the hospital and finds me gone she could call Anteil and send him right over here. That would be approximately one o'clock. So maybe I don't have so much time after all.

Getting up from the couch he stood for a moment. God, I'm weak, he thought. Wow. Unsteadily, he walked from the living room into the bathroom. There, with the door shut, he opened his parcel. He seated himself on the toilet seat and loaded the gun.

Carrying the gun in the pocket of his coat he went outdoors, on to the patio. The day had become warm and the sun made him feel stronger. He walked to the fence, opened the gate, and stepped out on to the pasture.

The horse, seeing him, started in his direction.

Thinks I have something for him to eat, he thought. Sugar cube. The horse picked up speed, jogging toward him and blowing excitedly.

Oh dear god, he thought as the horse stopped a few feet away from him, eyeing him. How can I? The fucking horse;

if they're so smart, why doesn't it run off? He got out the revolver and released the safety catch. Better the horse first, he decided. Lifting the revolver—his hand was shaking wildly—he aimed at the horse's head and compressed the trigger. There was no recoil, but the sound made him tremble. The horse shook its head, pawed, and then turned and galloped off. I missed him, he thought. I fired right at him and missed him. But the horse suddenly fell forward as it ran; it pitched over, tumbled, and lay on its side, with its legs twitching. The horse screamed. Charley stood where he was, looking at it. Then he shot it again, from a distance. The horse continued to kick, and he started toward it, to fire again at close range. But by the time he reached it, it had stopped kicking. It was still alive; he could tell by its eyes. But it was dying. Blood ran down its head, from the wound in its skull.

In the pasture the three ewes watched.

He walked toward the first one. For a while it did not budge; he had gotten almost up to it before—as always—it ducked its head and began trotting off, its wide sides sticking out like packs. This one had not had its lambs. He raised the pistol and shot at it. The ewe bucked and picked up speed. It turned slightly to one side, erratically; catching sight of its head, he shot at that. The sheep fell head over heels, its legs flopping.

With less trouble he approached the second ewe. She had been lying down, and as he reached her she scrambled to her feet. He managed to shoot her before she had gotten entirely up; her weight, the weight of unborn lambs, held her back.

Now he had the trouble of the oldest ewe, with her lamb. He knew that she would not run because she was accustomed to having him approach her. He walked toward her, and she did not stir. She kept her eyes fixed on him. When he was still a few yards off she bleated loudly. The lamb let out its thin, metallic cry. What about the lamb? he asked himself.

He hadn't considered that. Well, it has to be included, he decided. Even though I never saw it before. It's as much mine as any of them. He raised the revolver and shot at the ewe, but by now he had run out of bullets. The hammer only clicked.

Standing there, he reloaded the revolver. Far off, the eucalyptus trees stirred with the midday wind. The ewe and lamb watched him and waited as he finished loading the gun and put the box of bullets away. Then he took aim and shot the ewe. It sank down on its knees and keeled over. At once he shot the lamb, before it could start making any racket. Like its mother it died soundlessly, and that made him feel better. He walked slowly back toward the house, conserving his strength. On the pasture, nothing stood upright; no shapes of cropping animals. He had swept it clean.

Where, he wondered, was the dog? Has she taken it with her? That made him angry. He passed through the house and out on to the front porch. Sometimes the dog spent its time down the street or across the street. Using the dog-whistle on his key chain he called it. Finally a muffled bark sounded somewhere in the house. She had shut the dog in, probably in one of the bedrooms.

Sure enough, he found the collie standing in the guest bedroom, wagging its tail happily to see him.

He led the dog outdoors on to the patio and shot it by putting the muzzle of the gun against its ear. The dog let out a screech, like a mechanical brake, so high-pitched that he scarcely could hear it. It leaped up and spun and fell down, scrabbling.

Next he walked down to the duck pen.

While he was busy shooting the ducks through the wire mesh he thought, Won't somebody hear all the gunshots and call Sheriff Chisholm? No, he decided. There's always hunters this time of year, bagging quail or rabbits or deer—whatever's in season.

Having finished with the ducks he searched about for the

chickens. The flock had gone off somewhere and he saw no sign of it. Damn them, he thought. He called them, using the sound that he and Fay made at feeding time, but no chickens appeared. Once, he thought he saw a red tail moving in the cypress thickets . . . possibly the chickens had gone up into the cypress trees and had roosted there, watching him. No doubt the noise of the shooting had sent them packing. Bantams, he thought. So damn crafty.

There was nothing left to shoot, so he returned to the house.

The business of shooting the animals had put him in a state of exhaustion. As soon as he had gotten into the house he shed his coat, threw the gun down, dropped down on to the couch, and lay on his back with his eyes shut. His heart surely was going to stop working entirely; he could feel it preparing to cease beating. God damn it, he prayed. Keep going, you motherfucker.

After a time he felt better. But he did not move; he continued to lie dormant, conserving himself.

Maybe two hours, he thought. By then I'll either be dead or strong enough to get back on my feet.

From outdoors, beyond the patio, he heard a sound suggesting that one of the animals was not entirely dead. He heard whimpers, but although he listened, he could not make out which animal it was. Probably the horse, he concluded. Should he go out and shoot it again? Of course. But could he? No, he decided. I can't. I'd fall over dead either going or coming. It'll have to die by itself.

He lay on the couch, listening to the faint sounds of the animal out on the pasture dying, and meanwhile trying not to die himself.


All at once the noise of a car engine woke him.

He slid his feet to the floor and arose, his heart pounding. He reached around him for the gun and could not find it.

Outdoors, beyond the windows, Fay appeared on the patio. In her long green coat she stood gazing off across the field, and then she stood on tiptoe, shading her eyes. She's seen the animals, he realized.

Her crying was audible to him. She turned, saw him through the windows. God damn gun, he thought; he still could not find it, where he had put it. Fay had an armload, her purse and some packages. She dropped them and ran on high heels to the gate. At the gate she had trouble; she could not get the latch undone. He ran across the room and pushed open the door to the patio.

By the barbecue pit, standing upright, was the long two-pronged fork that they used to lift the broiling steaks. He grabbed that and hurried toward her. Now she had gotten the gate open. On the far side she paused to kick off her shoes. Her eyes were filled with wariness. When he had gotten almost to her, she loped away, facing him, not taking her eyes from him. If I had the gun, he realized, she'd be dead now. He reached the fence and passed on through the open gate, on to the field.

Fay, not speaking to him but speaking past him, called in a sharp loud voice, "You stay there."

The kids, he realized. Half-turning his head he saw them, standing together at the corner house. Both dressed up in their red coats and nice lace-edged skirts, two-tone shoes. Their hair brushed. Staring at him, staring and staring. Neither of them crying.

Backing away from him, Fay called to the children, "Go on away. Go up the road to Mrs. Silva's. Go on!" Her voice got that commanding tone, that harshness. Both children at once jumped forward, toward her, automatically going to her. "Go on up to Mrs. Silva's!" Fay called to them, gesturing toward the road. This time the children understood. They disappeared around the corner of the house.

He faced his wife.

"Oh," she said, almost with delight; her face shone. "I

see—you shot them." She had backed to the dead horse and had cast a quick glance. "Well," she said, "my goodness."

He continued a few more steps toward her. She moved back the same distance; the distance did not change.

"You motherfucker," she said. "You daughterfucker. You fatherfucker. You turdface. You shithead. You—" She went on steadily, never taking her eyes from him. She kept herself under control by cursing at him. And he kept on advancing toward her. Of course, she retreated equally. With her wariness.

"Call me anything you want," he said.

"I'll tell you what I'll call," she said. "I'll call Sheriff Chisholm and have you put in jail. I'll get the police here. I'll get you sent away. You nut. You madman. You sick person."

Back and back she went, never letting him get closer than ten feet from her. Now she had gotten her wind back; he saw her twist her head, measuring her distance from the barbed wire fence behind her that marked the edge of their land. Beyond the fence the ground sloped sharply, into trees and shrubs and eventually to marshy ground and a fast-moving stream. Once, he and she had pursued the Muscovy duck down on to the marshes; the duck had taken refuge among the roots of willows, and it had taken them all day to close in on her. His feet at the time had sunk down six inches with each step . . .

I haven't got it, he said to himself. Now she was moving more quickly; she was getting ready to leap the fence. Like an animal. Eyeing it first. Being sure. One hop and over. And then off at the speed of light.

But still she retreated step by step. She was not near enough to the fence to turn her back to him.

He began to hasten.

"Ah," she said, with excitement. And at once she turned and leaped the fence; her body spun and she was on the far side, still spinning, getting her balance. She fell to her knees, splashing in the mud and cow flop. At once she was up and off. Shows me her heels, he thought, going on to the fence himself and stooping down to crawl between the wire.

It took him a long, long time to get across. And, on the far side, he could scarcely stand upright.

There, not ten feet away, she stood watching him. Why? he wondered. Why didn't she run off . . .

Again he approached her, holding the long fork toward her. She resumed her slow backward walk.

Why? he asked himself again as he slipped a little on the wet slope. And then he realized why. The children and the Silvas stood in the land behind the Silvas' house, watching. Four people. And now a fifth person, an elderly man, joined them. He understood. She wants them to see. God, he thought. She's making them see me. She'll never run, never get away; she wants me to keep on, keep on. All the proof. Here. Here I am. Out in the field, pursuing her with this fork. Realizing that, he waved the fork at her.

"God damn you," he yelled at her.

She smiled her quick reflexive smile.

"I'll kill you," he shouted.

She backed away, step by step.

He turned and started toward the house. She remained where she was, not going any farther away and not following him. At last he reached the fence again. He crept between the wire and into his own field. We were on the Bracketts' property, he realized. She still is. Standing on Bob Brackett's field, his forty acres of swamp that we had an option on once and then let go.

When he got to the patio he looked back. Three men, starting from one of the houses up the road, were coming steadily toward him across the Bracketts' field. Fay hung back beyond them.

Opening the back door he crept into the house. He locked the door after him and threw down the barbecue fork. And the dead animals, he realized. Proof. All that dead stuff out there. And everybody heard me say it. The doctor. Anteil.

The kids saw me hit her, that day. Hell, they all know.

On the floor by the couch he found the gun. He picked it up and stood holding it. Meditating. Then he seated himself on the couch. The men had halted by the fence; they could see him through the windows, sitting on the couch with the gun.

He saw Sheriff Chisholm with them, telling them to go back. Sheriff Chisholm passed by the side of the house and was gone from sight. He'll get me in two shakes of a lamb's tail, he thought. He knows his business. Fucking rustic farmers.

Putting the muzzle of the gun into his mouth he pulled the trigger.

A light came on. Instead of sound. He saw, for the first time. He saw it all. He saw how she had moved him. Put him up to this.

I see, he said.

Yes, I see.

Dying, he understood it all.

# 17

The business of burning my things was dirty. And it wasn't
the first time. They did exactly the same thing during World
War Two and even before that. It's a pattern. Probably I
should have expected it. Anyhow, I was able to salvage my
geological collection. Naturally none of the samples making
up that exhibit had been consumed.

The day that Charley Hume killed himself I had been
feeling depressed since getting out of bed. Of course, at the
time I did not know the reason for my depression. Mrs.
Hambro in fact remarked on my unusual mood. I spent the
day outdoors working in the Hambros' terraced gardens, one
of the tasks I had undertaken as a means of repaying them
for their hospitality. In addition, I did similar work for the
other members of the group, including tending various animals that they owned, such as cows, goats, sheep, chickens.
My experience with Charley's animals indicated that I had a
natural bent in that direction, and I even considered taking
a course in animal husbandry over at Santa Rosa.

Meanwhile, of course, I kept up my spiritual life through
my contact with the group. And Mrs. Hambro had introduced

me to other sensitive individuals living down in the Bay area.

My depression became so acute by four in the afternoon that I gave up working and instead went and sat on the front steps of the Hambro house and read the newspaper. Not too much later, Mrs. Hambro drove up and parked and got out in a state of excitement. She asked me if I had heard the news that something dreadful had happened at my sister's house. I said I hadn't heard. She didn't know what it was—she had gotten the news in a roundabout way—but she had the idea that Charley had either killed Fay or had died of a second heart attack, or something on that order. Sheriff Chisholm was up there, and a number of cars from out of town, and what looked like County officials; anyhow men in business suits and ties had been seen walking around in front of the house.

It occurred to me that possibly I should go over there, since Fay was my sister. But I did not. After all, she had thrown me out. So I remained at the Hambros' the balance of the day, eating dinner with them that evening.

At eight-thirty, we got the news from Dorothy Bently, who lived down the road from Charley and Fay. It was really terrible. I could hardly believe it. Mrs. Hambro thought I should go over, or at least phone. We discussed it, and then Mrs. Hambro called a special meeting of the group to consider the whole situation and to see what significance it had in the cosmic program that was unfolding.

The group, after discussing it, came to the conclusion that the death was a symptom of the anarchy and dissolution attending the last agonies of the Earth before it became superseded. But we had still not decided whether I should go over. We put Marion Lane into a trance—Mrs. Hambro doing the actual hypnotizing—and she said that probably I should try to get in touch with Nat Anteil and find out if Fay wanted to see me. Because of the data that I had turned over to the group concerning Fay and Nat, the group had taken an active interest in their situation, viewing it as a manifestation on an earthly plane of certain super-terrestrial forces. None of us had been clear as to the nature or plan of these forces; we did not expect the goal to be revealed until the very end. That is, until toward the end of April, 1959. Meanwhile we had all kept in touch, as we did with everything else going on.

Using Mrs. Hambro's library phone I called Nat Anteil. We had found that when we used that phone—as contrasted to the extension in the kitchen or the living-room—we got better results. It was the luckiest phone in the house, and in a situation this grave I wanted everything favorable in the universe to be at work.

However, I got no answer to my rings. No doubt Nathan was over at the Hume house.

The next day I called Fay's number several times, and at last got an answer. She said only that she was too busy to talk and would call back; thereupon she hung up, and did not call back. The next contact I had was a printed announcement, mailed by her, of the services.

I did not attend the services, because it seems to me, as Pythagoras says, the body is the tomb of the soul and that by being born a person has already begun to die. The physical attribute of Charley which would be on display at the mausoleum was of no consequence to a person like myself who is concerned—not with this world—but with the real, that is, the eternal. Charley Hume, or the essence of him, the soul, the spark, had not been extinguished; it still existed as it always had, although now we could not see it. As Mrs. Hambro phrased it, the corruptible man must put on immortality, and I thought that was a good way of putting it. So I did not feel that Charley had left us; he was still hovering in the sky near Drake's Landing. And it would not be very many more days before the rest of us joined him—a fact he was ignorant of when he took his own life.

During this time speculation throughout the Point Reyes—Tomales Bay area concerned whether Nat and Fay would stay together or whether Charley's death would cause them to break up through remorse. At first the issue seemed in doubt. Neighbors along their road, especially Mrs Bentely, reported that Nat was not spending much time at the Hume home. The children had been taken out of school temporarily, so they could not be asked. But then his car was seen going back and forth once more, and the consensus was that they were once again resuming their relationship.

The item published in the Baywood *Press* merely mentioned that Charley Hume of Drake's Landing had "taken his own life," due apparently to despondency over ill-health. The article mentioned that he had had a heart attack and had been just released from the hospital. It did not mention Nathan at all, only that "he is survived by his widow, Fay, and his two daughters Elsie and Bonnie." The headline read:

## C.B. HUME ENDS OWN LIFE

The group felt that a much fuller account could have been given, and I prepared a complete factual presentation, describing Fay's relationship with Nathan fully, and informing the public at large that the real cause of Charley's death had not been despondency over ill-health at all but his having discovered that during his period in the hospital his wife had cheated on him with another man. However, the Baywood *Press* declined to publish this; in fact they did not even acknowledge receiving it—although, to be perfectly fair to them, I must admit that we were careful not to give our names or box numbers in case there was any legal action taken regarding use of the mails, etc.

However it did not matter whether the Baywood *Press* chose to publish the complete account or not, since everybody in the area knew the real story anyhow. It was the main topic of discussion at the post office and the grocery store for weeks on end. And certainly, in a democracy, this is right. The public should know the facts. Otherwise it can't judge.

In reference to the element of judgment, it was our observation that the average opinion in the area ran fairly strongly against Fay and Nat, and quite often we heard words of censure—although, of course, these were not delivered to either of them, and certainly not to the children. The Bluebirds continued to meet under Fay's guidance at the Hume household. Fay still attended the dance group, and none of the women either resigned or withdrew their children. The only overt action taken in reprimand of Fay and Nat was that some residents ceased waving to them when their car passed, and two or three mothers that I know of declined to permit their daughters to be picked up by Fay to play in the afternoons at the Hume house. But of course that had begun before Charley's death; it took place as soon as the group promulgated the original dramatized presentation that I made available to them. Mrs. Hambro had had it mimeographed and mailed out to the list of residents that she had gotten from the Republican Party in Marin County, so persons as far away as Novato had been fully informed.

I don't think that either Nat or Fay were too conscious of this public disapproval, since they had had so many problems of their own to settle. For a fact I know that they were concerned with the two children hearing something unpleasant on the playground, but when this did not transpire, their apprehension diminished. Outside of that, they seemed more interested in how to arrange their own lives, and I did not blame them for being wrapped up in that; they certainly had overwhelming moral and practical problems to cope with.

A week or so later I received a letter from an attorney in San Rafael named Walter W. Sipe, informing me that I was wanted at ten in the morning on April 6th in his office on B Street. It had to do with the C.B. Hume estate.

Mrs. Hambro felt very strongly that I should be there; she not only urged me to go but promised to drive me down. So on that morning, having put on a coat and slacks and tie of Mr. Hambro's, I was driven down by Mrs. Hambro and let off at the lawyer's office building.

In the office I found Fay and the two girls and some adults that I had never seen before. Later I learned that some of them had worked for Charley at his plant in Petaluma and some were relatives of his who had flown out from Chicago.

Nat, of course, was not present.

We were given chairs, and after we had seated ourselves the lawyer read us the will that Charley had made out. I could make little or no sense out of it. It was not until days later that I understood what it meant. Legal language being what it is, I am still not sure about certain details. In any case, the gist of the disposition of his estate was this. Mainly, he was concerned about his two daughters, which was understandable. Since he had had a good deal of distrust of Fay for years—which I had recognized already—he had started a process of withdrawing capital from his plant and putting that capital into stocks and bonds in the children's names. This had all been done before his death. The plant, then, was not worth nearly as much as might have been thought; in fact, it had been bled to the bone.

Under California Community Property law, one half of all assets acquired during the marriage belonged to Fay. Charley, in his will, could not dispose of that. But the stocks and bonds no longer belonged to either him or Fay; they belonged to the children. So he had gotten most of his assets out of his and Fay's hands, and into the girls'. In addition, he had instructed that the bulk of the estate be put into a fund to be administered by Mr. Sipe for the girls' benefit, and that at their twenty-first birthday the fund be turned over to them.

So not only did the girls own the stocks and bonds but they also got his share of the plant in Petaluma. The stocks and bonds, although belonging to them, were to be kept in trust by his brother, who had flown out from Chicago. He was to make funds available to the children according to their need. The children were to be allowed to live with their mother, and about that Charley had a lot to say.

All he had left to Fay was the Buick—that is, his half since the other half already belonged to her. She, of course, already owned one half of the house under California law, and one half of all the personal property in the house. Charley could not dispose of that. But here is what he had done with his half. He had willed his half of the house to me.

To me. Of all the people in the world. So Fay owned one half and I owned the other.

As to the personal property that was his, he had willed that to the children direct.

He had left as much to me as to Fay, unless you include the Buick, which was not worth much.

In the will was a long stipulation regarding tenancy of the house. Neither Fay nor I could forcibly exclude the other from the premises. We could, however, come to an agreement regarding sale of the house or use of the house. Each of us could sell his share to the other, for instance. Or rent it to the other for a sum to be named by the Bank of America at Point Reyes as reasonable. He had also set aside various small sums, derived from their joint bank account, half of which was his to will. He had almost a thousand dollars to be used for psychiatric help for me, if I chose to use it, and, if not, it was to be turned over to the girls. And he had left money for funeral expenses.

His having committed suicide had voided his insurance policies, so Fay got nothing out of them.

When it came down to it, he had left everything to the girls and nothing to Fay. And her property under California law consisted only of her half of the house—on which there was a large mortgage to be paid off—and her half of the plant, which did not amount to anything like she had expected, since the plant had been bled over a number of years. Of course, she could get an attorney and go to court and claim that a good deal of the stocks and bonds actually belonged to her, since they had been bought with her money as well as Charley's. And she could challenge the will in other ways, claiming, for instance, that he had willed her the Buick which was not his to will, since she had actually bought it before the marriage. A will which contains provisions of that sort can be tossed out, I understand. But Charley had written a clause in concerning her contesting the will. If she did so, the administrator of the children's share of the estate—that is, his brother Sam—was to take action against her in court on the grounds that she was an unfit mother, and the girls were to be taken away from her, and his family appointed guardians. Now possibly that provision could not hold up, it being punitive. But even by investigating it she risked having it enacted, and evidently Sam declared himself willing to go through with the requirements of the clause. Charley had gone to some lengths in the will to describe— although vaguely—her relationship with Nat, and he also mentioned me specifically as a witness to this. There was no doubt that the house and funds left to me were in the nature of an inducement to me to cooperate fully in the "unfit mother" clause if Fay did challenge the will; at least I so construed it.

She did not contest the will, although for a time she and Nat discussed it. I know they discussed it, because I was present. How could I not be? Almost at once, as soon as I had transportation, I moved back into the house with Fay and the children, and, of course, with Nat Anteil, to the extent that he was staying there. And this time they could not throw me out, because it was as much my house as hers. And it was not Nat Anteil's at all; he had no legal right to be there, as I had.

So when Claudia Hambro drove me back there in her station wagon, along with my possessions, she was driving me back to my own house.

...

When I walked in the front door, Fay and Nat were flabbergasted to see me. Without saying a word—they were that affected—they stood around while I unloaded the station wagon and said good-bye to Claudia. In a voice loud enough for them to hear I took pains to invite Claudia and her husband and the rest of the group over, to use the house as a meeting place or just to visit. Then, waving to me, she drove off.

Fay said, "You mean you'd just walk right in? Without discussing this whole business first?"

"What is there to discuss?" I said, feeling wonderful. "I have a legal right to be here, as much as you." And this time, I didn't have to take up residence in the utility room, like a servant. Nor did I have to do their unpleasant tasks for them, such as emptying the trash or mopping the bathroom floors.

I felt on top of the world.

The two of them remained in the living room while I began fixing up the study; that was the room I had elected as my bedroom. Neither of them made a move to interfere, but I could hear them talking in low, grumpy tones.

While I was hanging my clothes up in the study closet, Nat approached me. "Come on into the living room and we'll discuss this," he said.

Enjoying myself, yet wanting to be at the job of getting my stuff arranged, I followed him. It was nice to seat myself there on the couch and not have to retire off somewhere in the rear while others conducted their affairs.

Fay said, "How the hell do you plan to make your payments on the house? There's two hundred and forty dollars due a month on this place, including interest. Half of that is yours to pay. One hundred and twenty a month. And that doesn't include taxes or fire insurance. How can you pay that?" Her voice shrilled with outrage at me.

Actually, I hadn't given much thought to that. The realization diminished my pleasure somewhat.

"By acquiring half the title to this place," Nathan said, "you acquire half the indebtedness. You're responsible for maintenance costs, utility costs, as much as Fay is. Do you know what it costs to heat this place? She's not going to pay them; that's a cinch."

"Fifty dollars a month," Fay said. "That's what your share of the heating bill is going to be. My god, it'll cost you another hundred a month for utilities—it'll cost you three hundred a month to own half this house. At least three hundred."

"Oh come on," I said. "It doesn't cost six hundred a month to maintain this house."

At that, Nat whipped out the big cardboard carton in which Fay kept incoming bills; he had also the checkbook and past stubs and bills. "That's what it comes out to," Nat said. "You know you have no money. Your part is going to lapse. How can it not lapse? You can't live here. It's impossible."

All I could think to do was smile at them, to show my lack of anxiety.

"You horse's ass," Fay said, her voice continuing to rise in accusation. To Nat she said, "This is just to pay him so he'll go into court and tell a lot of lies about you and me— good god, Charley must have been out of his mind; he must have been a paranoid at the last, there, in the hospital, believing all that crap."

"Take it easy," Nat said to her. Of the two of them he seemed to me the more rational. "You better sell your equity right now," he said to me. "Before it's encumbered with indemnities." On a piece of paper he made out figures. "You've got approximately a seven thousand dollar equity," he said. "And you'll have to pay inheritance tax on that— did you realize that?"

I said, "You mean, you people buy my share of the house?"

"Yes," Fay said. "Otherwise the bank'll be taking your share and you'll wind up with not one god damn cent out of this." To Nat she said, "And then we'll be living here with the Bank of America."

"I don't feel like selling," I said.

Nat said, "You have no choice."

To that, I said nothing. But I continued to smile.

"There's a bank payment due right now," Fay said. "One of them. One-fifty-five. Do you have half of that? You have to have. It's your share. Don't imagine I'm going to pay your share of it, you—" She called me a name vile beyond belief. Even Nat looked embarrassed.

We argued to no avail for at least an hour, and then Fay went off into the kitchen to fix herself a drink. Meanwhile, the girls had come home from playing with some friend of theirs. They both seemed quite glad to see me, and I played the airplane game with them. Fay and Nat watched with dark countenances.

Once, I heard Fay said, ". . . gets to play with my kids, and what can I do about it? Nothing." She hurled her cigarette at the fireplace, and it missed and landed on the floor beyond. Nat went over and got it. She paced around and around the living room while he sat gazing somberly at the floor, occasionally crossing and recrossing his legs.

When I got tired of playing with the girls I sent them off to their rooms to watch tv, and then I joined Nat and Fay in the living room. I seated myself in the big overstuffed easy chair that had been Charley's favorite. Putting my hands behind my head I leaned back and made myself comfortable.

After some silence, Fay said suddenly, "Well, I'll tell you one thing; I won't live in this house with this asshole around. And I won't have him playing with my kids."

Nat said nothing. I pretended not to hear.

"I'd rather give up my share of the house," Fay said. "I'll sell it or give it away."

"You can sell it," Nat said. "It shouldn't be hard."

"What about now?" she said. "Right now? Tonight.

How'm I going to sleep here?" Glancing at Nat she said, "God, we can't make a move; we can't even eat a meal or take a bath—nothing."

"Come on," Nat said, standing up and motioning to her. Together they went outdoors on to the patio and stood together, far enough from the house so that I couldn't hear them.

The upshot of their discussion together was that they decided to leave the house entirely and move over to the smaller house that Nat rented, the one which he and Gwen had lived in together. As far as I was concerned, that was fine. But what about the girls? That house was too small for four people, even two adults and two children. At least, that was my understanding, from what I had heard. It had only one bedroom, and then one small utility room in which he had done his school work late at night. Plus of course a living room and bathroom and kitchen.

They took the girls that night, at about nine, and drove off with them. Whether they stayed at Nat's house or in a motel I don't know. In any case, I prepared to go to bed alone, in the empty house.

It gave me an odd feeling that night as I changed from my day clothes into my pajamas and prepared to get into the guest bed in the study. After all, this had been Charley's study, where he had spent a good deal of time. Now he was dead, and his wife had gone off, taking his and her daughters, leaving no one in the house but me. All of them gone. All of them had left this house which they had gone to so much trouble to build. And who was I? For a time, as I lay in bed, I felt confusion. I wasn't actually one of the persons who owned this house . . . at least, who owned it in a real sense. Perhaps I owned a legal share of it, but I certainly had never thought of it as mine. I might as well have had someone point to some movie theater or bus station and tell me that I owned a share of it. In some respects it was like when as a child I had been told that, as an American citizen, I'd someday "own" a part of every public bridge and dam and street . . .

I had lived well in this house, for a short period of time. But not because of the house itself; more, because of the good meals and the warmth. Now, if I wanted warmth, I would have to pay for half of the bill that came as a result. And I would be buying my own food, as clearly as I had to buy it when living in one single rented room in Seville. Nobody would charcoal broil t-bone steaks on the outdoor grill and hand me a piece free.

And the animals were dead. Except for the banty chickens. Now, at night, the banties had gone into their shed and gone to sleep. No ducks. No horse. No sheep. Not even the dog. Their carcasses had been dragged off for fertilizer.

The house and the land around it was absolutely silent. Except that now and then I heard quail whirring around in the cypress trees. I heard the quail calling like Oklahoma teenagers to each other; ah-h-whoo-whoo. A sort of Okie yell.

And then, lying by myself alone in the dark, empty house, hearing the refrigerator in the kitchen turn on occasionally, and the wall thermostats open and shut, I felt one thing. Fay and the girls and the animals had left, but someone besides myself remained. Charley was still in the house, living there as he had always lived there since the house had been built. The refrigerator that I heard was his. He had supervised putting in the radiant heating. The different sounds were made by things that belonged to him, and he had never left them. I knew it. It wasn't merely an idea. It was an awareness of him, just as at any previous time, during his stay in the physical world, I had been aware of him. By sight, smell, sound, touch.

All night long I lay being conscious of him in the house. He never left, even for a moment. It was constant; it never dimmed.

# 18

At seven o'clock the next morning the telephone woke me up. It was Fay calling from wherever they were staying.

"We'll buy your equity in the house," she said. "Here's what we can give you. One thousand dollars cash and the rest in the form of monthly payments of thirty-eight dollars. We sat up half the night discussing it."

I said, "The only thing is that I want to stay here."

"You can't," she said. "Did it occur to you that everything in that house belongs either to the girls or to me? And if we want to we can keep you from using the refrigerator or the sink—you can't even use the towels in the bathroom. You can't even eat off the dishes in the rack on the drainboard. My good god, you can't even sit down in a chair—that bed you're sleeping in doesn't come with the house; that's part of the personal property, and he only left you his share of the house. The sheets on the bed. The ashtrays!" She went on and on, working herself up. "And how are you going to eat? I'll bet you think you're going to walk into the kitchen and open up a few cans and packages of food. Do you think that food is yours? It isn't. And if you eat one bite of it, I'll sue you. I'll take you to court and sue you!"

I hadn't realized it. What she said was true. "There's a lot in what you say," I said. "I'll have to get my own furniture."

She said, "I think I'll have the movers up from Fairfax and move everything out of that house."

"Okay," I said, taken aback and having difficulty thinking.

"You idiot," Fay said. "All you've got in this world is that empty box of a house—half that empty box of a house. And we can keep up our share of the payments with what we're getting in from the factory." She hung up, then.

I dressed and combed my hair, and then I went into the kitchen and stood wondering if I should fix myself breakfast or not. Suppose while I was eating it, Fay appeared with the sheriff or someone? Wouldn't I, in a sense, be stealing the food?

Unable to decide, I at last gave up the idea of eating breakfast. Instead, I went outdoors and down to the chicken pen to throw grain to the banties.

How empty the duck pen was without the ducks. The trough remained, the porcelain sink that Charley had put down for them, and the drainage system that he had been working on. There was even a duck egg left over, half-buried in the weeds that the ducks had made into a nest. And, in the garbage can, half a sack of egg-gro. Almost fifty pounds of it.

I wandered on, to the stable that Charley had built for the horse. There was the saddle hanging up on the wall, and all the other equipment that had gone with the horse. Over three hundred dollars worth of stuff.

Returning to the house I seated myself on the floor, near the fireplace, and thought. I spent most of the morning deep in thought, and at last I came to the conclusion that what I had to do was find a way of bringing in enough money to make my monthly payments on the house, including what I had to pay on the taxes and insurance. Also, I needed to have enough money to buy food, because it was now clearly apparent that Fay and Nat would not give me any of theirs. I had had the half-formed notion that we could go back to something like the old system, with me doing babysitting for them—although not the dirty work, the scrubbing part—and them supplying me with what would be an equitable amount of supplies such as food and the like. However, that was off.

After figuring I came to the conclusion that I would have to earn almost five hundred dollars a month in order to keep up my end of the house, and this did not include either unusual medical bills or house repairs. Anyhow, I could make the payments, eat, buy some clothes, etc., and acquire some second-hand furniture.

I therefore got out on the road and hitch-hiked to Point Reyes Station. There, I started looking for a job.

The first place I tried was the garage on the corner. I told them that I wasn't a mechanic, but that I had a scientific disposition and was good at analyzing and diagnosis. They told me they didn't have any openings, so I went on across the street to the market. There was nothing there, either, even a job such as opening crates and putting out the merchandise on the shelves. I next tried at the big hardware store. They said that the only person they could use was one who could drive. After that I tried at the post office for the job of postal clerk, but there they told me that a federal civil service exam was required. I tried the other garages and gas stations, the pharmacy, the coffee shop—at least there should have been a job of dish-washer open—and the dress shop, even the little free library. No work was available at any place. I tried the feed store, the big building-supply yard, and finally the bank.

The man at the bank was very helpful. He recognized me as Fay's brother, and we sat down at his desk and talked for a long time. I explained my situation, why I wanted work and how much I had to have. The man told me that it was next to impossible to find work at any of the retail businesses in the area because they all did such a limited operation. My best bet, he said, was either the dairy ranches out on the Point or down at Olema at the mill, or over at the gravel works on the Petaluma road, or the RCA station out on the lighthouse road. If I could drive, he said, I could probably get a job driving the school bus, but that was obviously out. In summer I could pick produce, but this was only April.

Of the various alternatives it seemed to me that a job on one of the dairy farms would be the best, because of my love of animals. Thanking the man, I hitch-hiked back on to the Inverness side of the bay and then, by means of several rides, managed to get out to some of the ranches. It took all day. The only job that was open was that of milker, and this reminded me of what Charley had said originally, that milking would be my best bet up here in the country.

Milking, however, although it sounded like interesting work, paid only a dollar thirty an hour, and this would not be enough for me to meet my expenses. In addition, I would have to actually live on the various ranches, and this would defeat the whole purpose of the job. So milking was out. Toward evening, feeling discouraged and tired, I started hitch-hiking back to town. Fortunately the people at one of the ranches were kind enough to give me a big lunch, otherwise I would have had nothing to eat all day. As it was, I got back to the house at nine-thirty in the evening, thoroughly depressed and tired, with no prospect of work.

I turned on the light in the living room, and, because the house was so cold, I lit a fire in the fireplace, even though I was conscious that the wood belonged to Fay and the children, not to me. Even the discarded newspapers which we always used to start fires did not belong to me, nor the milk cartons that we saved out of the garbage. Only the stuff in the study that I had carried with me from the Hambros'.

Thinking about it, I wondered if possibly anybody in the group might be able to help me find a job that paid five hundred a month. I therefore took a chance and telephoned Mrs. Hambro. Although she was sympathetic she seemed to feel that there was no chance that I'd find a job paying anything like that much; she pointed out that in a farm area wages were generally lower than in the city, and even for San Francisco, five hundred a month was a pretty high salary.

At ten, while I was seated before the fire, the phone rang. I answered it. Again it was Fay, calling from wherever they were staying.

"I came by during the day," she said. "Where were you?"

"Out," I said.

Fay said, "Are you going to get psychiatric help?"

"I haven't thought about it," I said.

"Maybe if you go see Doctor Andrews you'll get more insight into your situation. Why don't you sell your part of the house? I talked to him today and he says that you identify with Charley and are getting revenge on us for his death. You hold us responsible for him killing himself. Is that why you won't sell? Good god, think of the children. They've lived in that house ever since it was built . . . we actually built it for them, not for ourselves. And that's virtually all the son of a bitch left me, except for that nothing factory that hardly makes enough to pay its own way. I have to have that house—half of it is mine, and you can bet your bottom dollar I'll never let my half go. Anyhow, you couldn't buy it from me. Could you? My god, you can't even pay the buck-fifty water bill."

I said nothing.

Fay went on, "I think we'll come over and discuss it with you. We'll see you in about fifteen minutes."

Before I could tell her that I was totally exhausted and about ready for bed, the phone had clicked. She had hung up. It never occurred to her to inquire whether I wanted to discuss it with her or not. That's the way she's always been; nothing will ever change her.

Even more depressed than before I sat waiting for them

to come. In a sense she was right; the children belonged in the house, and since she refused to live with me, the children would not be living here unless I moved out. She, of course, considered it her house, and to a degree it was. But certainly it was not her house in the sense that she meant it: that it was hers and no one else's. The fact of the matter was that the house belonged to Charley, and that he had divided it between her and me, with the obvious idea that both of us would live here. Charley assumed that since Fay and I were sister and brother we would be able to live together. What he thought Nat Anteil would do I have no idea. Possibly he did not realize that Anteil's wife had left him and that their marriage was over. He may have assumed that the relationship between Fay and Nat was only a passing affair. In that, he was not alone; none of us had thought of it persisting. Had Charley come back and not killed himself—nor Fay— then no doubt her assignations with Anteil would have come to an end. He had only to return to the house to put an end to the situation—at least, to keep them from physically coming together. Of course, the bond between them might continue, and that was why he did what he did. He had wanted to punish her for what she had done. I think he was right. She deserved whatever she got. However, at the end, she had outsmarted him and gotten him to kill himself instead. Even though he had drawn up a will that excluded her from the body of his estate, she still had her life, her half of the house, her children, and the household goods—even the car. And all that remained of Charley was the eternal presence that pervaded the house, the presence that I felt so keenly all the time I was there.

In fact, even now as I sat trying to see a way out of this dilemma, I sensed Charley around the house, in each part of it in proportion to the extent that he had inhabited that part while physically alive. Especially in the study, where he had worked at night . . . I felt it there the most. Not so much in the children's rooms or even their bedroom. And not at all in Fay's work room, where she did her clay modeling. Her creative stuff.

What he hadn't realized was that if he had killed her, nobody would ever have had a happy moment again. Think what the effect would have been on the children. Their lives would have been blighted. He himself would have nothing left ahead of him but death from his heart condition, unless he had planned to kill himself, too. Nat Anteil had already given up his wife, seen his brief marriage to her end, and, with Fay dead, what would there be in store for him? Who would have gained?

The nihilism of what Charley did is shown in his killing of the animals. That part affected me the most; I had the greatest difficulty understanding it.

Surely he hadn't hated the animals as he hated Fay; he couldn't possibly have thought that the animals had betrayed him—although of course the dog had learned to greet Anteil rather than to bark at him. To follow the logic of that, however, he would have had to kill his own daughters, since they both like Anteil, and he would possibly even have had to kill me, since the girls like me very much. Maybe he planned to. Anyhow, the sheep cared for nobody on earth, and the ducks, to the extent possible with their limited minds, kept a loyalty to him. After all, it had been he who built their pens.

After thinking it over steadily, I came to the conclusion that he had not known he was killing the animals, that he had only been conscious that when he got back to the house after being in the hospital, *there would be some great change,* which he himself would bring about, and that this change would affect all the living creatures there. He shot the animals to show that what he did mattered. He could do something that couldn't be undone. And yet, even deciding this, I felt then—and still feel now—that the actual reasons for his actions are beyond my scope. I don't understand his kind of illogical, semi-barbaric mind. It was not a question of scientific reason; it was brute instinct. Perhaps he identified the animals with himself. Possibly he was already beginning on the path of killing himself, that he knew in some part of his mind that he would never kill Fay; that it would be he who would end up getting shot, not she. Or possibly he hadn't even wanted to kill her, that he had only gone through the motions. Possibly he had meant to kill himself all the time, from the moment he bought the gun.

In that case, she was not to blame. At least, not as much.

But a confusion like this always results when the unscientific individual is involved. Science is baffled by the unreason of the hoi polloi. The moods of the mass can't be fathomed; that's a fact.

While I was studying this entire situation deeply, and waiting for Fay and Nat, I heard their car drive up. So I got to my feet and went to the front door to turn on the driveway lights.

Only one person came from the car. It was Nat Anteil; my sister hadn't come along.

"Where's Fay?" I said.

Nat said, "Somebody had to stay with the girls." He entered the house and shut the door after him.

His explanation, although reasonable, didn't convince me. I had the intuition that she couldn't bring herself to set foot inside the house as long as I was still there. And that made me feel just that much worse.

"Sometimes it's easier for two men to discuss a business matter," Nat said. "Without a woman."

"True," I said.

We sat down facing each other in the living room. Looking across, past the fireplace, at him, I got to wondering how old he was. Was he older or younger than I? About the same age, I decided. And look how little he had done with his life. A marriage that hadn't lasted a bit. Involvement with a married woman that had ended in the death of an innocent man. And, from what I had heard, a fairly insecure economic position. The only thing he had over me was that, to be very honest, he was much better looking than I. He had that sweet, open face, roundish, and jet-black hair which he kept cut short. He was tall, too, without appearing scrawny or bony. In fact he looked to me like a tennis player, with very long arms and legs, but at the same time keeping himself in good physical condition.

Also, I had respect for his intelligence.

"Well," I said, "this is a difficult situation."

"No doubt of that," Nat said.

We sat for a time in silence. Nat lit a cigarette.

"You don't want to be a dog in the manger," he said. "It's indisputable that you can't raise the capital to buy Fay out, and even if you did you couldn't afford to live here; the cost of keeping this place going is enormous. It's a completely impractical house. Personally, I'm not anxious to see Fay keep it. It's too costly to heat. I'd rather see her sell it and move into a smaller place, possibly an older house."

"But she has her heart set on living here," I said.

"Yes," he said. "She likes it. But if she had to, she could give it up. I think in the long run she'll want to give it up. After she's had to keep it running without Charley. In some respects, it's more a liability than an asset." Getting to his feet, he wandered around the living room. "It's nice. It's really a marvelous house to live in. But it'd take a really well-off person to maintain it. It's a constant drain. A person could wind up a slave to it, trying to keep it going. I don't think I'd ever want to do that; I hope to hell I don't get in that position." He did not seem to be especially talking to me; I sensed that he was actually thinking out loud.

I said, "Are you and Fay going to get married?"

He nodded. "As soon as I get my divorce from Gwen. We'll probably get a Mexican divorce and remarriage. There's no waiting period."

I said, "Since Charley didn't leave her very much, won't

you have to go to work full time to support her and the children?"

"There's the trust fund to support the kids," he said. "And she'll be getting enough from the factory and her property in Florida to maintain this place."

"I really don't want to give my share up," I said. "I want to live here."

"Why?" he said, turning to face me. "My god, it's got three bathrooms and four bedrooms—you'd be living alone, one person in this huge house. This place was built for five or six people to live in. All you need is a rented room."

I said nothing.

"You'll go out of your mind here," Nat said. "All alone. When Charley first went to the hospital, Fay almost went crazy alone, and she had the girls to keep her company."

"And you," I said.

To that he had no comment.

"I feel I have to stay here," I said.

"Why."

"Because," I said, "it's my duty."

"To what?"

"My duty to him," I said, letting it slip out before I realized what I had done.

Without difficulty, he grasped whom I meant. "You mean because he left half the house to you, you feel you must live here?"

"Not exactly," I said. I didn't want to tell him that I knew that Charley was still in the house.

Nat said, "Since you can't do it, it doesn't matter whether it's your duty or not. As I see it, your choice isn't whether to give up your share. It's whether you'll sell it and get something for it, or simply lose it and get nothing. With a thousand dollars cash and thirty-eight dollars every month you could establish yourself very nicely in town. Rent a nice apartment, buy clothes, eat out in good restaurants. Go out in the evenings and have a big time. Right? And meanwhile you'd be using the money he left for psychiatric care. And if you had psychiatric care you'd be a lot better off. Let's face it."

He had picked up that phrase, "let's face it," from my sister. It's interesting how one person's vocabulary affects another person. Everyone who ever had anything to do with her winds up saying that, and also, "in my entire life." And, "my good god." Not to mention the really foul language.

"I just don't want to leave this house," I repeated. And then, suddenly, I remembered something that I had forgotten. And it was something that Nat did not know. Or if he did, he did not accept.

The world was coming to an end in a month. So it didn't matter what happened after that. I only had to stay here a month, not forever. Then there would be no house.


I told Nat that I couldn't decide, that I still had to think it over. He went back home, and I sat by myself in the living room, for most of the night, considering.

At last, about four in the morning, I came to a decision. I got into the bed in the study and slept, sleep being something I badly needed. Then, the next morning, I got up at eight o'clock, took a bath and shaved, dressed, ate some Post's 40% Bran Flakes and toast and jam—which wasn't very much to take—and then set out along the road toward the Inverness Wye. There was one job-possibility that I had overlooked that I wanted to try. At the Wye was a vet's, not one that worked merely with sick dogs and cats, as the ones in town did, but with sheep and cattle and horses as well as smaller livestock. Since at one time I worked for a vet's, it seemed to me that I might have a chance, here.

However, after I had talked to the vet, I discovered that it was a family-run affair, the doctor and his wife and ten-year-old son and father. The ten-year-old boy did the feeding and sweeping that I had in mind, so I started back toward Drake's Landing.

At least I had explored every possibility.

Approximately at twelve-thirty in the afternoon I got back to the house. I right away telephoned Nat Anteil's number.

It was Fay who answered. Evidently Nat was either at work or doing his homework.

"I've come to a decision," I told my sister.

"My goodness," she said.

I said, "I'll sell you my half of the house for the thousand dollars down and the rest in payments, if you'll let me live in the house for the next month. And I have to be able to use the furniture and food and everything, so I can really live there."

"It's a deal," Fay said. "You horse's ass. You better not eat any of those steaks in the freezer. None of the t-bone or sirloin or New York cut. There's forty dollars worth of steaks in there."

"Okay," I agreed. "The steaks don't count. But I can eat any other food I find. And I want the money right away. Within the next day or two, no longer. And I don't have to pay any of the utility bills for the month."

"There's things we need," Fay said. "All the children's things. Their clothes—good god, my clothes, a million things. I don't want to move all those things out and then move them back in again. Why do you have to have it for a month? Can't you go back and stay with those nuts the Hambros?"

So even though she had agreed she was trying to get me out. I felt the futility of trying to make any rational agreement with her. "Tell Nat that I agree," I said, "if I can stay a month. I'll work it out with him. You're too unscientific."

After a few more exchanges she said good-bye, and we both hung up. Anyhow, I considered that I had agreed, even if it wasn't in writing. The house would be mine until the end of April—or, more accurately and realistically, until April twenty-third.

# 19

At nine in the morning, Nathan Anteil met his lawyer in the corridor outside department three of the San Rafael Courthouse. His witness was with him, a plump, scholarly man who had known both him and Gwen for a number of years.

The three of them left the courthouse and went across the street to a coffee shop. In a booth they sat discussing what the lawyer would want done and how. Neither Nat nor his witness had ever been inside a court of law before.

"There's nothing to be nervous about," the lawyer said. "You go up on the stand and then I ask you a lot of questions that you answer by saying yes; for instance, I ask you, isn't it true that you were originally married October 10, 1958, and you answer yes; then I ask you, isn't it true that you've been a resident of Marin County for a period in excess of three months, and so forth. I ask you isn't it true that your wife treated you in a manner involving cruel and unaffectionate behavior that caused you acute humiliation in public and before friends, and that her treatment had the result that you suffered mental and physical privation, resulting in inability to perform your job and that the result of this was that you could not carry on your life and meet your obligations in a way satisfactory to you." The lawyer droned on, gesturing with rapid, sharp flutters of his right hand. Nat noticed that the man's hands were unusually white and small, that his wrist had no hair on it. The nails were perfectly manicured, and it even occurred to him that this was almost like a woman's hand. Evidently the lawyer did no physical work of any sort.

"What do I do?" the witness said.

"Well, you get up on the stand after Mr. Anteil; they'll ask you to swear the same oath, at the same time as he. Then I'll ask you, isn't it true that you've lived in the County of Alameda for three months and in the state of California for over a year; you say yes. Then I ask you, isn't it true that in your presence you saw the defendant, Mrs. Anteil, behave toward Mr. Anteil in a manner that caused him acute humiliation, and that because of this you saw him become mentally distressed and suffer both physical and mental privation that resulted in him having to consult a physician, and there was noticeable change in him that caused you to remark that he didn't seem—" The lawyer gestured. "That he no longer seemed to be in the same good health and that he was visibly suffering as a result of Mrs. Anteil's behavior toward him." To both of them, he said, "See, we have to establish the result of Mrs. Anteil's behavior. It isn't sufficient to declare that she treated you badly—for instance, that she slept around or boozed or something—but that you actually suffered a noticeable change as a result."

"A change for the worst," the witness said.

"Yes," the lawyer said. "A change for the worst." To Nat he said, "I'm going to ask you isn't it true that to the best of your ability you tried to preserve this marriage, but that your wife showed in clear tangible fashion that she had no interest in your health and happiness, that she stayed away from the home for prolonged periods of time, showed obvious reluctance to inform you of her whereabouts during these prolonged intervals, and in general did not behave in the manner that a dutiful spouse would be expected to."

Sipping his coffee, Nat thought to himself that this was going to be a terrible ordeal; he did not know if he could do it, when the time came.

"Don't worry," the lawyer said, touching him on the shoulder. "This is just a ritual; you get up there and chant the proper formula and then you get the thing you want—a divorce decree. You won't have to say anything but yes; you just answer yes to the questions I ask you, and we'll be out of there in twenty minutes." He looked at his watch. "We should be getting back there. I don't know about this judge, but they usually like to get started right at nine-thirty." He was from Alameda County, and Nat had gotten him because once he had represented him and Gwen in a property dispute with some neighbors. Both he and she liked him. He had arranged the property settlement for both of them.

They returned to the courthouse. As they went up the steps, the witness discussed some trivial matters with the lawyer, having to do with the economic factor behind the decisions of courts. Nat did not listen. He watched an elderly man who sat on a bench with his cane in his lap, and a group of shoppers walking along the street.

The day was warm and clear. The air smelled good. Around the courthouse building, painters had thrown up canvas and ladders; the building evidently was undergoing alterations. The three of them had to stoop under ropes as they entered.

As his lawyer and witness entered the courtroom, Nat said to the lawyer, "Do I have time to go to the men's room?"

"If you hurry," the lawyer said.

In the men's room—a remarkably clean place—he took a pill that Fay had given him, a tranquilizer. Then he hurried back to the courtroom. He found his lawyer and witness on their way back out; his lawyer took hold of his arm and led him into the corridor, frowning.

"I was talking to the bailiff," he said in a low voice. "This judge doesn't permit the attorney to lead."

"What does that mean?" Nat said.

"It means I can't ask either of you questions," the lawyer said. "When you get up there, you'll be on your own."

"You can't prompt us?" the witness said.

"No, you'll have to tell your own stories." The lawyer led them back toward the courtroom. "We probably won't be first. Listen to the other cases and try to judge from them what you should say." He had the door open, and Nat entered ahead of his witness.

Presently he found himself seated on a bench, like the pew of a church, watching a middle-aged woman on the witness stand telling how a Mr. George Heathers or Feathers had spilled coffee on Mrs. Feathers at a barbecue party in San Anselmo and that instead of apologizing he had called her a fool and a bad mother in front of ten people.

The witness became silent, and then the judge, a gray-haired heavy-set man in his late sixties, wearing a pin-stripe suit, made a grimace of distaste and said, "Well, how did that affect the plaintiff? Did it cause any change in her?"

The witness said, "Yes, it caused her to become unhappy. And she said that she could not stand to be around a man who treated her that way and made her miserable."

The case went on to its end, and then a second one, very similar, took its place, with new women and a new attorney.

"This is a tough judge," Nathan's lawyer said to him out of the corner of his mouth. "Look, he's going through the property settlement. He's really giving trouble."

Nat scarcely heard him. The tranquilizer had begun to take effect, and he gazed out of the window of the courtroom at the lawn. He saw cars going by along the street, and the windows of the shops.

To him, his lawyer whispered, "Say you had to go to a doctor. Say she made you physically sick. Say she was away for a week or more on end."

He nodded.

On the stand, a young, violently-nervous dark-haired woman was saying in a faint voice that her husband had hit her.

Nathan thought, Well, Gwen never hit me. However she had that fool in the kitchen with her that night when I got home. I can say that she was in the habit of going out with other men, and that when I questioned her as to who they were and what they did, she abused me and insulted me.

To their witness, his lawyer whispered, "You listen to what Mr. Anteil says and take your cues from him."

"Okay," their witness said.

She caused me distress and humiliation, Nathan thought. I lost weight and started taking tranquilizers. I lay awake at night worrying about money. She borrowed money and didn't tell me about it. When she didn't come home at night I had to call around to everyone we knew, thus notifying everyone that I had no idea where my wife was at night, or whom she was with. She ran up huge gas bills on our credit cards. She hit me, scratched me, called me dirty names in front of all kinds of people. She made it clear that she preferred the company of other men to me, and that she had little or no respect for me.

In his mind he rehearsed.

Not so much later he found himself up on the stand, facing the rows of empty seats and the few people. Slightly to his left and below him his lawyer stood tensely, holding a sheaf of papers and speaking very rapidly to the judge. Their witness sat ill at ease in the first chair of the jury box.

"Your full name is Nathan Ruben Anteil?" his lawyer said.

"Yes," he said.

"And you live in Point Reyes in Marin County?"

"Yes," he said.

"And you have been a resident of California for a period greater than one year, and a resident of Marin County for a period greater than three months? And you are the plaintiff in this dispute asking a divorce between you and Mrs. Anteil in the Superior Court of Marin County? And that the marriage between you and Mrs. Anteil ceased for all practical purposes on or about March 10, 1959, and that at this time you and she are no longer living together?"

He said yes to each question.

"Would you tell the court," his attorney said, "the reasons why you seek a divorce from Mrs. Anteil."

Now his lawyer stepped slightly back. The courtroom was a little noisy, because, in the rear, a lawyer was consulting in low tones with his client and two people in the front were talking and rustling. Nat began to answer.

"Well," he said, "the reasons are that for the most part—" He paused, feeling the fatigue and languor brought on him by the pill. The sense of weight. "Are that she was never at home," he said. "She was always out somewhere and when she came back even though I asked her where she had been, all she did was vilify me and tell me it was none of my business. She made it abundantly clear that she preferred the company of other men to mine."

He tried to think what else to say. How to continue. All he seemed able to do was gaze at the lawn beyond the windows, the warm, green, dry lawn. He felt terribly sleepy, and his eyes started to shut. His voice had trailed off, and only with great effort could he resume any sort of speech.

"It seemed to me," he went on, "that there was nothing but contempt for me in her all the time. I could never depend on her to back me up in anything. She went her own way. She never acted like a married woman. It was as if we weren't married in the first place. The result of this was that I couldn't earn my living. I got sick and had to consult a physician. Doctor Robert Andrews," he said. "In San Francisco."

The judge said, "What was the nature of this illness?"

Nathan said, "What would be called a psychoneurotic complaint." He waited, but the judge had no comment. So he resumed. "I found myself unable to concentrate or work, and my friends all noticed this. This went on for a long period. At one time she stood on the front porch and shouted abuse at me that even the town's minister heard. He happened to be getting ready to visit us."

That had been the day that Gwen had moved her things out. Some neighbor had evidently realized what was happening, that their marriage was breaking up, and had called Doctor Sebastian. The old man had come by in his 1949 Hudson just at the height of the argument between them; Gwen, on the front porch with an armload of towels, had screamed at him that he was a no-good bastard and that as far as she was concerned he could go to hell. The old man had gotten back into his Hudson and driven off. Apparently he had given up any idea of trying to help them, either because he realized that it was too late and he could do no good, or because what Gwen had said was too much for him. He simply was too frail to stand the stress.

Anyhow, Nathan thought, as he gazed out at the warm lawn and the sunlight, the shops and people, she finished packing her things and then I drove her and them to her family's house in Sacramento. I even gave her back the snapshots of her that I carried in my wallet.

The courtroom was silent, waiting for him to go on. Waiting to see if he had anything more to say about the breakup of his marriage.

He said, "It was intolerable to me to be treated that way, as if I was second in importance to other men. I found strange cars sometimes parked in front of my own house, and when I got home I found men sitting there and that I had never in my life seen before. And when I asked her who they were she became so enraged and vilified me so completely that even the other man became embarrassed. He asked to leave, but she told him to stay."

How strange it feels, he thought. To be up here, telling these things.

"Anyhow," he said, "she had rages in which she deliberately destroyed objects that were of importance to me."

While she had been packing her things she had come across a plaster cat which they had won at Playland. She had been holding it, wondering how to pack it, when he had told her that he considered it his. At that point, she had turned and thrown it at him. The cat had broken against the wall behind him.

"She had these violent rages," he said, "where she couldn't control herself."

His lawyer nodded to him—impatiently, it seemed to him—and he realized suddenly that he had finished. Getting to his feet he stepped down. His lawyer called their witness, and Nathan found himself seated in the first chair of the jury box, listening to their witness tell how he had come by the Anteil house and found only Mr. Anteil at home, and how, on frequent occasions, when he had found them both together, he had been forced to listen to what he considered unfair and humiliating tirades on the part of Mrs. Anteil, directed at her husband.

The judge signed the paper; he and the lawyer exchanged a few words; and then Nathan and their witness and the lawyer walked up the aisle and out of the courtroom.

"Did he grant it?" he asked the lawyer.

"Oh sure," the lawyer said. "Now we go down to the clerk and get a copy of the interlocutory decree for you."

As they descended the stairs, the witness said, "You know, Gwen's about the most mild-mannered woman I've ever known. I felt funny up there talking about her 'tirades.' I never heard her raise her voice in my life."

The lawyer giggled at that. Nathan said nothing. But he felt a sense of release, a lifting of the burden of the court action. They entered the clerk's office, an immense, brightly-lit place in which rows of people worked at desks and file cabinets. At a counter which ran the width of the room, persons conducted their business with the many deputy clerks.

"Well, it's over," the witness said, while the lawyer got the papers.

Was there any truth to what I said? Nathan wondered. Some truth. Part true, part made up. Strange to lose sight, blend it together. No longer know what had happened, merely talk, tell what seems appropriate. Aloud, he said, "Like the Moscow Trials. Confessing to whatever they want."

Again his lawyer giggled. The witness winked at him.

But he did feel better. Dread of the ordeal . . . that was over, like the school play. Public speaking in assembly.

"Good to get it over," he said to his lawyer.

"Boy, that old man is a tough one," his lawyer said, as they left the clerk's office. "Not letting me lead—he probably didn't have a good bowel movement and felt like getting back at the world."

Outdoors, in the sunlight, they parted company. Each of them said good-bye and went off to his own car.

The time was ten-forty. Only an hour and ten minutes had gone by since the court had been called into session.

Divorced, Nathan thought. Over and done. Somebody else up there, now.

Reaching his car he got into it and sat.

Strange story to tell, he thought. When was she ever away from the house? Only when we broke up.

I should feel guilty, he thought. Getting up there and letting all those lies come out of me, that mishmash. That uninspired recitation. But his sense of release overcame any guilt. God damn, he thought. I'm so god damn glad it's over.

All at once he felt doubt. How can it be over? You mean I'm no longer married? What happened to Gwen? I don't understand it. Where did it go? How could a thing like this happen?

It isn't possible, he thought. What do you mean, I'm no longer married?

He stared out the car window. It doesn't make sense, he

thought. Dismay, as if he were about to break down and cry, started everywhere inside him, appeared on all sides, throughout. I'll be god damned, he thought. It just can't be. It isn't possible.

This is the most awful thing that ever happened to me, he thought. It's weird. It's the end of me, of my life. Now what am I going to do?

How did I ever get into this situation?

He sat watching the people go by, wondering how a thing of this sort could have come about. I must have let myself get mixed up in something horrible, he thought. It's as if the whole sky is a web that dropped over me and snared me. Probably she's the one who did it; Fay arranged all this, and I had nothing to do with it. I have no control of myself or anything that's happened. So now I'm waking up. I'm awake, he thought. Discovering that everything has been taken away from me. I've been destroyed, and now that I'm awake all I can do is realize it; I can't do anything. It's too late to do anything. It's already happened. The shock of getting up there and telling that account made me see. Mixture of lies and bits of truth. Woven together. Unable to see where each starts.

At last, putting the key in the ignition, he started up the car. Soon he was driving from San Rafael, back to Point Reyes Station.

At his house he saw her, in the front yard. She had found a bucket of gladiola and tulip bulbs that Gwen had brought up from the city to plant; wearing jeans and sandals and a cotton shirt she was busy with a trowel, digging a shallow trench for the bulbs along the front walk. The two girls were not in sight.

As he opened the gate she heard him and turned, lifting her head. As soon as she saw the expression on his face she said,

"You didn't get it."

"I got it," he said.

Laying down her trowel she stood up. "What an ordeal it must have been," she said. "My god, you look really pale."

He said, "I don't know what to do." It was not what he had intended to say, but he could think of nothing else.

"What do you mean?" she said, coming up to him and putting her thin, strong arms around him.

Feeling her arms, the authority and conviction of her, he said, "Hug me."

"I am hugging you," she said. "You asshole."

"Look where I am," he said, gazing past her at the remaining bulbs. She had planted most of them already. At one time the bucket had been full. "You've got me in a terrible spot. There's nothing I can do. You really have me."

"Why?" she said.

"I have no marriage."

"Poor baby," she said. "You're scared." Her arms pressed harder against him. "But you did get it? He granted it?"

"They have to grant it," he said. "If it's properly presented. That's what the lawyer's for."

"So you're divorced!" Fay said.

"I have an interlocutory decree," he said. "In a year I'll be divorced."

"Did he give you any trouble?"

"He wouldn't let the lawyer lead," he said. "I was on my own." He started to tell her about it, how the session had gone, but her eyes got that rapt, faraway expression; she was not listening.

"I meant to tell you," she said, when he halted. "The girls baked a cake for you. A celebration. One candle. Your first divorce. They're indoors now, quarreling about the icing. I said they better wait until you got home and ask you what kind of icing you wanted on it, if any."

He said, "I don't want anything. I'm completely exhausted."

"I'd never go into court in a million years," she said. "I'd rather die; you couldn't drag me into court." Letting go of him she started toward the house. "They've been so worried," she said. "Afraid something might go wrong."

"Stop talking," he said, "and listen to me."

She slowed to a stop; both her speech and her motion toward the house ceased. Inquiringly, she waited. She did not seem tense. Now that he was back, having gotten the decree, she was relieved; she did not seem to have paid any real attention to what he had said.

"God damn you," he said. "You never listen. Don't you care what I have to say? I'll tell you what I have to say; I'm pulling out of all this, the whole darn business."

"What?" she said, in a faltering voice.

He said, "I've gone as far as I can. I can't stand any more. When I got out of the courtroom I realized it. It finally came to me."

"Well," she said. "My goodness."

They stood facing each other, neither of them saying anything. With the toe of her sandal she kicked at a lump of dirt. Never before had he seen her so downcast.

"How did the Sparine work?" she said finally.

"Fine," he said.

"You were able to take it before you went in? I'm glad you had it. They're very good, especially for something like this that overtaxes you." Then, rallying, she said, "I don't see how you can leave me. What would happen to you? This is the worst possible time. You've undergone a dreadful traumatic situation these last couple of weeks. We both have. And this divorce business, this having to go into court, was the ultimate." Now she was attentive; her voice became quiet, and her expression changed to a tough acuteness. Taking hold of his arm she stretched him toward the house. "You haven't had anything to eat, have you?"

"No," he said. He held back, refusing to let her budge him.

"You're really furious at me, aren't you?" she said finally. "This is the most hostile you've been toward me."

"That's right," he said.

"I suppose the hostility must have been there all the time, buried in your subconscious. Doctor Andrews says it's better to say things like this if you feel them than not to." She did not sound angry; she sounded resigned. "I don't blame you," she said, eyeing him, standing very close to him and gazing up into his face with her head cocked on one side, her hands behind her back. Perspiration, from the heat of the day, shone on her throat; he saw it as it appeared and evaporated and reappeared. It pulsed there. "Can't we talk about it further?" she said. Instead of becoming childish she had become deeply rational. "A decision this serious should be discussed. Come inside and sit down and have lunch. Anyhow, where are you going to go? If someone has to go, good god, this is your house—you can't let us stay here if you feel about me the way you do. We'll go to a motel. I mean, that's no problem."

To that, he said nothing.

Fay said, "If you leave me you won't have a god damn thing. Maybe there are character traits in me that should be changed—that's why I go to Doctor Andrews, isn't it? And if there're things wrong with me, can't you tell me the right way to act? Can't you put me in my place? I want you to tell me what to do. Do you think I respect a man who I can push around?"

"Then let me go," he said.

"I think you're nuts to go," Fay said.

"Maybe so," he said. Turning around, he walked away.

From behind him, Fay said in a firm voice, "I promised the girls that we'd take them down to Fairyland this afternoon."

He could scarcely believe his ears. "What?" he said. "What the hell is 'fairyland'?"

"Down in Oakland," she said, facing him with composure. "They heard all about it on Popeye. They want to see King Fuddle's castle. I told them when you got back we'd go."

"I never said that," he said. "You never told me."

"Well," she said, "I know how you don't like to be bothered."

"God damn you," he said. "Committing me."

"It'll only take a couple of hours. An hour from here."

"More like two," he said.

"You should never break a promise to a child," she said. "Anyhow, if you're going to walk out on us and leave us, you should want to do something so they'll remember you. Do you want them to have a last impression of you not giving a damn about their interests?"

He said, "It doesn't matter what last impression they have of me, because you'll manage to tell them something about me that'll make me look so weak and awful—"

"They're listening," she said.

On the porch, the two girls had appeared. They had their cake on a big plate. "Look!" Bonnie called down. Both girls beamed at him.

"Nice," he said.

"Well," Fay said. "Is this too much to ask of you? Then you can walk out on us."

The girls, obviously paying no attention to what either adult was saying, called down. "What kind of icing do you want? Mommy said to wait and ask you."

He said to them, "You want to go to Fairyland?"

At that, they both came racing down the steps; the cake was put aside on the railing, abandoned.

"Okay," he said, above the clamor. "We'll go. But let's get started."

Fay stood watching, her arms folded. "I'll go get a coat," she said. To the girls, she said, "You both get your coats."

The girls scampered back into the house.

To Fay he said nothing. He got into the car, behind the wheel. She did not join him; she waited for the girls. As she waited she got her cigarettes from the spot at which she had left them, lit up, and did a little more digging.

• • •

The howling of the children made him weary. Everywhere kids raced and screamed, in and out of the bright, newly-painted storybook buildings that made up the Oakland Park Department's idea of Fairyland. He had parked quite far from it, not being sure exactly where it was, and the walk alone had worn him out.

Bonnie and Elsie appeared at the bottom of a slide, waved at him and Fay, and scurried to join the other children at the stairs leading back up.

"It's nice here," Fay said.

In the center of Fairyland, Little Bo Peep's lambs were being fed from a bottle. A middle-aged woman's voice, amplified by loudspeakers, told the children all to come running to see.

"Isn't that funny," Fay said. "We come all the way down here to see lambs being fed. I wonder why they feed them from bottles. I guess they think it's cuter."

After the girls had finished with the slide they wandered on. Now they had found the wishing well and were fooling with it; he only vaguely noticed them.

Fay said, "I wonder which is Fuddle's castle."

He didn't answer.

"This is tiring," she said. "I guess you already had enough for one day."

Presently they arrived at the refreshment stand. The children had orange drink and hot dogs. Just beyond that they saw the ticket window and station house of the little train. Its narrow track ran into and out of Fairyland, passing among the trees beyond. On their way to Fairyland from the car they had noticed the track; in fact they had followed it to the main gate of Fairyland, which of course was on the opposite side from them. They had to walk all around it.

As they trampled along, looking in vain for the gate, Fay had said to him, "You know, you're a schlimozl."

"What's that?" both girls had demanded.

Fay said, "A schlimozl is a person who always gets up to the ticket window at the ballpark just as the last bleacher seat is sold. And he doesn't have enough money with him to buy a reserved seat."

"That's me," he said.

To the girls, Fay explained, "You see, he parked on the opposite side from the entrance, and we had to walk all around. Now, if I had been driving I would have parked and we would have gotten out, and there we would have been. Right at the entrance. But a schlimozl always has bad luck. It's an instinct with him."

Yes, he thought. It's true about me. There is a bad luck that gets me into things that I don't want to be in, and then it keeps me there. It holds me there. And nothing that I do can get me out.

"It's just my luck," Fay said, "to marry a schlimozl. Maybe our luck will balance out, though."

Now, he stood with her and the children, lined up to buy tickets for the little train. His legs ached and he wondered if he could live through it, the waiting in line for tickets and then, after getting tickets, the waiting for the train to return and take on passengers. At this moment the train was off somewhere in the park, out of sight. A whole raft of children, who had already gotten tickets, waited eagerly on the platform beyond the ticket window.

"It'll take at least half an hour," he said to Fay. "Is it worth it?"

Fay said, "This is the main event. Isn't this what we saw them all doing? They have to ride on it."

So he waited.

After a long time he was able to reach the ticket window and buy tickets for all four of them. Then he and Fay and the girls pushed on to the platform. By now the train had returned; children and their parents were spilling out of it, and the conductor was pointing the way out. A new load ran to the cars and began to board. The cars were small and irregularly-shaped. The occupants' heads were forced almost to bump, as if by entering the car they became ancients nodding and dozing.

"In a way this Fairyland is a disappointment," Fay said. "I don't think they give the children enough to do; they can't actually go into those little houses—all they can do is look at them. Like a museum."

His weariness and lethargy kept him from commenting. He no longer felt related to the noises and movement around him, the swirl of the children.

A conductor came along the platform, collecting tickets. He counted aloud. When he reached Nathan he stopped, saying, "Thirty-three." Then he took Elsie's ticket and said to Nathan, "Are you all together?"

"Yes," Fay said.

"Well, I hope I can squeeze you all in," he said, taking her ticket and Bonnie's and Nathan's.

"How many can you get in?" Fay said.

"It depends on the number of adults," the conductor said. "If it's mostly kids we can keep squeezing them in. But an adult is another matter." He departed with the tickets.

"I guess we get in," Fay said. "He took our tickets."

Theirs had been the last tickets collected. Behind them, a family of five fretted and worried.

They won't get on this time, Nathan thought. They'll have to wait. He gazed off past the refreshment stand at the sturdy house that the third little pig had built.

When the train returned, he and Fay and the children moved with the others through the gate and on to the outer platform, along the track. As the cars became empty the new passengers clambered on. The conductor began shutting the wire doors of the cars. At the gate, the family with tickets were stopped. "No," the attendant said. "You can't get on if you have tickets."

How weird, Nathan thought, seeing a small boy whose

ticket had not been collected standing hopefully at the train, holding his ticket up. Here, if you have a ticket, you're barred. If you don't then you can get on. The girls and Fay hurried toward the rear car, along with the others. His feet dragged; weighed down, he fell behind them. Children squeezed past him and hopped up into the cars.

When he arrived at the last car he found that Fay and Elsie had already found places. The conductor started to close the wire door, and then seeing Bonnie, said to her,

"Room for one more."

Lifting her up, he handed her to Fay, inside the car.

Around Nathan, the other children without tickets disappeared into the cars. Only a few remained, and then only he remained on the platform. Everyone had been seated but him. The wire door on Fay's car had been locked and the conductor was starting away. Suddenly seeing him, the conductor said,

"I forgot about you."

Nathan found himself smiling. Behind him, beyond the gate, the waiting people waved and shouted with sympathy. Or was it sympathy? He did not know. He found himself walking along with the conductor, back up the length of the train, toward the engine. The conductor prattled away, telling him how he had happened to overlook him. At the first car the conductor peered in and then said,

"Here. You can get in here."

He clambered up, pushed through the little entrance, and found himself facing four Cub Scouts in blue uniforms. They stared at him as he tried to seat himself on the bench. At last he said to the first Cub Scout, "Why don't you move over?"

The scout at once moved, and he was able to seat himself. His head brushed the roof of the car, and the angle was such that he had to hunch forward. He sat no taller than the scouts; only larger, more awkward, filling up more space—as the conductor had said. The wire door was locked and then the conductor signaled to the motorman.

After a series of noises the train jerked and began to move.

Under Nathan's feet the floor drummed; the train vibrated steadily, without variation. They moved away from the platform and the waving, shouting people. Almost at once they found themselves out of Fairyland, among oak trees and grass.

Seated so far up in the train, he could look out at the tail of the engine and, beyond that, the area toward which they were moving. He saw the track ahead of them, the slopes of grass, a road to the right. Beyond the road were more oak trees and then the lake. Now and then he made out the sight of picnickers. They glanced up at the train, and once, the Cub Scout next to him started to wave and then nervously changed his mind. No one in the car spoke. The noise of the wheels was so constant that no one expected it to stop; they all sat patiently riding, gazing out, contemplating.

On and on the train went, always at the same rate of speed.

The unvarying noise and vibration and pace of the train took the fatigue out of his legs. Cramped as he was he began to feel more at peace. The oak trees lulled him. The inevitability of the train's progress . . . always ahead of them he saw the track, the two rails, and there was nothing else the train could do but follow it. And nothing else that any of them could do but remain where they were, cooped up in the little irregular cars, locked in by their wire doors, hunched and huddled in whatever postures they had first assumed. Their knees touched; their heads almost touched; they could not even look at one another unless luck happened to have put them facing that way. And yet none of them objected. No one complained or tried to stir.

How odd I must look, he thought to himself. In here with these Cub Scouts in their blue uniforms. One bulging, misshapen adult crowded in where he shouldn't be. Where several children should be, on a child's train, in a child's amusement park. Did the City of Oakland anticipate me? Certainly they had not. This is the luck of the schlimozl, he thought. Put up forward here, away from Fay and the girls. Riding alone here while they ride together in back.

But it stirred no real emotions in him. He experienced a relaxation of physical tension; nothing more.

Is that all that is wrong? he asked himself. Merely the accumulation of tensions, worries, fears? Nothing of lasting importance? Can the constant vibrations of a children's train soothe me and take away whatever it is that confronts me? This sense of dismay and doom . . .

He no longer felt the dread, the intuition that he had been moved against his will into a situation built for another person's use.

He thought, There is certainly no hope left of getting away. And it isn't even terrible; it's possibly funny, if even that. It's embarrassing. That's all. A little embarrassing to realize that I no longer control my life, that the major decisions have already been made, long before I was conscious that any change was occurring.

When I met her, or rather, when she looked out of her car window and saw me and Gwen . . . that was when the decision was made, assuming that it ever was. She made it, as soon as she saw us, and the rest was inevitable.

Probably she will make a good wife, he thought. She will be loyal to me, and try to help me do what I want to do. Her passion toward controlling me will ultimately subside; all of this energy in her will fade. I will make substantial changes in her, too. We will alter each other. And someday it will be impossible to tell who has led whom. And why.

The only fact, he realized, will be that we are married and living together, that I will be earning a living, that we will have two girls from a previous marriage and possibly children of our own. A valid question will be: Are we happy? But only time will tell that. And not even Fay can underwrite the answer to that; she is as dependent as I am, in that final area.

He thought, She could bring about everything that she wants and still be wretched. Out of this I could emerge as the prosperous one, the peaceful one. And neither of us can possibly know.

When the train had finished its trip and was returning to the platform he saw the people lined up for their ride. The Cub Scout next to him plucked up his courage at last and waved; some of the people waved back, and that encouraged other scouts to wave.

Nathan waved, too.

# 20

With the money I received from my sister as cash payment for my equity in the house I opened a checking account at the Bank of America at Point Reyes Station. As soon as possible—after all, there wasn't much time left—I set out to buy the things I needed.

First, I paid two hundred dollars for a horse and had it brought to the house by truck and let loose in the back pasture. It was almost the same color as Charley's horse, possibly a little darker, but the same size, as far as I could tell, and in as good physical shape. It ran around for a day or so and then it calmed down and began to crop grass. After that it seemed perfectly at home.

I then set out to buy sheep, the black-faced kind. With this I had more trouble. In the end I had to go all the way to Petaluma for them. I paid about fifty dollars apiece for them, three ewes. As far as lambs went, I was undecided at first. Finally I came to the conclusion that he hadn't considered the lambs his, so I did not get any.

Getting a collie like Bing was really hard. I had to take the bus down to San Francisco and go shopping at various kennels before I found one that was the same variety. There are all sorts of collies, costing different prices. The one resembling Bing cost almost two hundred dollars, virtually as much as the horse.

The ducks cost me only a dollar and a half apiece. I got them locally.

My reasoning was that I wanted everything set up the way it was supposed to be. It seemed to me that there was a very good chance that on April twenty-third Charley Hume would come back to life. Of course, this was not a certainty. The future never is. Anyhow, I felt that this increased the chances. According to the Bible, when the world ends the dead arise from their graves at the sound of the last trumpet. In fact, that's one of the ways that the end of the world is known to be coming, when the dead arise. It's a piece of strong verification of the theory. During the month that I lived there in the house I felt his presence grow more and more real, as he neared closer and closer to the moment of his return to life.

I felt it especially at night. Beyond any doubt he was close to resuming his existence in this world. His ashes—he had been cremated, according to the terms of his will—had been sent by error to the Mayfair Market, and there Doctor Sebastian had picked them up (the clerks at the Mayfair had telephoned him and explained the situation) and had driven them out to Fay. She had taken them into the ocean. So when he returned, he would do so in the Point Reyes area, and with his house exactly like it had been, with the horse and dog and sheep and ducks, all of which had belonged to him, he was sure to arise there.

In the afternoons, when the wind from the Point was strongest, I could go outdoors on to the patio and actually see the bits of ash in the air. In fact, several people in the neighborhood remarked on the unusual concentration of ash in the air near sunset. This gave the setting sun a deep reddish color. Beyond any doubt, something of vast importance was about to happen; you could feel it, even if you hadn't been warned.

Every day that passed put me into a greater state of excitement. Toward the end of the month I was hardly sleeping at all.

When April twenty-third arrived I woke up while it was still dark. I lay in bed awhile, so keyed-up that I could barely stand it. Then at five-thirty A.M. I got out of bed and got dressed and ate breakfast. All I could get down was a bowl of Wheat Chex, incidentally. And a dish of applesauce. I lit a fire in the fireplace in the living room and then I began walking around the house. I didn't know exactly where Charley would first be seen, so I tried to cover every part of the house, be in each room at least once every fifteen minutes.

By noon I was so conscious of him that I kept turning my head and catching a glimpse of him out of the corner of my eye. But at two o'clock I had a distinct feeling of let-down. I had a cheese sandwich and a glass of milk and that made me feel better, but the sense of his presence did not become any stronger.

When six o'clock came, and he still hadn't come back to life, I began to become uneasy. So I telephoned Mrs. Hambro.

"Hello," she said, in that hoarse voice.

I said, "This is Jack Seville." (What I meant, of course, was Jack Isidore.) "I wondered if you'd noted anything definitive."

"We're meditating," she said. "I thought you would be with us. Didn't you catch our telepathic message?"

"When was it sent out?" I asked.

"Two days ago," she said. "At midnight, when the lines are strongest."

"I didn't get it," I said in agitation. "Anyhow, I have to be over here at the house. I'm waiting for Charley Hume to come back to life."

"Well, I think you should be here," she said, and I noticed

a real hint of crossness in her voice. "There may be a good reason why we aren't getting the expected results."

"You mean, it's my fault?" I demanded. "Because I'm not there?"

"There has to be some reason," she said. "I don't see why you have to stay there and wait for that particular person to come back to life."

We argued awhile, and then hung up with less than the most amiable feelings. Again I began pacing around the house, looking this time into every closet, in case he returned and found himself shut in where he couldn't get out.

At eleven-thirty that evening I was really getting worried. I again telephoned Mrs. Hambro, but this time got no answer. By a quarter of twelve I was virtually out of my mind with worry. I had the radio on and was listening to a program of dance music and news. Finally the announcer said that in one minute it would be twelve midnight. He gave a commercial for United Airlines. Then it was twelve. Charley hadn't come back to life. And it was April twenty-fourth. The world hadn't come to an end.

I was never so disconcerted in my entire life.


Looking back on it, the thing that really gets me is that I had sold my interest in the house for next to nothing. My sister had gotten it away from me, taking advantage of me the way she takes advantage of everyone. And I had restocked the place with a horse and dog and sheep and ducks. What did I get out of it? Very little.

I sat down in the big easy chair in the living room, feeling that I had reached the really low point in my life. I was so depressed that I could hardly think; my mind was in a state of complete chaos. All my data rattled and made no sense.

Out of it all I realized that there was simply no doubt. The group had been wrong.

Not only had Charley Hume not returned to life but the

world had not come to an end, and I realized that a long time ago Charley was right in what he said about me; namely, that I was a crap artist. All the facts that I had learned were just so much crap.

I realized, sitting there, that I was a nut.

What a thing to realize. All those years wasted. I saw it as clearly as hell; all that business about the Sargasso Sea, and Lost Atlantis, and flying saucers and people coming out of the inner part of the earth—it was just a lot of crap. So the supposedly ironic title of my work wasn't ironic at all. Or possibly it was doubly ironic, that it was actually crap but I didn't realize it, etc. In any case, I was really horrified. All those people over in Inverness Park were a bunch of cranks. Mrs. Hambro was a psycho or something. Possibly even worse than me.

No wonder Charley left me a thousand dollars for psychoanalysis. I was really on the verge of the pit.

Good god, there hadn't even been an earthquake.

Now what was there left for me to do? I had a few more days left to me in the house, and a couple of hundred dollars of the cash that Fay and Nathan had given me. Enough money to get back to the Bay Area and relocate myself in a decent apartment, and possibly be able to find a job of some sort. I probably could go back and work for Mr. Poity at One-Day Dealers' Tire Service, although he had gotten all he could stand of my crap.

So I wasn't really so bad off.

Of course, it's unwise to go overboard in blaming myself. I had had a theory, which couldn't be verified until April twenty-third, and therefore until that time it couldn't positively be said that I was out of my mind for believing it. After all, the world might have come to an end. Anyhow, it did not. All those people like Fay and Charley and Nat Anteil were right.

They were right, but thinking about them I came to the conclusion, after a long period of hard meditation, that they were not a hell of a lot better than me. I mean, there's a lot of rubbish in what they have to say, too. They're darn near a bunch of nuts in their own way, although possibly it isn't quite so obvious as in my case.

For instance, anybody who kills himself is a nut. Let's face it (as Fay says). And even at the time I was conscious that his killing all those helpless animals was an example of the lunatic brain at work. And then that nut Nathan Anteil who just got married to a very nice girl and then dumped her as soon as he got mixed up with my sister . . . that isn't exactly a model of logic. To get rid of a sweet harmless woman for a shrew like Fay.

As far as I'm concerned, the nuttiest of all is my sister, and she's still the worst; take my word for it. She's a psychopath. To her, everybody else is just an object to be moved around. She had the mind of a three-year-old. Is that sanity?

So it doesn't seem to me that I should be the only person who has to bear the onus of believing an admittedly ridiculous notion. All I want is to see the blame spread around fairly. For a day or so I considered writing to the San Rafael newspapers and giving them the story in the form of a letter to the editor; after all, they have to print that. It's their duty as a public service. But in the end I decided against it. The hell with the newspapers. Nobody reads the letters to the editor column except more nuts. In fact, the whole world is full of nuts. It's enough to get you down.

After thinking it all over, and weighing every consideration, I decided to avail myself of the clause in Charley Hume's will and take the thousand dollars worth of psychoanalysis. So I collected all my things that I had around the house, packed them up, and got a neighbor to drive me down to the Greyhound. A couple of days before I had to I left the house that Charley and Fay had built—Fay's house—and started back to the Bay Area.

As the bus drove along I considered how I would locate the best analyst. In the end I decided to get the names of every one of them practicing in the Bay Area, and visit each of them in turn. In my mind I began putting together a questionnaire for them to fill out, telling the number of patients they had had, the number of cures, the number of total failures, length of time involved in cures, number of partial cures, etc. So on the basis of that I could draw up a chart and compute which analyst would be the most likely to give me help.

It seemed to me that the least I could do was try to use Charley's money wisely and not squander it on some charlatan. And on the basis of past choices, it seems pretty evident that my judgment is not of the best.